A CHILD
WENT FORTH

ALSO BY BOSTON TERAN

God Is a Bullet

Never Count Out the Dead

The Prince of Deadly Weapons

Trois Femmes

Giv — The Story of a Dog and America

The Creed of Violence

Gardens of Grief

The World Eve Left Us

The Country I Lived In

The Cloud and the Fire

By Your Deeds

A CHILD
WENT FORTH

BOSTON TERAN

Library of Congress Control Number: 1-5700842511

ISBN: 978-1-56703-067-9

Published in the United States by High Top Publications LLC, Los Angeles, CA
and simultaneously in Canada by High Top Publications LLC

Special Thanks to LET US BREAK BREAD TOGETHER... THERE WAS A CHILD WENT FORTH by Walt Whitman... JUMP JIM CROW... WHEN THE PIGS BEGIN TO FLY... MY OLD KENTUCKY HOME and HARD TIMES, COME AGAIN NO MORE by Stephen Foster.

Map image courtesy of Barry Lawrence Ruderman Antique Maps—www.RareMaps.com

Image of Girl—Print#N269, Hugh Mangum Photographs, David M. Rubenstein Rare Book & Manuscript Library, Duke University

Photo of Boy—Courtesy of Charlene Crandall

Cover and interior design by Alan Barnett Design

Printed in the United States of America

To the writers and artists, whose inspiration has made this and all other Boston Teran works possible

ACKNOWLEDGMENTS

To Deirdre Stephanie and the late, great Brutarian...to G.G. and L.S....Mz. El and Roxomania...the kids...Natasha Kern...Janice Hussein, for her fine work.... Charlene Crandall, for her brains and loyalty...And finally, to my steadfast friend and ally, and a master at navigating the madness, Donald V. Allen.

BROOKLYN

CHAPTER 1

"Every artist dips his brush in his own soul and paints his own nature in his pictures. I learned this from you, Mister Beecher. And what is the great canvas of our age? It is America, sir. And the country we paint together will determine the future of this great nation. This is what I teach my son, and what encompasses all that I have learned from your honored self."

Zacharia Griffin then looked at his son with such love, and smiled in that telling way as only he could. They sat in the private office of Henry Ward Beecher, the most famous evangelist of the day. The boy and his father had traveled all the way from Topeka to the Plymouth Congregational Church in Brooklyn with a letter signed by the most important abolitionists of Kansas. Theirs was an urgent plea to solicit financial aid from the famous Christian foot soldier for their fight against slavery.

Zacharia Griffin brushed his boy's hair back. "We never know the love of a parent till we become parents ourselves," he said.

Mister Beecher, that kindly soul, sat at his desk with folded hands and nodded intently, hearing his own prized words being recited back to him. "Handsome boy," said the evangelist.

"Looks like his mother. The tragic soul. Has her good heart and nature. And like her, reading is already a passion."

The boy sat there in his polished shoes and neat suit. He had never been in a room of any kind with such beautiful woods and cut stone. He was overwhelmed and a little bit frightened.

"What is that book you have there?" the good evangelist said to the child.

The boy held it out for the older gentleman who took it.

"He already has a fascination about growing up to be a writer," said the boy's father.

"A noble profession," said Mister Beecher, "when committed to a noble heart."

The boy, of course, had no such idea about being a writer. Or at least, he didn't know it at the time.

The book looked to have journeyed many hard miles, the pages being severely dogeared, the binding in places torn loose. But when the evangelist saw the embossed title, how moved his features became. "Ahhh," he said, "Uncle Tom's Cabin." It was his own dear sister's work, and he nodded profoundly.

He stood and came around the desk and he handed the book back to the boy and he took the boy's hands in his own. "What is your full Christian name?"

"Full Christian name?"

The boy looked to his father.

"It is Charlemagne Ezekiel Griffin," said the father. "But we call him Charlie."

"Well...Charlemagne Ezekiel Griffin...Like a vineyard, or a vine, they are tenderly sheltered, nourished, and trained, are wisely instructed and restrained, and bear rich and abundant fruit."

The boy's father nodded in agreement, and there was a look the boy recognized. A look perceptible to no one but himself most probably, that seemed to be totally in tune and in time with all that was going on around him. A look that spoke of such human authenticity, with just a touch of private glee, that the boy had come to know meant…the fleece was on.

• • •

Mister Beecher called for an attendant. An old black gentleman named Louis was asked to escort young Charles to the kitchen. "Fill the boy a nice plate," said the evangelist. "And make sure there's plenty of gratitude to go around." This would give Mister Beecher and Zacharia a chance to talk privately.

The boy had one stiff leg and walked with decided difficulty. Louis led him down a steel circular stairwell. The boy had to clasp the railing and refused Louis' help when offered.

"Thank you," said Charlie, "but I can do it." There was quiet shame in his voice.

"How did it happen?" said Louis.

"How did what happen?"

"Your leg."

"Nothing happened. My father…well…he's like to say God borned me like this."

A place was set at a table in the kitchen. Not at the table where the blacks who worked for the church ate, but at the one for the handful of whites who were part of the ministry.

Charlie sat alone and quietly watched the kitchen help as they went about their business, crossing and crisscrossing the scullery, talking in hushed tones, respectful with their glances. A boy about

Charlie's age, twelve or so, came over and excused himself and then said, "We're praying for you." Charlie knew then word had gotten around, as it always does, one whisper at a time.

Zacharia and Ward Beecher were upstairs in that cool, dark, secluded office to discuss Bleeding Kansas and the popular sovereignty law, which stated slavery in that state was to be decided by the vote of those who lived there. And so, in the most practical sense, violent confrontation was born. Free staters went to war with pro-slavery border ruffians.

"The cost of freedom, is freedom itself," said Zacharia. "God's will is to be determined by he who has the best armed encampment."

It was money—that was what those who signed the letter were asking for. Money to buy arms Zacharia could negotiate for and deliver through a network of underground sympathizers.

CHAPTER 2

"THE PIOUS ARE GOD'S SACRED MARKS. Put here on earth to be served up like supper," said Zacharia. "You should have seen that fanatic clergyman come to terms with his own goodness once he got you out of that room." Zacharia now did a railing imitation of that evangelist for his son. "If we mean to free this world of its crime of slavery, guns are more important than bibles."

Zacharia drank from his Washington and Eagle flask. "Thank God for hypocrisy. He's going to talk to some of his abolitionist friends. He should have four thousand dollars within days for me to buy arms." He looked at the letter he'd created with its forged signatures, then he tossed it across the room. "Charlie, my boy... goodness is the building block of humanity's downfall. If there's one thing you remember for when you're a writer, it's that—"

"I never said I wanted to be a writer!"

Charlie was sitting on the bed trying to free himself of that damn brace of leather and iron that his father had built for him to wear so he'd pass for a cripple. The boy's leg was black and blue and cut and, it ached so, and he was angry.

"That's just another lie you made up there at the church," said Charlie.

"Yeah," said Zacharia. "I forget sometimes what I make up and what's the truth. No matter. As long as you can successfully lie your way out of a lie…you'll fare well."

The boy tossed the brace so it would land near his father's feet to hint of his anger.

Zacharia had rented a room in a small waterfront hotel off of Hudson Avenue and within blocks of the ferry that would take them back to Manhattan and the trains when it came time to escape west.

The blocks were lined with refineries and shipyards and mill houses, and the Brooklyn Gas Light Works lit the night sky outside their window. The bars were rough and loud and peopled with hard cases and seamen and prostitutes. There was no shortage of the poor in the streets and gangs of homeless youth and louts sleeping off a drunk in some muddied alley. And there was always a game of chance to be found and the unintended consequences they engender.

Zacharia went to the window, sat on the sill, and sipped from his flask. He was looking out into a waterfront darkness while Charlie watched him silently. The boy could read that stark and declarative expression from what was already years of experience following his father's footsteps across a nation of back alley gambling dens. His father's eyes got all fiery and glistened as if touched by lighted oil, and the stare seemed ceaseless and rather desperate.

Charlie knew his father had the hunger then and that he was already imagining secret pleasures there on the night streets waiting for him. The drinking halls with their money wheels and drunken laughter and brothels with their rinky pianos and dice games and sallow faced girls lurking in shadow. My inheritance, thought the boy, will be the memory of coal smoke, stale beer and bawdy house perfume. I know the clatting of the roulette wheel like some men know the rhythms of their own body. His father would often say.

And it was so true, it made the son sad, because it was their life.

"I think I'll tumble out for a while," said Zacharia. "You rest up here."

His father stood and tucked away the flask and started for the door, but Charlie was quick to say, "You're not taking all the money we have left with you?"

The look his father gave the boy flashed with anger, and then hurt. "Not exactly a master of faith, are you?"

"I only know what I learned from you."

Zacharia didn't appreciate being so pointedly observed by a boy, but his better angels got hold of him, and he threw out his chin and reeled off a laugh, and then he brushed his long straight black hair back off his forehead.

He reached for a slim packet of bills he had pocketed, licked a thumb, and counted off a few worn dollars which he tossed on the bed. It was then he noticed a medallion attached to a horsehair rope one can wear around their neck. It was lying next to the copy of Uncle Tom's Cabin.

"What is that?"

"A medallion. It was given to me by a boy who worked in the kitchen. They believe you're going to do what you told Mister Beecher."

Zacharia heard the conflict in his son's voice and brushed past it. He took up the medallion and made a show of looking it over. It was some kind of white jasperware. He had to look closely because the image on it was chinked. He held it to the oil lamp. It was a black man there, in chains and down on one knee. There was etched writing along the rim that he could not read or did not care to read. He tossed it down without a word.

CHAPTER 3

THE BOY IN THE CHURCH KITCHEN who had talked with Charlie had called to him later, to get his attention, whispering, "Hey…you boy."

He was half hidden in a doorway to the church cellar and motioned for Charlie to come over. Charlie was not sure he should and looked about secretly, but the boy was so intent, and Charlie's curiosity had the best of him. In the shadow of that doorway, the boy said, "The old man wants to give you something," and he pointed down in the darkness.

The basement was made of stone walls, and it had the damp, musky smell of a dungeon. Much was stored there and stacked high, with a thin labyrinth of walkways to get around. There were huge trunks, old furniture, workman's tools, used brick, and the remains of an altar crucifix twice the size of a man, that leaned against a stone pillar.

"What does the old man—"

"Ssssshhhh," said the boy.

They waited in silence, they waited in blackness. They stood close together. Charlie could hear the people walking above through the hollow bones of the building like strange ghosts, and he followed their steps with his eyes. The Christ on the cross was a shadowy figure that looked down upon them, then there was a sudden wisp of light across his features, and Charlie saw it was a battered, broken face, a tortured face, the chiseled wood harshly mistreated and for a moment—a frightening, ill feeling moment—Charlie saw his mother there, the memory of her in her misery staring at him from her asylum bed.

A lantern descended the creaking stairway. It was the old gentleman, the one named Louis. He made his slow way across the oppressive cellar. He set the lantern down on a trunk by the two boys.

"Give me your hand, son."

Somewhat tenuously, Charlie put out a hand. The old man took it in his own and placed there in the open palm the medallion on the horsehair rope.

Charlie, at first, didn't know what it was. The white jasperware shined so in the light and the black figure that stood out, he was to realize, was a slave in chains kneeling on one knee.

"What is it?" said Charlie.

"A medallion for you to carry and keep tucked away. But if you or your father should find yourselves in trouble and with nowhere to turn, you show this to our people. Do you understand? Not a white person, now. Not unless you know *to your bones* certain they have the same feelings as Mister Beecher.

"And this too. Not all of our people will know what this is… until they look at it. Of the ones that do, most will help. Some might be too afraid to help, but they will never do you harm."

Charlie was holding it close to the light. Could see there was writing along the rounded edge.

"You can't see well enough to read in this light what's written there."

From the floor above, someone called out for Louis.

He squeezed Charlie's hand around the medallion.

"You'll see black folks in Brooklyn wearing them in your travels. On the road, if need be, show it to black folks…but secret like. I wish we could do more for the journey."

When the old man closed Charlie's hand around the medallion, the boy felt utter shame, for he knew what the journey truly was. It's called the confidence game. From Find the Lady to Thimblerig, with a bum leg thrown in as a topper. He felt such shame, he could not look at the old gentleman, for whom this had absolute meaning.

The shame felt like a curse of birth, or a black sickness on his being. He wanted to hand the medallion back to that kind fellow, but felt that would expose him for the liar he was, so he took it and said, "Thank you."

Louis slowly climbed the stairs, his name being called again and again from somewhere in that stone rectory. The two boys remained where they were with the lantern.

"Louis got that medallion when he was in England," said the boy.

"He was in England?"

"It's a hundred years old, that medallion…so Louis says."

Charlie looked the medallion over now as if he were handling a piece of history. "Can you imagine that?"

CHAPTER 4

CHARLIE LAY ON THE BED on his back looking up at the medallion suspended there from its horsehair rope. It was a pretty darn thing with that flue of light from the oil lamp upon it, floating so like some airy cloud. He would give it to his mother when next they met. They would be taking her out of the asylum then, with the money they confiscated here. He knew it weren't clean or legal or right, but they would not tell her they came upon it this way. He and his father had already decided that. It would be like they hustled it in some shill game. No less, no more.

He remembered about the words etched into the rim of the medallion and he rolled over and held it close to the lamp and really studied it. His fingers went from word to word while he squinted to sight the words better...Am-I-Not-A-Man...Am-I-Not-A-Brother.

He didn't quite understand, but no matter. He would put the medallion around her neck, and she would be so thrilled. She would take her boy in her arms and she would be crying because she would know—even though the knowing would be difficult because she had been sick—the beauty of her son's affection: that he had come all this way just for her. And she would fill the empty space that surrounded him forever with her love.

It grew to be a long night in that grubby room. He read some of *Uncle Tom's Cabin* but there sure weren't exactly youthful adventures in it like *The Three Guardsmen* with their swords and darings.

The woman next door started singing like she did most nights along about this time. He could hear her through the shoddy wall planking, serenading her baby. She lived there with a worthless bummer of a man and loudest and most complainingest son of a bitch ever created from the muds between heaven and hell.

Such a beautiful voice she had, it stirred Charlie with feelings like a smoky dream might or the rain falling on faraway branches. He was taken with loneliness and he turned down the lamp wick and lay there imagining this was his own mother singing there.

He thought of God sudden like, and would have asked for some favor, but there were so many favors to be had and how does one come down to choosing? Besides, God would have to have his head on backwards granting favor to such a low and larcenous being as himself.

• • •

Outside his window a woman laughed, a little too loud and tinny as far as Charlie was concerned. Then came Zacharia with that rooty voice of his. Charlie was lying in bed and leaned up now and looked over the rim of the sill very careful like. And there in the yellow stream of a gas lamp, his father and a woman in a cotton dress and tired out shawl stood close together. The woman being coyly suggestive was a sign Charlie recognized. The boy knew his father had every intention of bringing her up to the room, then disappearing his son, so he could get between the woman's knees.

Zacharia was putting forth the charm but Charlie knew that

woman wouldn't surrender to sweet words or easy laughter, not to kindness either for that matter, but only to the weightly feel of a seated Liberty dollar.

"Mister Griffin. Excuse me, sir."

Upon hearing that familiar voice, Zacharia turned to find his son there on the hotel stoop.

"Mister Griffin," the boy repeated.

Zacharia scratched at the stubble on his chin in quiet wonderment, trying to ascertain what in hell was going on.

"Your wife asked me to come down, sir…and tell you the baby is not well." Charlie pointed upstairs. "She's singing to him now."

Sure enough, you could hear the singing.

"She needs you, sir. She asked me to get you up there quick as a cat."

Well, the lady with Zacharia was brandishing a stare that was the second coming of rage. She turned and started off, but Charlie grabbed at the small purse she was carrying. By the time she reacted he was pawing through the damn thing.

"Well I'll be—," cried the woman.

"I just wanted to make sure you hadn't already clipped him."

He handed her back the purse, which she tore from his grasp. "Straight out of some savage garden, aren't you?"

"Yes, ma'am."

She walked off into the Brooklyn night, leaving a trail of invective behind her that was mighty impressive.

Zacharia went and sat down on the hotel stoop. "What was that sham all about? You mind telling me?"

"I didn't feel like sleeping up on the roof so you could get between her knees."

"Well," said his father. From his coat pocket Charlie's father took out a knotted up handkerchief weighted down with silver. "I hooked up with a colored fella tonight and worked a shill with him. Very slick." He tossed the handkerchief to his son. "Add that to your estate. I was going to get you your own room, by the way."

Charlie headed inside, counting out the silver.

"When you act like this Charlemagne...you cause me great concern."

They lay in the dark sharing the one bed. The moon above the Brooklyn Gas Works, the hotel silent, father and son, together with their secret thoughts.

"Pop, I want to ask you. If we get the money—"

"If? Where's your sense of enlightenment, boy?"

"We goin' straight to Cincinnati, right? No side roads?"

"I've been wearing out the pages of *Phelps Traveling Guide* plotting out the route."

"I wonder how Mother is getting on?"

"Seeing you," said his father, "will be like Christmas, Thanksgivin', and her birthday all snowballed into one."

"I talk to her sometimes." Charlie hesitated. "I tell her we're coming. Not to lose hope."

Zacharia clasped the boy's shoulder.

"Been thinking about where we'll all live?"

"The asylum's in Cincinnati," said Zacharia. "And Porkopolis *is* the gateway to the West. Plenty of itinerants, German breweries, and gambling. Perfect for our line of work."

Charlie lay on his back with his hands clipped together behind his head. "You never had it against black folks, did you?"

"No. Why do you ask?"

"You don't hate 'em in any way?"

"Prejudice is a dangerous thing, son, when you're in the gaming racket. Disrupts the thinking."

THE VESTRYMAN

CHAPTER 5

THE VESTRYMAN would have been the last person on earth anyone, let alone Mister Beecher, would have suspected of such dark intent. But due to the unfortunate nature of his character, John Briner was tormented by quiet hatreds that forcibly powered his life. During the financial crash of '37, as a very young man, he had to forfeit his family property in the Bedford Hills section of Brooklyn for debt, a debt incurred by his penchant for ill advised gambling. He had gone to members of the church vestry at first, including Beecher, for private solicitations, but to no end. His habits precluded any such charity or good will.

Briner then sold the property to one James Weeks to pay that debt. Weeks, a black man, began a community there for colored freedmen and their families. It became known as Weeksville, and over time the property increased to a fine value.

That those of the same race close to Briner had failed him, and in succession he was forced to sell his inheritance to a black man festered in Briner to almost religious heights. Yet, over the years he performed his church duties admirably and with resolve, for his own advancement and stability, of course, as he still gambled when and where the opportunity arose.

Among the crass that he drank with and gambled with, he was a joke. "Hey," they would say, "maybe you can find some nigger to buy your boots for another turn at the wheel." Or, "How 'bout your teeth? Maybe some nigger will buy your teeth…then they can chew you to death with 'em."

It was left to Briner to collect and ultimately deliver the money that Mister Beecher had solicited.

And so a plan was put into being. Briner went to meet with two men at Blackwell Tavern down near Buttermilk Creek. A sordid place built on docking one could see the tide slopping up against the pylons through the rotting floorboards. And the stench from what was tossed into that creek defied all practicality for the drinking establishment's location.

Briner knew a rough who worked as a hardcase for a Ward Boss. A huge cracker of a man, some say the largest in Brooklyn, with a chest like a beer keg, and a mind to match. He was cool and arrogant and known as Billy Tule, though no one believed for a minute that was his rightful Christian birth name.

That night Tule brought a confidant along he introduced to Briner as only Handy. He was a Negro and Briner was not sure he could be trusted in this particular matter because of his race. But Tule, in a private conversation, gave Briner a little history on the fellow.

Handy, you see, was a runaway slave who had both his thumbs amputated on orders from the overseer where he lived as a slave. The thumbs had been axed off by a colored man, the best friend of old Handy. Yeah. The overseer had decided the thumbs were to be taken because of a personal slight the overseer believed he had suffered. And so Handy's friend was told to chop off the offending appendages or else this would be done to him by none other than Handy himself. And so Handy was made a cripple.

In the quiet months that followed the incident, Handy lay in wait, brooding and plotting. When the time came, he murdered his once friend. He then went about the business of slitting the overseer's throat in his sleep. And then, moving about the darkened house of the overseer, he murdered the overseer's wife, his daughter, and the slaves who attended him.

Tule also told Briner, as if this were a mark in Handy's favor, he was an alcoholic and an expert with knives in spite of the debilitating handicap.

CHAPTER 6

WORD CAME FROM BEECHER the next day, and Zacharia was most shamefully exuberant, prancing about the hotel room like some ridiculous piper at how well the fleece was going down.

They were to meet at the Gloucaster family home. Beecher would be in attendance. A cashed bank draft would pass hands, and there was to be a farewell meal and a prayer session for their success.

Charlie was perched on the window sill taking in all this foolishness, and said, "Do I have to wear the brace again?"

"Sorry, son. No miracles until we have our hands on the money."

"Then we go straight to Cincinnati."

The smile on his father's face smoothed out a bit and the boy, always vigilant for signs, felt a whisper of concern. "Cincinnati… right?"

"Even God couldn't convict me of lying about that."

The Gloucasters, it turned out, were a fine black family living in a fine house in a good downtown Brooklyn neighborhood.

The husband was a Presbyterian minister and his wife, Elizabeth, had gone from being a domestic for a Quaker family to one of the city's most successful businesswomen. "The queen of tidy profits" is how she was called in some quarters, but in others—those of a mind akin to John Briner—the woman was a foul nigger bitch with the blood of the Jew lender running through her veins. Add to that enmity, the fact the Gloucasters had entertained in their home many people of influence who were engaged in the fight for freedom, from Frederick Douglas to John Brown.

Zacharia put on quite a show, from sweeping humility at being in such company, to a purposeful pride that he was even an insignificant player in this grand cause.

Charlie, on the other hand, watched in silent amazement. He had never lived in a house so nice; he had hardly ever been in a house so nice. And to realize this was the home of black people. All the black people he knew lived in rural shanties with leaking roofs and filth, or waterfront hutches not fit for rats. And how many lived on the dodge, their homes being the woods or fields where they slept and shat.

He stood there politely being introduced to the Gloucaster children, one by one, with their neat clothes and good manners and their aura of happiness.

It all touched a nerve and the natural weakness of life crept in. He was a homeless boy, a nothing, on the dodge with a larcenous father, living from one scam to another.

We drink from bitter waters and so drown in the process. He was suddenly jealous of these children and their life. A heartsick jealousy that consumed and poisoned him to the point where he was fraught with anger.

When John Briner arrived with the leather satchel, Charlie was genuinely glad to shill them of the money. And as a moment presented itself where he could be alone with his father, Charlie whispered, "They're rich. This is the kind of place people rob." And Zacharia winked at the boy and eyed the paper currency, as if to say, "That's what we're doing."

Funny, Charlie should have felt joy at that moment, but he did not. He felt shame, no matter what direction he turned.

Before they sat down to the meal, the Reverend Gloucaster gathered everyone up, adults and children alike. He had them form a circle there in the sitting room, except for his oldest daughter. She went to the piano and sat. The Reverend then requested all go to their knees and take hold of the persons' hands beside them. Charlie, having that bad leg, was given a chair to sit on as a humane courtesy. Then, with his daughter in accompaniment, the Reverend led them in song.

> *Let us break bread together on our knees,*
> *Let us break bread together on our knees.*
> *When I fall on my knees with my face to the rising sun,*
> *O Lord, have mercy on me.*
>
> *Let us drink wine together on our knees,*
> *Let us drink wine together on our knees.*
> *When I fall on my knees with my face to the rising sun,*
> *O Lord, have mercy on me.*
>
> *Let us praise God together on our knees,*
> *Let us praise God together on our knees.*
> *When I fall on my knees with my face to the rising sun,*
> *O Lord, have mercy on me.*

Everyone knew the song, except for Charlie and his father, and sitting in that chair while they sang away, the boy came to feel like some fragment of a person and a pure embarrassment, something disembodied, a cast out, but from what he did not know.

He had been staring at the carpet, avoiding the eyes of those around him, when he chanced to look up. One of the Gloucaster children, a girl about his own age, was stealing a glance at him. He tried to read her expression. Was she inwardly appalled by what she saw? Charlie Griffin...the lame heathen. When they made eye contact, the edges of her mouth began to crinkle. Was that a sign there was sympathy in her heart for his plight? Maybe it was simple pity. He wished some celestial life saver to just come along and whisk him right out of the room.

CHAPTER 7

TULE AND HANDY had taken up their station in an empty lot beside a boardinghouse a few doors down from the Gloucaster home. Briner had pointed out Griffin and his crippled son, and the two men waited in turn where they could watch without being seen. Handy nursing a flask and Tule, his Meerschaum pipe carved in the likeness of a lewd woman and a snake.

"I don' know why we's sittin' here," said Handy. "Let's lie in wait in theyz hotel room. Do the killin' there."

"What if they bank the money when they leave here and are carryin' a draft?"

"I takes the boy. Plier out a couple of his big teeth. Show the damn bloody things to his daddy. That'll bring 'em religion. We be countin' out cash, soon enough."

"I don't think they'd be lingerin' in Brooklyn," said Tule. He drew on his pipe. Motioned with it to make a point, as was his way. "Which means they'll probably ferry to Manhattan for the railroads."

"Possible."

"I say the killin' is done in Manhattan or some point beyond. Too close to here and so soon leavin' the nigger house might 'rouse suspicions. I don't believe Briner would do so good with that. He's short on sand."

"What difference?" said Handy. "Youz gonna kill Briner anyways. A blind cat can see that."

The discussion went on no longer, for Handy saw a flock of niggers gathering up on the Gloucaster porch to make their goodbyes to Zacharia Griffin and his crippled son.

Missus Gloucaster came up to Charlie, and said, "Would you mind if I put my arms around you and wish you a proper good-bye? Or would that be too impertinent?"

"No ma'am," said Charlie. "That would be…fine. I guess."

The lady came forward. She embraced the boy tightly, patting his shoulder, and she whispered to him, "When you're feeling low, or frightened, remember…God is present in all things." She then stood away and saw the boy's hair hanging down his forehead, and in a motherly moment, brushed it back.

• • •

They hadn't covered three blocks when the pain of that brace was enough, and Charlie pleaded, "I need to get this thing off."

"The brace? Now?"

"It's carving me up."

Zacharia took to looking back up the street. Just their luck will have one of the Gloucaster kids come running along, or maybe Beecher passing in that overdone carriage of his.

"You want to hex us?"

"I want to be done with it."

"At the hotel," said his father, as he shoved the boy forward.

In their room, Charlie couldn't shed that torture device fast enough, and for the last time, too. His father sat on the bed and opened the leather packet with over four thousand dollars inside. He wanted to see the money one more time.

"Come here and get a feel for it, boy."

Charlie was more intent on ridding himself of that wool suit.

"Throw me your coat," said Zacharia.

The plan was to beat it out of Brooklyn on the quick to Manhattan and the trains west. Charlie was getting back into old road clothes. He tossed his father the coat.

It was a worn thing that Charlie wore, all frayed to hell and not worth a shit. Zacharia had already unseamed the collar and the lining along the border spine and shoulders. He began to take bills from the leather packet, create smaller pads of them, and place them in the lining of the coat, arranged just so you'd never know anything was there. He went to sewing the lining back in place. Then, joking, said, "We got this thing just about sewed up, don't we?"

They would ditch their nice suits and get back to their filthy rags so no one would suspect they were carrying anything of value. They'd be just a couple of road paupers. American itinerants on the move across the nation, like a generation around them.

While Zacharia went about all that sewing, the boy gathered up his few possessions and packed them in his haversack, wrapping them in a sheet of sailcloth he used as a slicker against the rain. *The Phelps Traveling Guide* lay on the floor by the bed, and Charlie scooped it up.

His father always had scraps of paper he'd written on stuffed into the damn thing and these fluttered out when Charlie snatched up the *Phelps*. He went about picking up the scraps and half sheets of stationery, when one note caught his eye. It was a traveling schedule, but it was not to Cincinnati and the asylum where his mother was housed.

"So," said Charlie, "you're willin' to be a deceitful man, even where I'm concerned?"

His father looked up from the sewing. It didn't take much to connect the boy's statement to that bit of stationery he was holding.

"You weren't planning on going to Cincinnati? And getting Mother out of that place? And making a home? And taking care of her proper, like people do? And seein' her well?"

"How can I tell it…How can I explain—"

"It's no business to you how much you hurt me with this. You can lie to me straight up. Just like you would a mark. That's what I am in this."

His voice had grown more and more strained. The boy was trapped between tears and rage. His father saw such despair in that face, as if all hope had died.

Charlie slung the haversack strap over his shoulder. He put on his cloth railroad cap and tucked it down tight. He was not listening to a word coming out of his father's mouth.

"I'll wait for you at the ferry," said Charlie. "Or maybe you'll just take off with the money on your own."

CHAPTER 8

CHARLIE WAS OUT OF THAT HOTEL and hauling it down to the ferry like something exploded from a cannon. Tule and Handy were loitering in an alley between the hotel and a tanyard fence beside it. The alley, from the smell of it, was a place where people conveniently relieved themselves.

"Dat boy," said Handy. "It wuz him."

Tule chased after that wraithlike vagabond with his eyes, watched him sprinting among the drays and freight wagons. "Our boy's a cripple," he said.

"Our boy'z the chigger that just run'd past."

"If you're right, boy, there'z gonna be a deadliest case of the colic going around in some quarters."

They waited. Their boots sticking to the muddy ground where people had pissed and shat. Finally Zacharia Griffin made his appearance. He was carrying a deplorable looking carpetbag and outfitted in shoddy clothes, topped off by a slouch hat a field hand wouldn't be caught dead wearing. "A sure far cry," said Tule, "from the uptown gent of a few hours ago commiserating with niggers and the like."

They followed after Zacharia to the ferry, moving among the foot traffic and pull horses. And this Zacharia, he was taking his own sweet time, like a man walking into the sunny disposition of the world.

Merchant wagons weighed down with haul and horse drawn carriages were loading onto the ferry when Zacharia arrived. Charlie was already on board the catamaran, leaning against the railing over where people fished from the deck. He was a solitary portrait to be sure and when he saw his father he was none too happy. He spit into the sound as Zacharia approached and tossed him the coat. "Put it on," said Zacharia.

Charlie obeyed without a look or word of acknowledgment, as Tule walked by with Handy following. They were looking the boy and his father over with muted stares. Then they took up a post in the doorway to the passenger cabin.

"I tole ya that chigger was da one," said Handy. "Look at 'em. Actin' like po' boys. Theze some checke'd bastards I don't mind tellin' ya."

"He was slick enough," said Tule, "to enlist a child to play cripple. That's some almighty."

"Got my eyes on da carpetbag. And feelin' da money."

The ferry bell rang and the steam engine started turning that center wheel and great flumes of water were being spumed up as they pulled from shore.

"I want you to witness something," said Zacharia.

He took from his pocket the crumpled paper Charlie had thrown at him. He struck a match with his thumb and put flame to paper. He held that scrap between two fingers as bits of burning ash were carried away on the wind. The boy was neither moved nor satisfied.

"You don't understand, Charlie."

"You think I don't see things," said the boy. "You think I'm just your own ignorant field hand, here to do your bidding. But I can have my heart broke as easy as the next fella, in case you didn't know."

The boy started away now, not wanting to expose any more of his pain or grief.

"I had my reasons, Charlie."

"And I have mine. And mine are better."

• • •

Charlie made his way among the travelers to the prow of the ferry to be free and clear of his father and escape into the salt air and sunshine, when he sees this character, for that is how he would best describe him, wearing a wide brimmed hat at a cocky angle and an easy fitting broadcloth shirt, reading aloud from this wisp of a book he had resting in one hand. His voice was giving the wind as good as it got.

"There was a child went forth every day. And the first object he look'd upon and received with wonder, pity, love or dread, that object he became. And that object became part of him for the day, or a certain part of the day, or for many years, or stretching cycles of years."

Charlie was but a few paces away, watching most curiously. "What are you doing, mister?"

The man had huge, intense eyes that gave the boy a studying. "I'm reading a poem."

Charlie looked about. There were people scattered along the railing but not a one showed signs of being his audience.

"To who?" said Charlie.

The man made a sweeping gesture with an arm. "The flood tide below me…those seagulls floating high there in the air…these men and women travelers in their usual attire…the ferry…that sun…those clouds racing to the west…the swift current and gladness of the river… that glorious place called Manhattan Island…myself…you…the soul."

When done, he just stood there bathed in the moment, smiling. A little strange, Charlie thought, but damn well spoken and clear voiced.

"What's your name?"

"Charlie."

"Short for Charles."

"Actually my birth name is Charlemagne. My mother named me that, but—"

"A regal name. But cumbersome for everyday living. Right?"

"I got rousted plenty in school for it, so I settled on Charlie."

"My name is Walter. I am known by Walt."

He put a hand out and the two shook like gentlemen.

"Know how to read?" Walt said.

"My mother was a school teacher in Ohio," said Charlie. "Taught me to read right proper. Until they put her in the asylum. That's where we're going now to get her out. Me and…my father."

"Got a favorite book? Every boy has a favorite. Cooper…*Last of the Mohicans?*"

"*The Three Guardsmen,*" said Charlie, perking up.

"Ahhhh…d'Artagnan. Yes. There is a d'Artagnan in every one of us. And if there isn't…there should be."

Charlie was close enough now to Walt to see the open book. There was an engraved picture printed on the frontpiece, and damn if it didn't look like Walt there.

Charlie pointed to it and Walt quietly admitted the likeness was him.

Well, thought Charlie, if this ain't a cage shaker. The wind blew and the air filled with a spray of fresh salt, and just talking with this gent, he felt washed clean for the moment of the bad thoughts that had been hounding him.

"It's an awful pretty day, Walt."

The light on the river burning against it like a high force had the boy captured in all its beauty and he looked to drink it all in, when what catches his eye…a hard looking black and the Goliath shadow beside him roosting by the passengers' station.

"Excuse me, sir. But I have to be catchin' up with my father."

As he started away, Walt called him back. Then, to the boy's amazement, he tore a page out of the book, folded the sheaf neatly and placed it in Charlie's haversack.

"What's that for, sir?"

Walt didn't answer really. He just said, "Good luck with you, d'Artagnan."

CHAPTER 9

THE TRUTH IS A POOR BEDFELLOW, you may sleep but there is little else. What Zacharia hated most about himself was that he failed to lie well enough. He had let the boy believe too much, allowed the child's mind to run away with new found hope. Of course, that hope helped to get Charlie to work hard perpetrating their confidences. But the worst that could happen was, at the asylum there being even the least hint of releasing the boy's mother to their care.

He felt suddenly ashamed, but the shame was for *not* being ashamed at having such thoughts. He was a selfish man, he knew that. He had even told his wife Beck—her birth name was Rebecca Moriarity, but he called her Beck—this very fact their first night.

The truth had been the worst poison of all, because it had no effect on her feelings whatsoever. There's nothing worse than misplaced honesty, and so all suffered.

He had been running a Find the Lady scam at a traveling carnival that had set up on the Cincinnati waterfront. Beck had recently graduated and was teaching her first time at an all black school in "Little Africa." A job cursed with hostility. They had met in the crisp night air with torch light and music and the rattling wheels from the games of chance. Everywhere the potent lure of excitement and a pure white moon. Attraction equals blindness, and now all he had left were flashes of memory and a twelve-year-old boy. The price and reward of being entrapped by innocence. It was the stuff of hokey melodrama, if the world don't mind him thinking so.

Charlie was suddenly beside him. Flushed and short of breath. "Two men," he said, "a huge fella and a black who's got no thumbs. Don't look now...they're back over by the far doorway."

"So?"

"I saw them in the alley by the hotel when we left."

Zacharia made this inconspicuous move, leaning down like he was checking something in his carpetbag, just enough to look past Charlie. The sun was high and hot on the deck, and he thought to himself, those two look like they might have left a few funerals in their wake.

"They ain't shopkeepers," said Zacharia.

"I think they're followin' us."

Zacharia kept his calm for the boy's sake, "You got a hot imagination...but we'll see."

CHAPTER 10

THEIR DESTINATION WAS THE TRAIN TERMINAL over on Chambers Street. The railroad followed the Hudson River up to Albany, then linked west to the Ohio border.

As they headed off the ferry, Zacharia made it clear, "I do the looking, not you."

They wandered up Water Street. The thoroughfares along the harbor were jammed with merchant wagons and drays and flat carts pulled by a single horse. It was a hot day and the men had merciless frank language for anyone and anything that held them from their way.

Zacharia intentionally drifted over to Pearl Street and then Beekman. Always with a watchful eye. The blocks there lined with wholesalers, grocers, ship repair businesses, foundries, printers, iron-mongers, hatters, upholsterers, sail makers, metal wares, commission merchants. The street was cast with the shadow of tenements where kids hung about the roofs spitting down on their enemies, and women looked out windows sooted from furnace smoke. Men on stoops drank ale and complained or played cards, and there were men filthy with hard labor and sweat while derelict men and grey looking desperate men went along the dusty roadway in search of something better or, at least, some scrap with promise. Charlie had never seen anything like this. Never experienced anything this immense. It was as if the whole world had been distilled down into a few square blocks.

The boy knew without knowing, his father's silence spoke well enough. "Why are they following? Do they know?"

Zacharia said nothing. But any profiteer who was even half sharp could figure it out. He and the boy were dressed as road tramps so not worth robbing. They had been marked like Cain, and with wicked efficiency. Not by Beecher or the Gloucasters—they had the cause in their souls. But by someone in a church pew close by. The hands of the vestry had something to do with that pair of dice following them. Briner…he'd seemed to be convivial in that nauseating way frauds have. Men with God in one pocket, and the devil in the other.

"Do unto others…," said Zacharia.

Charlie asked what his father had said, but Zacharia shrugged him off. The boy drew closer to his father the longer this went on. Anger aside, there was blood on the line, family to stand with. He kept in step now with his father's shadow.

"It'll be all right," said Zacharia.

They then turned into Broadway, and the whole world changed.

• • •

The street was a merciless jam of omnibuses with well to do passengers and fancy carriages driven by horses at least as temperamental as their owners. A hotel took up a city block over there, a new city hall where a photographer was taking pictures with salted paper over here. A steepled church adorned one corner, a vaulted auditorium where they gave away cigarette cards of its elegant entryway near another. And everywhere, endless posters painted in eye grabbing colors on wood about plays and shows where one could see everything from world renowned artists to an underdressed female chorus. A litany of ostentatiously attired women showing off or shopping cruised the sidewalks, and tailored men on horseback matched them guile for guile.

Such a grand aura out of filthy streets. Zacharia would have done anything, given anything, surrendered or sold anything to be part of such beautiful madness because he could feel the gullibility of the world there to be had. The thievery behind the smiles spoke to everything that was him. If circumstances were different this would be home, but there was devilment to deal with.

Something up the block caught his eye. It looked to be a mob, and Zacharia said, "I'm in the grips of an idea, boy. So come on and be quick."

Charlie hustled off after his father.

"Where we goin'?"

Zacharia pointed. A short march up Broadway there were women, hundreds of them, maybe as many as a thousand, all of them with their small babies, all of them crowding the entry to a five story building. And painted onto the facade in God's most garish lettering—BARNUM AMERICAN MUSEUM.

CHAPTER 11

It was a scene all right, straight out of some funny paper madhouse—young matrons and their precious little ones flocked all the way out into the street, and no shortage of tourists either or cynical city gawker. Charlie followed his father right into the heart of all that pent up motherhood, and shouted, "What is all this?"

Zacharia pointed to a line of posters by the entry and the boy had to rise up on his toes to get above all the jabbering craziness, to see:

NATIONAL BABY SHOW
THE CROWNING ACHIEVEMENT OF MOTHERHOOD
CASH PRIZE FOR WINNERS

"What are we doing here?"

"Here," said Zacharia, "is where we wait for that pair of dice. And I confront 'em."

The boy thought his father was just making talk, but far from it. He had that cold eye of decision. He then took up a spot in that sea of mothers with their babies. Babies in carriages, babies in cribs, in rockers, babies sleeping in their mother's arms, or googling foolishly, babies sucking on sugar tits, babies crying, being cooed by their mothers, or staring at who knows what while their mothers sized up the competition.

Zacharia found himself a little street space and kneeled down. He set his carpetbag in the dusty road. He opened it and carefully slipped out the pocket Colt he carried there. He tucked it into his belt inconspicuously where he could keep it concealed by his coat. He saw Charlie had a look of grim concern, and he tried to disarm the boy with a story.

"You know this Barnum. He's quite the hustler." Zacharia closed the bag and stood. "He had this colored fella he claimed had discovered a weed and if you took it as a tonic it would turn you white. Well...Barnum put this colored fella on exhibition and people paid every day to come and see him turning white."

"Is there such a thing?"

Zacharia grinned with mischievous joy. "Nothing can turn a fella white unlessin' they're born white. It was a hoax boy. A confidence scheme. Barnum made a fortune. The colored fella, I bet, got run out of town on a rail. That's more of Barnum's shenanigans up there."

Zacharia pointed to rows of posters on the building facade... Tom Thumb, The Smallest Man in the World...The Maine Giantess...The FeeJee Mermaid...Chang and Eng the Siamese Twins... The trunk of a tree where the disciples of Christ sat.

"This is the greatest con job in the world, Charlie... this town would be perfect for you and me. After we get your mother...maybe we come back here and challenge the fates. It's something to think about anyway."

There was a tone in his father's voice that Charlie easily recognized when his father either had too much jack, or was being dragged through the sorrows.

Charlie caught sight of the two now well back in the street—
"the dice" as his father called them—the tall one a shoulder above
the heads of the women. The man was waiting on an omnibus to
pass. With dust kicking up in a trail of its wheels, he started forward.
He was scanning the crowd, with the black following. That one wore
a black coat, black pants, and a grimy shirt, and didn't he look like
the devil's own undertaker?

"Let's give them the money," said Charlie.

"Not listening, boy."

A woman had gotten up on a soapbox and took to addressing
the crowd with staunch vehemence. "This whole pitiful excuse for
a contest is not only a human shame, but a social disgrace. It is
unfair and prejudiced." She had a high pitched scratchy voice that
pretty quick got people's attention, but engendered no heartfelt
solicitation. "Where are the Negro babies?" she said. "Where are the
Chinese babies...the dark skinned babies...the obviously foreign
babies...Or what Mister Barnum calls the unhealthy babies. And
what is an unhealthy baby? Could it be his secret phrase for 'poor'
baby? And that this contest is his attempt to aggressively appeal to
the more well to do, as a means of making money. I ask you ladies to
help me shut down this ill hearted venture."

The woman had a small cadre of followers, but beyond that, she
faced a pretty harsh climate of catcalls and stormy verbal disdain.

Just to cause trouble, Zacharia whistled and applauded for the
poor, dear soul. He winked at his boy. He too now saw his hunters,
spreading out, trying to see their way through the crowd.

Zacharia tapped the boy on his shoulder. "You know," he said,
"I've been pretty much of a wreck as a father. "I've had moments of
high tide, but mostly...Here's what I need you to do." He reached

into his pocket and flipped the boy a quarter. "You go in like you're seein' the exhibition. Find an exit around back. Head right for the depot. I'll meet you there. If I'm not there by the time the train leaves—"

"Won't do it."

"This is part of the hustle, boy. You take the train till you get to a stop called Poughkeepsie. You get off there and wait."

"Leavin' you ain't good!"

Zacharia pulled the boy by his collar to him. He brushed the boy's coat like he was his personal valet. "You know…you're a better man than I am already. And at our age. Most of the time anyways. Of course, you can't let that dull the edge."

"Just give them the money."

CHAPTER 12

CHARLIE OBEYED HIS FATHER, even though it tore at him. He loved his father more than he was infuriated by him, but sometimes the boy just forgot. His father had that way of making Charlie disbelieve there was a heart beating under all that duplicity.

Charlie paid his quarter and joined a stream of patrons entering the museum. The last he saw of his father, he was moving through a jam of baby carriages with their little bundles of joy.

When Zacharia stepped into the street Tule spotted him right off and he whistled to Handy then pointed. To say the two men were surprised to see an unconcerned Zacharia approaching them didn't quite nail it. They came to a halt about half a dozen paces apart with horse carriages and riders moving all around them. A steady stream of rising dust to catch their words.

"I'd have put on a clean shirt and full suit, but I didn't expect to be in such elegant company," Zacharia said.

"You're quite the confidence man," said Tule.

"It was Briner, wasn't it?"

"And that business with the boy. You shucked them, all right."

"Never put your faith in the vestry," said Zacharia. "Some old Israelite should have writ that up in Proverbs."

"Where is the boy?" said Tule.

"What are you? A factory thug? Tavern pimp? And this thing here." Zacharia jerked his head toward Handy. "What cage did you loose him from?"

"Who ya' talkin' like dat?"

"You're no freedman," said Zacharia. "You're a runaway. Look at those hands. You sassed your master and he clipped you. Then you skedaddled it north. I'll bet there's wanted posters of you from here to creation. So if you don't want me to start howlin'…mind your manners."

"You better watch yourself," said Tule. "This nigger's got some bad blood in him. And he might take it out on your boy."

Zacharia spit in the road.

"Just give us the money," said Tule.

"He bein' too slick," said Handy. "Let's ass't the boy. Now… where is he?" He looked about like he might be anywhere. He even bent down as if to be looking for tracks. Then he made like he was smelling the air, really working his nostrils. "Handy's nose says he at the rail station. Just ov'r cuppel streets."

"You're God's own genius, aren't you?" said Zacharia.

"Just the money," said Tule. "You keep it, you're a wanted man. A cell in the Tombs is the best you can expect."

A couple of gents on horseback came trotting right among them. No excuse-me's, no polite anything. Tule took to cursing after them.

Zacharia tossed the carpetbag at Tule's feet. That huge head of his with its shabby beard stared down at it. "How do I know it's in there? And you don't have it belted to you?"

"You start by squatting down and opening the damn thing."

He took a long deep 'sizing up the situation' breath. "I hope for your sake you're a bad liar."

He took the chance. He squatted down over the bag and as he did, he said to Handy, "Be watchful, boy."

There was a moment when Tule had to avert his eyes from Zacharia to get hold of the lock clasp. It was then Zacharia pulled the pocket Colt from his belt, cocked the hammer, and fired into the face of one Billy Tule.

Tule was surprised all right. A shocked gruff sound came up out of his throat. It was a dead man sound. But the hammer jammed. There was a faulted click you could hear on the dry air. Nothing more. Only Zacharia standing there with an extended arm.

In that heartbeat, Handy was on him. He carried a Lagniappe scalping knife with a nine inch blade and a handle he'd whittled down so he could grasp it right with his four fingers. It was a native weapon made of the finest iron that he'd robbed off a white man he'd murdered for his clothes.

Before Zacharia could recock the hammer and fire another shot, Handy had jammed the blade right up through the musculature under the ribs, and the heart of one Zacharia Griffin was shorn open. He sunk to the street dead like all the bones had been pulled from his body.

Charlie was heading up Ann Street when he heard screams from the direction of the museum. He stopped to look back past the rattling wagons to see where men were rushing across the intersection, and Charlie knew absolutely that he'd lost him.

Tule had gotten hold of the carpetbag and was sprinting up Broadway. In the moments before anyone realized there was a murdered man lying there in the dusty street, Handy had used his knife to tear away Zacharia's shirt, then his belt, and lastly his trousers. He caught up with Tule at a dead run and the two men slipped into an alley across from the depot. Trying to catch their breath Tule looked through the bag while Handy kept watch to see if anyone was in chase.

A rolled up suit, an extra shirt, socks, a pair of drawers, a pipe. Tule cast one after another aside until all that was left…Tule laughed in disgust. He held up a small family Bible with a few yellowing envelopes tucked between the pages.

"This is all of it," said Tule.

Handy grabbed the bag. He had to look for himself to believe it was true. Cursing his fate, he cast the bag aside. "Dat dead man—"

"The boy," said Tule. "He has the boy carryin' it. And he comes right up to us."

THE MANSION
OF HAPPINESS

CHAPTER 13

HIS LIFE NOW WOULD BE FOREVER ALTERED. His life would be everything up to this moment, and then everything after this moment. The split would be as obvious as the demarcation of a fence, a wall, a river, or the path of a fire. And it would be as dramatic and painful and life changing as the split in the very nation itself.

Charlie knew going back to see would be dangerous, he knew having to see would be devastating. But his heart demanded it even above his will to resist the desire, with a force liken to the inexorable turning of the earth.

There were people screaming in all directions out in front of the Barnum Museum. Women cried, women hid their children's faces from a scene of stark violence, attendees of the museum rushed about trying to mitigate this catastrophe, men pointed in the direction the killers had run, while others crowded around the place where the body lay in the street.

The sun burned so hot suddenly upon the boy's face, so hot upon his eyes, he could not really see. Had it been that blazing and bright a few minutes ago? He felt swimmy headed, like when he had a fever and his body seemed to be moving beyond his will.

The crowd separated momentarily to allow two policeman access who had come upon the scene. The boy recognized the dead man's brogans, the canvas trousers, the shoddy road coat. It was his body where blood spread out in the dust…the husk of his body anyway—but it was not his father. Not the man, not the heart and soul of the man, lying there in the brilliant midday.

● ● ●

The terminal was on Chambers Street and Charlie knew they might well be lurking there. He also knew, from having seen with his own eyes when he arrived in the city with his father, how trains leaving the terminal were pulled along slowly by a dummy engine, and led by a man on horseback giving notice of its approach by waving a flag. It would be easy for the two who murdered his father to board there and search the cars.

The train would cross town after that till it reached the river. It was there the dummy engine was replaced by a real locomotive to begin its ride following the waters of the Hudson up to Albany. It might make the most sense to board over there, once the locomotive had been coupled and the train was really moving.

His heart was either racing, or so constricted he could not breathe. He was afraid and he was alone and he was being hunted. He looked back over his shoulder in dire fear and he had to keep wiping the sweat from his eyes time and time again. He stopped strangers, one after another, and asked how best to get to the terminal by the river because he could not hold a thought in his head as there was only the image of his father's lifeless body sprawled across the gateway to his thoughts.

I am alone—the phrase took on monumental proportions. It dwarfed the world around him, which was already beyond his conception. There then came over him a sense of loss so profound that it felt as if he might be turned into measureless dust.

He could try and hand the money over in an attempt to save himself. To escape the dark will of a world that could be unforgiving to his plight. But something inside him rebelled at the thought. He did not understand, or even sense what that something was, he just knew that it was.

There were long shadows across the Hudson when Charlie made the river. The Palisades on the far shore already a dark battlement. He took up a spot about two blocks north of the terminal. There was a shantytown of sorts on a slope, and high weeds that rose all the way to a dock that had burned and was now just charred rubble where some local nasties were drinking and flinging bottles. Charlie burrowed down in the high weeds and watched. His *Phelp's Guide* told him the next passenger train out of there was the one to jump. He'd slung up on trains before with his father, so he knew the play of it.

He watched a woman at shantytown setting her laundry on a line. She had a couple of small kids with her. The sheets were like shiny flags in the failing sun. He closed his eyes. He had not cried. He realized how hungry and thirsty he was. He put his head down to rest and soon after he felt a slight tremoring in the warm earth.

It was the train. The boy sat upright and he was primed as a rabbit searching for predators. He could feel the train picking up speed. It wasn't long before the black face of that locomotive came shouldering up the tracks, the rattling of the iron wheels growing louder and louder. He was half up now, his brogans digging in against the earth to give him a quick start and as soon as the shadow of that hulking beast was on him, Charlie came out of the brush like a shot.

And the trap was sprung.

He heard them before he saw. He was just yards from the passenger cars shuttling past. They were on both sides of the track—Billy Tule and Handy—and they were coming on at a punishing pace. Charlie reached out for the stair guard but his shoes caught in the rail ties and he stumbled and lost his grip. With arms flailing he righted himself. He could hear them screaming, their voices louder, ugly, enraged, vile, desperate.

He reached out toward the last car. A wall of latticed sunlight in his eyes as it swept past. Fueled by abject fear, by mad determination, by the sight of the two men hounding up his back, he stretched out for the railing and this time he held fast, this time he wrapped one arm around the other, and this time he pulled himself aboard.

CHAPTER 14

CHARLIE STOOD ON THE PLATFORM holding tight to the railing while the colossus of the city receded into streams of deepening shadow. Tule was a huge man carrying too much weight and he began to falter and so fell well behind Handy. Charlie could hear Tule shouting, "Just get on that damn train…Don't lose him now…Leave word for me at the stations…I'll be on the next train…You hear, boy?"

Tule came to a violent stop and threw up his hands. And Handy, that black man with his black coat and black trousers was something wraithlike and wild fast, arms churning, body driving forward, lean, strong, young. The train was gaining speed, topping up over twenty miles an hour, but that bastard was gaining ground. The puffs of dust off the padding on his soles coming faster and faster.

Charlie could hear the breath pounding out of Handy's lungs. He backed into the passenger car. The last car on a train was the segregated car, and this one had its share of black folks. Workmen, travelers in poor but clean suits, a family, an old man dozing. They were staring at Charlie as he backed his way up the aisle, wondering where this white child had come from, and what in creation was he doing in this car.

The back passenger door opened violently. In the trundling doorway, like something deadly sinister, stood Handy.

"Ya not fas' enough, boy."

The blacks in the car had turned to see this coal faced stranger now stepping his way up the aisle, grabbing the backs of seats as he came on.

"Da piper, boy…Ya hear da piper?"

Charlie backed out of the car, jumped to the next and cleared the entry just a sweep of the arm ahead of Handy. The conductor was collecting tickets from a flock of whites traveling up the Hudson. Charlie came to sit so the conductor was between him and Handy.

The conductor looked the black man over.

"What are you doing in this car, boy?"

Handy's tongue moved across his dry lips.

"I'm talking to you, nigger."

"Nothin," said Handy.

"Damn right, nothing," said the conductor. "This car ain't for you. Now, git."

Handy's glance went from Charlie to the conductor. He was an older man, a short man, a heavily girthed man, pasty skinned, with loose flesh around the jaw. Handy could dispatch this bastard in one cold hard second.

"I won't tell you again, nigger."

Handy kept staring at Charlie who sat there all quiet, hands folded across his lap, a look of pure calm, unconcerned. Charlie was shaking inwardly though, but sure, at least for the time, that he was safe.

One of the men in the car stood. "You want some help tossing this buck from the train?"

"I can handle it," said the conductor. He took a step closer to Handy. "Prove the slave catchers aren't after you. Or you're not on some wanted poster. Let's see your papers."

Handy noticed a slight flicker around the edges of Charlie's mouth. If that was a smile—

Handy reached for his coat pocket. He removed an envelope and from it, took two sheaves of paper. One he handed to the conductor, who opened it, and read:

Thomas Jefferson Stone Freedom Paper
To all whom these presents shall come,
Greetings, I, William Jacobs, Notary Public
by Authority of New York State...

He read on. It was duly certified, duly recorded. The letter stated that Thomas Jefferson Stone was five feet eight inches tall, about twenty five, of firm build and extremely dark complexion, with a scar across the back of his neck.

If they only knew that Thomas Jefferson Stone was a rotting pound of flesh in some Brooklyn grave. That Handy had scoured the back street taverns and whorehouses where blacks congregated and found himself a boy about the right age and the right height and the right complexion. And one night, while they lay up together in some hovel on foundry row, Handy stove in that nigger's head with a wrench and pocketed the boy's life. The only little blemish was the scar on the back of the boy's neck which Handy recreated with an artified slash from one of his prized knives.

"Let's get a look at that scar," said the conductor.

Handy bowed his head, and bent the neck.

The conductor said, "Up."

Handy lifted his head. He tried to keep the rage in check at having to be so obedient.

He saw Charlie there, who had escaped his wrath, staring at him.

He thinks he mighty smart, thought Handy. He don' know there ain't no distance he travel I ain't gonna be dere.

The conductor tapped the stumps with the freedom certificate where once upon a time were Handy's thumbs. "How come the certificate doesn't mention those?"

Handy passed the conductor the second letter, which he looked over. The tracks were pretty rough along this stretch and he had to hold the seat backs to keep his balance:

To Whom It May Concern:
I, William Tule, assistant to Edward Lane, representative
of the 12th Ward, Brooklyn, New York, here do verify that
Thomas Jefferson Stone lost both thumbs in an accident
while in the employ...

It too was duly notarized, and duly recorded.

He handed back the letter. "Back to your car. And be quick."

CHAPTER 15

CHARLIE THOUGHT OF TRUMPETING IT to the conductor how this Thomas Jefferson Stone took part in the murder of his father on a New York Street. But he realized with an almost feral instinct born of his life that if he said as much there'd be questions, and those questions would lead to some hard interrogating that would eventually end on the doorstep of what his father and he had done. And what could Charlie expect after that?

Life in some New York reformatory most probably. And he'd heard from other boys on the road about life in a reformatory. He'd seen the hollow stares and tearful hatreds as boys relived their horror stories about acts committed upon their person that Charlie did not even understand.

No...there'd be no 'fessing up. He'd leave it to his own devices to be shed of one Thomas Jefferson Stone and get to his mother in that Cincinnati asylum.

Charlie edged up in his seat to get a look at the man hunting him. Handy stood on the platform of the segregated car. Charlie could just feel the dark stirrings underfoot. This was a night beast that would die in the hunt, no doubt about it.

Handy entered the segregated car. The blacks there wanted no trouble and avoided looking at him.

"Any ya shits got lik'r?"

He looked from face to face.

"I got money." He slapped his pocket. He started down the aisle slowly, giving off a gruff menace.

"Ya all good Christ'ns."

He kicked on the back of the seat where the workmen were gathered. They all meekly shook their heads.

"Da masta got ya all train'd."

He had nothing in common with these niggers, and wanted nothing to do with them. Then he spotted two old men seated together talking. One in a suit and wire rimmed glasses...no drinker there. But the other...

"You," said Handy. "Yel'ow eye. Ya got booz. Ya a drunk. Get it out, boy."

The old man didn't want trouble and reached for a straw suitcase. From it came a pint flask. Handy reached in his pocket and tossed the old bum a little silver. He then walked back up the aisle and leaned against the car door from where he could keep watch on the boy, and plot his taking.

• • •

Charlie sat alone looking out the passenger car window. Muted light against the glass. A single ferry crossed the solemn waters of the Hudson, framed in the window for a flashing moment. There, then gone. Only his reflection left there to tell the tale. The image of his father in his own face. The deeply set eyes filled with memories. The impact of what had happened left him desolate. He looked away. A suffering weariness stole over him. He clung to one single thought—How do I shake the hunter? How do I elude that beast?

Looking about the car—men playing cards, smoking, one curled up on the seat dozing, his hat pulled down over his face—Charlie took notice of a woman sitting across the aisle. She was an attractive lady who'd be right about his mother's age. Well dressed, eyeglasses with tinted lenses, her hair up in a stylish bun.

She offered him a quiet smile. He doffed his railroad cap like a gentleman should.

She motioned for him to come and sit across from her. He was unsure, but did so reluctantly. He kept his haversack close.

She reached for a small biscuit tin on the seat and opened the top. "The gentleman that works for me, in the segregated car, always makes too many sandwiches when we go on the train. Would you care to indulge?"

He took off his cap and stared into the tin. A neat stack of petite sandwiches awaited.

She saw he was hesitant. "They'll go to waste," she said.

"Well…thank you, ma'am." He reached into the tin. "My stomach has been raisin' a yell."

"What's your name, if I may ask?"

"Charlie Griffin."

"And mine is Missus Emmaline Watters."

She put her hand out to shake. Charlie wedged the sandwich between his teeth and shook her hand.

He posed quite an image she privately smiled at.

"I'm traveling back home to Albany," she said. "What about you?"

"Goin' to Cincinnati."

"You're rather young to be traveling all that way alone."

"I've done a lot of traveling. I came here from Kansas."

"I stand corrected," she said. "What's in Cincinnati?"

"My mother. She's in an…asylum."

"I see," said Missus Watters.

She let him eat after that and then she offered him more food. He tried to be polite and say no, but his eyes told another story. She pressed the tin his way. That was all the persuasion he needed.

"Where's your father?"

He stopped eating and just sat there. It looked to her like he was drifting. "My father…is dead."

He'd never said it before. He'd heard himself say the words. They sounded like they came from a boy he knew a long time ago.

"It's hard being so young and alone," she said.

"I'm learning, ma'am."

They sat quietly after that. The boy ate halfheartedly. She felt pity for him, and concern. She wanted to ask him why the men she'd seen from the railroad car platform were chasing him, but she felt the timing injudicious.

They rode past small bits of town seen through the trees along the windy riverbank. A man in the seat behind them said to a friend, "That's Sing Sing Prison." Charlie looked out the window. Squat grey buildings in the dusk. Plaintive clouds, men moving about in chains. A sight to forget.

They stopped at Peekskill and the conductor notified the passengers the train would be laid over for twenty minutes for track repair, and they might get off and stretch their legs.

This, thought Charlie, might be an opportunity to escape into the countryside.

In the station Missus Watters introduced Charlie to an older black gentleman who worked for her. His name was Augustus. It was he, said Missus Watters, who had made the sandwiches. Outside the station people were milling about. Charlie went to get a drink of water from a pump, but making sure it was when people were there. He drank, but was studying the woods, a road that led to the river, where he might exact an escape.

"No escap'n me, boy."

Charlie looked up.

"I can seez in da dark. Go day'z wit no sleep."

Charlie wiped his mouth. He knew enough to not give in to fear.

Handy pulled his coat way back to show the boy the knives he had sheathed to his belt. "M'sta Handy wit da knife. G't to have da money. Or I cut ya skrot'm off."

To hear, to see. The knives with their long sheaths. The raw smell of booze coming from that open mouth. A row of mean white teeth. Eyes burning with clarity. It was a window into hell he had not imagined. This was the terrible that had taken his father, and Charlie was overcome with the sudden and catastrophic violence.

"Know what da skrot'm is, boy?"

Charlie remembered and repeated something he'd often heard his father say. "Yeah…it's where you keep your brains."

He started back to the station, but Handy blocked his path just enough to be threatening, but not enough to rouse suspicion.

Missus Watters had been keeping her eye on Charlie, while Augustus explained what had happened back in the segregated car. She listened while she watched the confrontation between Charlie and the other black play out, framed as it was in the station doorway.

"Augustus," said Missus Watters, "that man means the boy harm."

CHAPTER 16

THEY SAT TOGETHER AS THE NIGHT FELL. Missus Watters noted how Charlie would look back toward the segregated car from time to time, where Handy remained pressed to the car door window, watching, like the very spectre of death itself.

Charlie put up a brave front, the lady saw that. She was trying to figure how best to broach the subject of the black who went by the name of Handy, and why he and another man were trying to run Charlie down outside the terminal.

"How would you like to pass some time playing a board game?"

The idea seemed to brighten the boy's mood. From a suitcase, she took out a box. "The Mansion of Happiness," she said. "Have you ever played it?"

He sat forward. He knew the game well. He even remembered the cover of the box, with its angelic ladies in a lush garden, and behind then a house beautiful. He'd played the game with his mother at a table in the weathered shanty, along a row of weathered shanties, a tiny rosette of light from a hanging lamp to frame their faces. A quiet, peaceful joy came upon him suddenly that he remembered having once upon a time. A joy touched with home, with love, with being safe.

Missus Watters set the open board upon the car seat. Each took a marker. She was about to set the teetotum down when Charlie reached for the spinner and began to play with it. "My mother said they used the teetotum instead of dice, to know how many squares you move, because dice were Satan and gambling."

"I remember this also," said Missus Watters.

"My father preferred dice when we played."

He and Missus Watters each took their turn spinning the teeto-tum and moving their markers along the circular track, ultimately trying to reach the Mansion of Happiness which, his mother had told him, was heaven.

But the game...it felt different now, somehow.

Along the way, if you landed on spaces of virtue called piety, truth, charity, temperance, you were rewarded and allowed to move a cer-tain number of spaces forward on your way to true happiness. Should you land on vices such as intemperance, cruelty, ingratitude, you were made to return to your previous station until it was your turn to spin again. And there were punishments for landing on certain spaces... Like being dunked in water...being pilloried...or even being sent to the house of corrections. How his father had howled at suffering these. He'd seemed to prefer the vices, thought them a pure joy.

The game had appeared so utterly simple and straight forward back then. He had believed the board, and what it said. Somewhere in the waters of memory was his mother, at the end of the game, as he'd completed the journey and achieved the mansion. She would get up and lean over his seat and cradle him in her arms until they were one. Not a word spoken. Only a silent kiss and the measureless feeling of completeness.

Charlie watched Missus Watters moving her marker along the board, stopping one space short of TRUTH. She had, the boy observed, a telling profile and such curly black hair.

She realized Charlie was staring at her. "What?" she said.

"How come you travel with this game?"

She looked out the car window. Far down a long dark slope, the drifting waters of the Hudson. A singular light burned near the shoreline, a campfire most probably. "I used to play it with my son," she said. "And now, I take it along when I go on trips. On the chance I meet someone…like you, who I can play it with."

Her voice, to Charlie, seemed touched by the forlorn. And he saw her hands, they were now clasped one over the other.

"Is your son home in Albany?"

"My son," she said, "is dead. He died with my husband two years ago."

CHAPTER 17

Charlie heard the words, "Holy Hell," come out of his mouth.

"Yes," said Missus Watters. "But not so holy."

"Is it wrong for me to ask…what happened?"

She sat back. It was quiet but for the clacking of the train wheels. "We were aboard a steamer…the Henry Clay. We were traveling from Albany to New York City."

She took to looking out the window. The very moorings of the night seemed to darken and reshape as the moon struck across the treetops.

It had been about three in the afternoon, she explained, when the Henry Clay was charting its course past Yonkers. Missus Watters was in the ladies' saloon below deck, chatting with the other women about the likes and dislikes of the day. Her husband had gone up on deck to walk the promenade, as many of the men did to escape the saloon talk of women. Her son wanted to go with him, to be one of the men.

"How fate rests on the turn of a moment," she said.

The fire started in the engine room, spidering along under the wood work by the boilers. It spread like a fury after that, up the

67

flues and through the center of the boat. The deck hulls burned like kindling and just as quickly flames rose up through the passageways to consume the canvas canopies that covered the promenade. By the time a deck hand reached the saloon to evacuate the women, the stairwell was black with smoke.

There were hundreds of people on board that August day and only two lifeboats. In a desperate attempt to save as many lives as possible, the captain turned the Henry Clay toward shore. It would be a harrowing mile to haunt the rest of his life.

The fire ravaged the center of the boat. Passengers were trapped forward, others were trapped aft. A forge of burning ash and black circling clouds made it impossible to see, and the air was like breathing in hot iron. To move through the flames forward or aft, impossible. Shouts above the roar of the burning hull to find loved ones and the savage cries of lost children a chaos of unbearable proportions.

Among those forward was Missus Watters. Pieces of her dress had been burned, the fabric strips of charred tatter. In a desperate attempt to get aft through the flames to find her husband and son, her arm was burned, her hair scored by fire.

The Henry Clay was beyond saving. There was little the captain could do but drive that steamer into shore in an attempt to save as many passengers as possible. The prow cut a twenty foot path through the sand where it crashed into a railroad embankment. The hull broke apart. Passengers were killed on impact or crushed by hull beams. The aft of the steamer rose up out of the water and was suspended there.

Water filled the engine room and waves of steam from the boiler shot up through the gaping hull scalding those on deck. The survivors that were forward jumped to the sand and saved themselves. The passengers aft were being engulfed by fire and smoke and those who could jumped into the Hudson. Some drowned because they could not swim, others were weighted down by the bulk of their clothes and perished. Survivors on shore were helpless to save children waving for help among the floating wreckage before they succumbed to the blackened tide.

Like so many others, Missus Watters walked among the wounded and the dead, slogging her way out into a lifting tide, calling her husband and son's names, searching the bodies carried on blanket stretchers, some so burned as to be almost unrecognizable. The only identification a watch or ring, a bracelet, a cameo, or a cross.

Missus Watters pulled at a delicate necklace she wore, and in her palm, showed Charlie a badly scarred crucifix. It will never be long ago, she thought, even when it is. It will always be now, even when it isn't.

Charlie sat there and listened like a quiet shadow, seeing nothing but her tender, suffering face, all kindness and gentility, and then without even realizing, he burst out crying.

He came up out of his seat and went to her and he wrapped his arms around her waist and buried his face there. He was sobbing so, a man a few seats ahead stood and looked back and Missus Watters made a hand gesture that it was alright. The man sat back down and there they both were in that darkened railroad car, two strangers connected only by the mysterious journey that is life.

She cradled Charlie, then bent down and whispered, "Are you crying for me?"

He looked up at her, his eyes red and runny with tears, his mouth trembling, the answer buried in feelings beyond his ability to bear.

She brushed slightly at his hair. She understood the vast sea of emotions even in the most stubborn heart. "Maybe, you're just crying for all of us. Is that possible? You're crying for all of us."

He looked up at her almost fawn like, and she thought, this poor suffering but brave soul caught in that powerless place between being a boy and a man. And so, she just let him cry, and cry he did until the crying softened and stilled and soon he was asleep against her.

She sat without moving after that, resigned and resting a hand upon his back and staring out into a black world of forest and stark moonlight. How many people, she thought, were trying to escape this very night, with only perseverance in the face of mortality to guide them?

CHAPTER 18

"HIDE DERE ALL YA CAN, BOY…ya nuthin' more dem a run'way nigga ya'self…an 'bout to be a catch'd."

Handy pressed to the door window like a vigilant prisoner in a cell trying to see into the length of the darkened railcar ahead, the lone pipe or cigarette all there was to light the way for his eyes.

Sipping from a pint of home brewed grain some black was selling at the train depot, mumbling to himself, drifting between hard threats and poisonous insinuations, Handy sees all of a sudden the white woman the boy had been lackeying up to come rushing out onto the platform, then stepping across to the segregated car. The Goddamn bitch, he thought, is coming in. Handy stepped back and there was a rush of night air.

Missus Watters seemed beside herself from what Handy saw. The steep pitch of her eyes desperate, as she called out, "Augustus."

He rose from his seat at the rear of the car when he heard his name, "Ma'am."

"He jumped from the train," she shouted.

"Who?"

"That boy."

Everyone who had been awake was aware when she entered. At this hour, a white woman, alone, in the segregated car, brought fear to their hearts.

"Did any of you see him jump?" She was walking down the aisle. "Did any of you see him jump?" She pointed out the windows. "A boy. He jumped from the train."

A number of passengers who had been asleep were surely awake now. The others were standing, some looking out the windows, others motionless, tentative, fearful that some unfounded wrath might come down upon them.

"The boy you were talking to?" said Augustus. "That boy?"

Handy silently made for the back of the car, bending, looking out the windows from one side to the other. The train had swept inland from the river by about half a mile or so. On both sides of the tracks were knotty stands of forest and dense brush that rushed by like malevolent shadows.

He was making for the rear platform but wasn't to be the first. Two of the black workmen were already there, like bookends searching both sides of the track line for any sign of the boy. And Missus Watters with them saying, "He's only a boy."

Handy, this poisonous being who had threatened the boy with his knives, had been taken. He had been turned fool by the boy, just as that boy and his father had made fools of Beecher and the Gloucasters. The boy had jumped from a moving train in the pitch of night with nothing but brass to outslick his hunter. And to that end, Handy pushed past the blacks on the platform, cursing them. He swung up onto the rail guard. A woman screamed out and one of the workman tried to grab Handy thinking he was accidentally going over when Handy swept his arm away and jumped.

He landed on the tracks in a crouch and held there, his eyes moving across the night like some great jungle cat. A quiet and still fury taking in the thick black pools of landscape around him. As the clacketing of the train wheels dimmed in the blue grey darkness, he waited, body taut, breathing slowly through his nose, watching, watching…

• • •

Missus Watters watched from the platform until Handy had disappeared into the dark wilds of the night.

"Do ya want me to get the conductor?" said Augustus.

"No," she said. "Take your rest."

She left the segregated car, but instead of taking her seat she opened the door to the next platform. The air was cooling precipitously as the tracks arced back toward the river. A figure was sitting there, all huddled up on the railcar steps.

"He jumped," she said.

Charlie looked up from the shadows. The boy took on a grin, all right. It could have been his father there, glowing in the ecstasy of a good play.

Charlie rose up. He had learned at the foot of a true confidence man. He had been taught what every pickpocket used in the affirmation of their trade. What every kid living on the street having to master the hustle knew if they were going to survive and be successful. They tag it as the art of distraction…to slip past the mark's defenses. There is nothing like the purity of emotional sleight of hand at exacting your will.

"Thank you for your help, ma'am," said Charlie.

As they headed back into the car, Missus Watters said, "At least he can't catch you now."

• • •

They sat together as miles of track unwound behind them.

Earlier, when Charlie had awoken from an exhausted sleep, sitting upright abruptly, forgetting where he was, he found Missus Watters there quietly watching him.

The first thing she said, "Whatever you have sewn into your coat...a man might not notice such a thing. But a woman, that could be another matter. They tend to look more closely. And I bet it might have something to do with that fellow back in the last car."

It was astonishing her being so direct...and right. Did she expect he would answer? He was in the throes of conflict but knew he had to meet her unremitting stare head on.

"When we left the thirty-fourth street terminal," she said, "I was standing on the car platform, which I had often done with my son. He loved watching trains leave the station. And this time I saw a boy running for the train. He'd come out of the brush, you see. And to my amazement he was being chased by two men. One fell behind, the other...made the train. And so did the boy. You...are that boy."

"Yes, ma'am," said Charlie, "I am." He sat back and pulled a leg up on the seat and wrapped an arm around the knee. "You're very smart."

"I have to be," said Missus Watters.

"So do I, ma'am."

His father used to tell him, "If cornered with the truth, never underestimate the power of a lie to get out of it."

As he considered what to say, how to shape the facts to comport with what he needed, wanted, something inexplicable came over him. This woman stranger with the sharply defined features and rich black hair had aroused in him feelings of deep kinship. A kinship he sensed she too felt, having lost a boy about his age and, there was the way she let him sleep across her lap. Telling details all.

This kinship made him willing to chance the idea he could tell her the cold, hard, shameful, deceitful, violent truth and still work it to his advantage.

And so he did. The Brooklyn scam, the letter signed by the Kansas abolitionists, Beecher, the Gloucasters, the damn leg brace, the jasperware with the slave on the horsehair rope. She listened with implacable calm, as if impervious to the facts, or that their reality was of no import, until he told her about the murder of his father on the streets in front of the Barnum Museum, with all those women and their babies. She struggled with that. A look of sheer pity playing out on her expressive face, and the fear of what act that Handy fellow in the segregated car might commit.

When Charlie was done Missus Watters had leaned forward, and all she said was, "What can I do to help you?"

CHAPTER 19

WHEN THEY DISEMBARKED IN ALBANY, there was a whispery mist over Castle Island that was drifting toward Farmers Turnpike. On the train, Missus Watters had written a letter to James Montgomery and placed it in an envelope. James Montgomery was one of the abolitionist names that Charlie's father had forged in the letter he gave to Henry Ward Beecher.

"On the chance," said Missus Watters, "that you go to Kansas." Then she did something that surprised Charlie. She offered him the Mansions of Happiness game. "I want you very much to have this."

"Ohhh…," Charlie shook his head no. "It was your son's."

She was not having it and took it upon herself to put the game box in his haversack. "It will be in good hands," she said.

A wagon pulled up to the loading platform at the far end of the station. It was being driven by an older black woman. She and Augustus exchanged words, and then he began to set the suitcases in the wagonbed.

Charlie put out a hand to shake and Missus Watters took it affectionately. "Ma'am, I want to thank you for everything you've done for me."

She smiled and nodded. He did not want to let go of her hand suddenly. He knew he would miss this woman so. That she had made a place for herself in his heart. She had appeared out of the devastation that was his like some unfathomable force of kindness. Asking nothing, giving all.

He stood there in his poor railroad cap and haversack and shoddy coat, a wily scrapper of a kid carrying a world of conflict on his back in that journey to manhood.

The runny grey air was closing over the loading platform and the lights of the town across the river like mournful, solitary eyes. She put her arms out and took the boy to her and she kissed the top of his head and the sides of his face time and again.

"Ma'am…I have to know something."

She regarded him thoughtfully.

"You never told me to give the money back. You never said I was wrong in what was done. I know it was. And you never, never—"

"God always has a plan."

"Excuse me?"

"There is a vast instrument at work in our lives. That much I've learned. You were on the train, I was on the train. And here we are now."

"Yes, ma'am."

She saw he did not grasp what she said. What it meant would come in time she believed. "You know," she said, "you can always come here and you'll have a place in my home."

"Thank you, ma'am."

"Would you come with me a moment? I'd like you to meet someone."

He followed her over to the wagon where Augustus and the old woman waited. Augustus had now taken the reins. Missus Watters said to the old woman, "I'd like you to meet a friend of mine. This is Charlie Griffin. He's going to Ohio…to see his mother. After that… who knows? He has a lot of decisions to make."

The old woman was sinewy, sharp eyed. She raised a hand in the gesture of a wave.

"Charlie," said Missus Watters, "I'd like you to meet my mother."

• • •

Charlie Griffin was on a train heading west. He sat alone in the last seat of the last car, before the segregated car. He had never met a person like Missus Watters, of mixed heritage, who could so perfectly pass for white. He had heard of such people in vile insults and crass jokes—some of which he did not understand—spewed out in the bars and bawdy houses he had traveled with his father.

And yet, what kept his mind busy was Missus Watters' goodness. She had never made a condemnation against him for what he'd done. And if anyone should have, or could have, it was she.

He was a tainted soul; he knew that much about himself. A raggedy swindler and masquerade artist, pickpocket and short con gamer. Goodness like he experienced in Missus Watters eluded him completely. And now, what did he have? He was alone, an almost orphan, his father lost to the streets of New York, with money sewn in his coat that he'd helped thieve. Shameful from the top of his head to the rivets in his shoes.

The hours passed. He went into his haversack for one of the sandwiches that Missus Watters had made Charlie take with him. Scrounging about, he came upon the poem that strange fellow on the Brooklyn ferry had actually torn out of his own book. It seemed that haversack was starting to fill with a collection of odds and ends he'd fetched along the way.

To pass the time, he read as he ate. He slouched back and hauled his legs up on the seat like some scruffy potentate.

There was a child went forth every day…

The phrases and ideas were foreign to him. It wasn't *The Three Guardsmen*. That got your blood up. But…he came upon a few lines that caught his eye:

> *His own parents. He that had father'd him and, she that had*
> *conceiv'd him in her womb, and birth'd him,*
> *They gave this child more of themselves than that;*
> *They gave him afterward every day—they became part of him.*

He set the pages down. Outside the window a verdant landscape stretching on to the horizon, beyond the far trees a sky touched with painterly clouds and beautiful long rivers of sunlight. But that is not what Charlie was looking for hidden there in the glass. He saw his father, oh, to be certain…in the finely lined eyebrows, the long straight nose, the full resolute mouth. But it was her he was trying to find. He smiled as if to create his mother in that smile, looking at him with joy.

Is remembering foolish? His father had almost always said as much. The past is old decayed bones; it's only now that is fluid and supple and alive.

Charlie just sat there watching, hoping she would appear to put his father's words out of his head. A boy does not always know in what ways he is being corrupted, by what deeds, what acts, what speech, what persuasions. And those who do, usually grow up before their time, grow old before their time, and some tragically die before their time.

He rested his head against the seat and silently told his mother one sweet promise after another like any boy would. And he let his imagination invite story after story in the hunt for happiness.

CHAPTER 20

HANDY HAD LEFT WORD FOR BILLY TULE at the depots all the way up to Germantown where he sat in view of the station by a ruined carriage. Nearby, a handful of blacks were waiting for the train by a sign that read– FOR COLOREDS—which had been nailed to a post by an open pit latrine in the trees.

This place was just another white outpost where blacks stood out like a rabid dog would in church on Sunday. Handy kept to himself in the dappled shade. A nice breeze cooling the nervous sweat from his back. Among the wanted posters on the station wall was one with a decidedly troubling description of the murderer. He'd taken a brazen chance and ripped away the poster. He'd then torn it into scraps and dumped it where the blacks shat.

One of the men waiting with the blacks wandered over to Handy and struck up a conversation.

"You makin' for Canada?"

Handy looked up from his pint bottle of homemade, glaring, and gave this stranger a suspicious looking over. He was young, workmanlike, in a soft way. A clerk probably. Handy wondered was he giving off signs he was a runner. "Why ya askin', boy?"

"A lot of us travelin' 'lone is makin' for Canada."

Handy sipped from his pint. "Git ya'self all safe en soun' in snow c'untry. Shit. Ya neva be safe 'til they turn'd ya inna gimcrack…Or ya dead."

Handy offered the young man the bottle and he threw his head back and took a crisp, deep swallow. He wiped his mouth on a coat sleeve and thanked Handy. Then he said, "Be ca'ful…you come 'cross too almighty."

The nigger, thought Handy, was right about that. Of course, a nigger can see things a white man can't.

The next train that entered the station saw Billy Tule come walking through a great wall of steam. Seeing Handy he guessed the worst.

"You lost him, didn't you?"

Handy told him the whole story. Motioned with the hand that held the bottle in that clumsy thumbless grip, two fingers snaked around the skinny neck.

"Think the boy really jumped?" said Tule.

Handy grinned. He said he wasn't sure, even when *he* jumped himself. But he knew how to find out. You see, he'd noticed the boy talking with a white lady at the Poughkeepsie station and that lady had herself an old nigger.

And that nigger was named Augustus, and Augustus was a real mouth flapper. And in his old man ramblings, Handy learned the white lady's name, and he learned the white lady lived in Albany. And one more thing he learned…the lady was a nigger passing for white.

• • •

Charlie was asleep on the seat like a vagabond, when a couple of brothers his age wandered in from another car hunting up a little adventure. In no time Charlie had snared them into a game of Mansions of Happiness. A two cent entry fee and—Winner take all - put a little extra spin on the game. One of the brothers had stolen a candy bag full of cheroots from a slow eyed hick of a tobacco farmer down in Chemung County who rolled and sold his own at the depot.

Huddled around that board the three boys viced and virtued to be first to the big mansion, taking turns puffing on a cheroot like they were rakish sharpies straight out of *The Three Guardsmen*. That was until the boys' father showed up in a furor, firing off a round of holy condemnations, and there Charlie was, abandoned and alone, with a bag of untapered cigars to add to his haversack.

In Buffalo there was a layover for the train that would take him on to Ohio and his mother. It was a new station, there just this year, down by the Erie Canal; the old one on Exchange Street having burnt to the ground. Now people didn't have to drag their luggage and haul their tired selves those few blocks from one train line depot to another, being as they were all housed now in the same place. Walking through the terminal Charlie picked up many conversations about the true nature of progress.

Outside the terminal were a handful of vendors selling goods and geegaws. Charlie snuck a few cents from a secret pocket and treated himself to a ginger beer and jerky, and he rambled over to a small crowd of people gathered around a fiddler and a boy in black face.

They were putting on some regular entertainment, the boy being done up in baggy pants and galluses and a floppy top hat. His face and hands all smeared with burnt cork so he was black as the bowels of Satan.

He couldn't have been but ten, and the man on the fiddle, did he roar away. The boy kicked and danced, his arms all wavy and spirited and his mouth a huge white chestnut of a smile as he sang:

Come listen all you galls and boys I's jist from Tuckyhoe,
I'm going to sing a little song, my name's Jim Crow,
Weel about and turn about and do jis so,
Eb'ry time I weel about and jump Jim Crow.

He took up a place where he could sit with his back against the station wall, sip his ginger beer, tear off strips of jerky, and just watch the show.

He had seen it before…all the jumpin' and patter, the wild exaggerated movements. But today some unseen presence seemed to be rising the curtain before his eyes, and the show looked mighty different. Mighty different indeed.

Oh I'm a roarer on de fiddle, and down in old Virginny,
They say I play de skyentific like Massa Pagannini.
Weel about and turn about and jump Jim Crow.

The boy was singing there in the throes of such sainted mockery—could it have been meant to be a boy liken to Missus Watters' son. The son lost to her in the burning of the Henry Clay. The son of the woman who'd saved his life with no expectation of reward. The woman who had offered him kindness, when his despairing soul so needed kindness. Who'd greeted his confession of a wicked act with only mercy.

Couldn't it have been the child of Missus Watters there, turned into a showboat coon to be laughed at? Her, who had befriended him with affection, who had offered him her home, when he was a homeless, heart bereft vagabond, who she so little knew.

He set his drink down. He pulled his legs up and crossed his arms over them and bowed his head so it came to rest upon his knees. A trembling reality took possession of him. And reality shows no favorites, it offers no favors, it simply is.

Traveling with his father, the world and its most hardened province always seemed a few miles yet down the road. Just off there on the lip of the horizon. You could see it, yes…like you could a phantom figure though hardly more than a dream. But it wasn't stirring in your life yet, it wasn't at contest with your soul.

At this moment, he saw in all that jumpin' and patter the cold hard reality of humiliation and hatred.

He stared down at the little patch of earth beneath him and wondered, "What am I, once I have seen this?"

CHAPTER 21

ZACHARIA GRIFFIN USED TO TELL HIS SON, "Where there is man, there is crime. You go back to the Garden of Eden and what do you got? Satan—the best damn pickpocket the world has ever known. He picked Eve's pocket, for God's sake, and the woman didn't have a stitch of clothing. Crime is as natural to man as breathing, and just as necessary. Without crime there would be no progress. It was crime, in fact, the confidence man, the gamer, the sharper playing the system, that kept the system in fine tune. Why the world owed the confidence man everything.

"And the greatest confidence job of all time was the Bible, and the churches that sprouted up out of its slickster pages. The Bible wasn't meant to keep you on your toes, it was meant to wreak havoc on your ingenuity, to leave you anxious and worried about the quick jaws of perdition. And it was all designed for one purpose. The collection plate. You didn't need to be a master pickpocket, the mark just turned their money over to you because they were hoping to buy salvation."

It was, Zacharia Griffin had thought, the most exquisite confidence play ever created. And that alone should guarantee its creators a seat in heaven, if there was such a notoriously oversold address.

Charlie sat there watching the fiddler and his boy stomping the boards, then he took to studying the crowd like he would his numbers in school and soon enough he specs out this girl, she had to be about sixteen. Neatly dressed, nothing special. She looked like a girl of good morals and good judgment. His eyes had the fix on her as she was deftly drifting from personage to personage that were crowded around the players making like she was listening to the music. A quaint smile until you noticed the darty eyes.

She stopped by a gentleman who had all the usual giveaways of a prize mark—a well tailored suit, highly polished expensive shoes, a watch chain, no mud around the bottom of the pant leg. And before you could say "Jack be nimble," her hand moved like a dainty viper and there went the wallet. She slipped it into a cloth bag and was off heading around the station. Charlie laughed to himself as he saw how the fiddler gave her a kind of glinty smile. He knew that smile, every good confidence man has it. The muscles around the mouth do their little victory lap. And he wondered, was the fiddler her father or was he getting between her knees?

Charlie was up right quick after that. The boy was running low on cash. He only had what little his father had given him that last night in Brooklyn. He'd been pretty prudent, spacing out his spending. He had promised himself never to touch the money sewn into the coat until he was there with his mother.

He followed the girl. She had stopped to get herself a soft drink and was in conversation with a lady and her child, acting the part of the nice young woman who had never been party to devilment. Well, Charlie slipped past her like a mist and pluck—

Next thing he was tugging at the gentleman's coat sleeve. "Excuse me, sir…you seemed to have dropped your wallet."

Charlie saw the usual flash of fear in the gent's eyes. First thing they always do is look to see if their cash has flown the coop. The more pitched the look of fear, the bigger the poke. Second thing they do, often but not always, is to give the good soul who returned the wallet a slight gratuity.

Charlie shuttled along through the station with fifty cents in coins bobbing in the palm of his hand. Not a great remittance, but not bad either for returning a pallet of leather. It was a little scam he'd worked from time to time perfecting the art.

He pocketed the money when who should come railing up alongside of him, and now she wasn't quite so genteel.

"Ya sniv'ln id'git, it were you what fleec'd me."

Charlie greeted her assault with a pose of stammerin' confusion.

"Ya thiev'n bastard, say sumthin'."

"Get yourself a better handbag."

• • •

The iron rails followed the southern shore of Lake Erie. Charlie sat alone and contented himself with watching the startling progress upon the earth and listening to the tales of the travelers. He often thought of his father, his chicanery and wild shenanigans, his shameless smile, and sometimes selfish hardness. He would never know where his father's body lay at rest and this plagued his heart. He hoped, if there were such a mansion as promised in the game, that his father had a pleasant room and that the lofty ones didn't come down too hard on him for being inclined to the shill.

From time to time Charlie would take the poem from his haversack that the gent with the cocky hat on the ferry had given him. He would read word for word, over and over again. It seemed that everything was part of the child in the poem... men and women in the street...villages at sunset...a drunkard staggering home... schoolmistresses...a barefoot negro girl...all kinds of flowers and seeds...schooners on the sea...apple trees...Charlie did not understand this, or even if it were possible. He knew that the death of his father was part of him. And his mother in the asylum, that too. He knew the kindness Missus Watters had shown was part of him. But the lightning there, far out upon the grey waters of the lake, could that be part of him? And the rain that came later and slashed across the train windows, how could that be part of him?

The questions made him weary, and he set the poem back in his haversack and lay upon the seat, and he slept through the lightning overhead and the thunder that followed. He slept through the cleansing power of the rain.

He slept until the sudden desperate shrill of the locomotive upon the night sky and the horrific grate of the iron wheels and the couplings crushing together as the train braked. The passengers were violently thrown forward in their seats. From the different cars could be heard the cries of women.

Charlie, like most of the men in the car, thrust his head out an open window to see. Up ahead there were flares along the track. Torches and kerosene lamps were fanning out upon the countryside.

The waves of steam from the locomotive obscured the scene as the train came to a stop, but it looked like there was an overturned wagon on the tracks and what could only be the vague shapes of human bodies.

CHAPTER 22

THE PASSENGERS WERE FILING OFF THE TRAIN. They were about a quarter mile from the Mad River depot and the town lights along the Sandusky Wharf. Through rising fumes of steam from the locomotive, Charlie saw it was a dead white man on one side of the wagon and a dead black on the other. There were sheriffs and deputies and townspeople in the half light of torches and lanterns in conflict with three men bearing shotguns or rifles. Charlie heard one of the passengers quietly tell another, "Slave catchers."

One of the three men with a shotgun shouted out, "I'll give fifty dollars to any of you folks who helps me to catch my niggers."

A confluence of townspeople tried to shout him down, but there were others who stood with the slave catchers, who returned verbal fire, holding up a torch and walking among the citizenry. "I have legal right to those runaways, and it's your responsibility..." meaning the sheriffs' "...my property is returned, and anyone helping them escape is prosecuted. And that man..." he swung the torch toward the dead white man, who now had a woman kneeling over him and weeping for his spent life, "...was breaking the law."

Sandusky was an important terminal in the underground railroad and served as a jumping off point to Canada. Charlie had learned all this when he and his father read *Uncle Tom's Cabin* together at night in the rooming houses of their travels as they prepared for the confidence scheme exacted against Ward Beecher.

In Sandusky, runaway slaves were hidden in the homes of abolitionists who then secreted them on board steamers such as the Island Queen that carried the runaways to Kelly Island. There, they changed over to smaller launches and sailed the short distance to Canada where they would land in freedom on a strip of beach at Point Pelee. There was danger in this, as the book, and news reports, liberally detailed. And there were deaths, such as tonight.

"There are four runaways to be taken," said the man wielding the shotgun. "Two bucks…and a bitch with a child. And I pay in good old fashioned silver."

Opaque figures carrying torches were led by a reluctant sheriff and his deputies through the high grass on both sides of the track. And don't think there weren't demands and pleas from those hoping for the blacks' escape.

The white corpse was being attended to as they began removing the carriage from the tracks. The black was left to his own people, some of whom were ordered off the train to assist in the grisly chore.

The air was filled with charry streaks of smoke from the torches and the heavy idling huffs of the locomotive as the hunters spread out in a vast circle and the sheriff was calling out into the darkness for the runaways to surrender, or God help them if they were spotted within rifle shot.

His father had taught Charlie that he must always look to see what others fail to, that the confidence man—the schemer, gamer— must observe what others dismiss. Because the art of distraction plays out in life where you least expect, and often, by sheer accident.

Brittle weeds, grass and rubble, a progression of cast asides strewn about that had built a railroad and so a nation, but amidst none of that, runaways desperate for their freedom. Charlie scanned the road where they were dragging the carriage from the tracks, but came away with nothing there either. Then something odd—the blacks in the segregated car.

They were not looking where the burning spotters made their way up the hillface toward a tree lined bluff. Nor were they watching the carriage and the dead being carted off. A few were looking at each other, talking, then pressing their faces to the glass and peering down.

Well, he thought, if that don't twist the spigot. There was a shadow beneath the railcar. A bundled blackness hugging the inside of the iron wheels.

Charlie walked over as calm and casual as could be—and don't think the blacks in the car weren't getting anxious. When he was close enough and sure not to be spotted, he squatted down.

And there was a woman with a small child tight against her breast, sweating, petrified, and the child even more so, a hand pressed to its gaping mouth, like poor creatures caught in a trap, knowing they would be devoured. And helpless in their almighty predicament against the sinful wrath that was upon them.

It shamed Charlie at that moment, them staring at him like that. He stood and walked around the back of the car to the other side. No one was watching down this end of the train. They were too busy having the black dragged off into the brush and dumped like so much trash.

There was a shallow ravine alongside the train that fed down to a stand of trees about a block from the wharf. Charlie wondered, was this where the woman was trying to get with her child. He bent down, "Ma'am…if you're going this way, come over to this side. I'll give you the word when it's clear. Come on now." She refused to move, whether it was fear or—"Ma'am…you can't spare the time being suspicious. They mean to have your hide…now git."

She crawled over the ties and was about a foot from Charlie, when a voice shouted, "Hey, boy…what gives back there?"

Charlie stood. It was one of the men with a rifle. He was beside the locomotive and he had his weapon in a position that said he meant business.

"Hear me, boy."

"Just lookin' sir, 'cause I sure would like to pocket that fifty."

No sooner did the man turn away than Charlie stomped a brogan in the dirt to signal. "Now, ma'am…git."

She was out from under the wheels quick as a cat and silent as a whisper. Her eyes and his met for what would be a lifetime in a flash, and Charlie watched her slip down that decline with the brush barely moving behind her till there was only the deep and lasting huff of the locomotive engine sitting in wait on the iron road of the country. And Charlie was left to wonder, would he have committed himself to such an act, had it not been for Missus Watters?

CHAPTER 23

Lest we forget
— Rebecca Griffin

THAT WAS THE HANDWRITTEN INSCRIPTION in the Bible that Billy Tule had taken from the bloody carpetbag of Zacharia Griffin.

The inscription so much mundane tripe, but the penmanship— it was small and quite refined. It spoke of education and class, and Billy Tule considered how it was so many women with refined penmanship ended up in the bed of such sorry bastards.

There had been a half dozen scribbled note papers in the Bible. Most were railroad schedules. Trains leaving for northern New York, Ohio, even Pennsylvania.

And there was a letter that intrigued him, so he read it over and over on the train ride to Albany.

Dear Mister Griffin,

With regards to your most recent letter. I'm sorry to say that your wife has shown little to no signs of recuperative progress. In fact, her repeated bouts of stupor seem immune to any and all forms of treatment. And so, we all here have deep concerns for her long term prognosis.

I heartily agree with your idea to try and convince your son not to come here. There is little to be gained. Though, I might add, seeing her boy could have a positive effect on Rebecca. At least we have seen such in certain cases, even if the return to normalcy is only temporary.

On a completely different subject. There is a photographer here and he is in the process of taking pictures of each patient and matching them with their case history. He is copying a study done recently in England. I will get an extra photograph of your dear Rebecca so you and Charlie may have one. She is such a fine, sweet, quiet woman. And, I must add, quite a lovely one.

The doctor who'd signed the letter, he noticed, had a hard to pronounce name. Probably one of those aggressive and ambitious foreigners who from the moment they get off the boat, believe this country is their own private preserve. Tule put the letter back in the Bible, and the Bible back in his pocket.

He sat in the train car smoking his pipe. There was no mistaking it. Griffin and his son were hustling it that morning to the depot. The boy jumping a train all but stamped it. And did the boy take just any train? Not a chance.

• • •

Missus Watters lived in a small, two story farmhouse on Ferry Street, within eyeshot of the brick buildings that were the Albany County almshouse. Her late husband had worked tirelessly to help run the home for the poor, the orphaned, and mentally ill, and his death was a great sadness to many.

The Watters' house stood far back from the road, cloistered in the trees, with a barn that was already a hundred years old and taken to dangerous leanings.

Missus Watters returned after dark with her mother. She noticed no lights on in the house, and the barn door left rattling with the wind. It was not like Augustus, whose daily rituals were precise to a fault.

She entered by the kitchen and lit a candle and set it on an old plate. Entering the dining room the candle's light blossomed across the ceiling, and there on the table an open whiskey bottle and dirty bowls from a recently eaten meal. From somewhere in the house the smell of burning tobacco, and Missus Watters said, "Stay here mother…please."

She followed the scent to the sitting room, and from the doorway, the burning wick fleshed out the walls from the shadows. There she discovered the black from the train, the one she knew now to be called Handy, sitting in what had been her husband's chair. Across the room was a second man. His huge bearing, far too big for the spinet chair where he rested.

"What are you doing here?"

The man hunched over the keys, knowing enough to approximate a tune, and went about wording through a song, *"I've got the gift of prophecy…as I will quickly show. The secret of the future…most infallibly I know. I'll give you a few straight tips…and I will prophesize. Of some strange things to happen…when the pigs begin to fly."*

Missus Watters tried not to become unsettled. "Where is Augustus?"

Tule answered by repeatedly hitting the same spinet key.

"Where is the boy?" he said.

"The boy left on the train."

"Where did he go?"

"I have no idea."

Tule just kept on with that unnerving play of the keys. Missus Watters saw that the light from the candle was tremoring. Tule saw it too. She tried to steady her hand.

"My boy there," said Tule. "Carries two knives. One is a genuine American Indian knife. Bad business those knives. The other they call a Damascus blade. It's about as long as a boot. And if you don't tell me, that nigger is going to kill your mammy there."

"Don't tell him."

Missus Watters turned. Her mother now stood just behind her at the rim of the light. An expression of battleworn defiance.

"Oh, Mother," said Missus Watters, knowing the old woman had given away too much by saying that.

"The boy's mother is in a hospital," said Tule. "An asylum. That's where he's going, isn't it?"

Seconds passed. The only sound Tule hitting the same ivory key. Handy got up and went for the old woman. No sooner did he shove past Missus Watters, than she broke for the stairwell. She threw the candle aside. The light went spiraling across the floor.

Handy was left to chase her in the blind. She got to her bedroom door and locked it before Handy reached the landing. She was at her desk in the dark swiping through her writing papers as he shouldered against the door.

The wood cracked around the hinges but didn't cave away and she found the paper where she had written down the address so she could write him as promised. By the time she lit a match and put flame to paper, Handy drove against the door with such violence, screaming, that the wood frame was shorn free and he clambered over the wrecked planking. He saw the paper aflame as she was holding it and hit her squarely in the face so hard she was thrown back against the wall and dropped to the floor stunned. The burning paper on the floor there beside her he stomped out the flame with a boot heel.

Tule was dragging the old lady partway up the stairs to the tune of agonized cries.

"I got sumthin'," Handy shouted.

Tule was holding the paper now blowing on the bits of edge that still burned.

CHAPTER 24

THE COMMERCIAL HOSPITAL AND LUNATIC ASYLUM of Cincinnati was a grim faced world of stone and brick and windows covered with canvas drapery, and even in the most stirring daylight it had a dark countenance where one was forever reminded of winter.

The day Charlie arrived the city was in the midst of violent protests. And there was a danger on the street for even the most innocent of citizens. A mayor was to be elected. And one of the candidates represented the American Party of nativists who believed the city was being overrun by foreigners. German Catholics whose allegiance was to the Pope, their German Jew brethren and an endless plague of darkies making their way across Ohio—all despoiling the soul of that great city.

The asylum was on Twelfth Street facing the Miami-Erie Canal. They'd nicknamed the canal "The Rhine" because the neighborhood on the asylum side was predominately German.

Charlie was on Twelfth Street Bridge staring at the building. Furnace smoke drifting across the gentle light of morning. He was nervous, to say the least, about going to see his mother. It had been three years. And time does funny things. After all that traveling, and waiting, and hoping, all the anticipation, just to get here, and now this. The fear he would not live up to some expectation, but he did not know what that expectation was. Charlie was carrying around a state of confusion. Torn, but why? Then the worst fear of all, like a collection of personal wounds—what if she doesn't love me anymore?

A gang of locals came shuttling past him, they were boozed up and looking for trouble. There were packetboats tied off at the canal, the boatman unloading their wares. The packets had the name of foreign owned businesses painted on the sideboards, and pretty quick, they were under a hailstorm of bricks and rocks and empty liquor bottles. The boatmen were being called down by that street gang as the Pope's ass lickers, thievin' Jew boys, and a nigger's bedmate.

There was no end to it, then one of the boatmen was hit in the face with shards of glass and cut up pretty severely. With catastrophe in sight, it took a few errant shots from a revolver to scatter that ratpack. Charlie could hear them all the way down the canal cursing like sewage and swearing revenge.

Had it been like this three years ago? Charlie didn't remember. He wondered could it be 'cause he'd been too young then to take notice? A considerable number of thoughts going around in his head gave way to one…the asylum, all still and quiet.

He took off his railroad cap and leaned over the bridge railing and caught sight of himself in the water. He took a hairbrush from his haversack and tried to get that mass of unkempt hair righted as best he could. He'd wished he'd kept that suit so he could look more gentlemanly.

On the way, Charlie had to pass by those packetboats. Among the rocks and bottles that had been flung across the canal, he noticed a white object. It looked like a pestle made of white stone and handsomely sanded, and he could just manage his fist around it. He dumped it in his haversack just for luck.

• • •

A woman in a plain frock and white apron sat at a desk in a poorly appointed atrium. The light as a door opened reflected off her gold rimmed glasses, and before her stood a raggedy young character.

"May I help you?"

"I'm here to see my mother."

The woman sat back, her angular face looking over this oddly self possessed yet tentative youth, this way and that.

"And your mother's name?"

"Rebecca Griffin."

Her forehead wrinkled at some private thought.

"Are you alone?"

"Yes, ma'am."

"And what's your name?"

"Charlie. Charlie Griffin."

"Sit please."

There was a bench she pointed to, and he sat as she walked down a long hallway. He was excited now, and he was sweating. He rocked back and forth some to try and calm down all that burning anticipation. In the silence to follow, he began to hear faint noises from the floor above. Human sounds, oddly pitched. They sounded neither right. Nor happy.

From down along another hallway the sound of wheels wobbly across a badly wooded floor. Two men, one pushing while the other pulled a confinement crib across the atrium. Charlie did not notice until a hand thrust from between the slatted bars, and he jerked back. The crib wasn't empty. He leaned down and saw there was a young man who looked to have half his hair plucked out and with eyes as big as seedpods. A rank odor from the cage where this thing was trying to grasp at the stale air.

"Charles Griffin?"

Charlie looked up at the sudden voice. A gauntish man in a suit and with a hermetic smile said, "How would you like to come with me?"

Charlie shrugged.

They sat in a small office. A roll top desk, precarious stacks of patient files. Pipe smoke and poor ventilation and patches of ceiling with water damaged rot. Dusty light filtered through the worn drapes.

"Where's your father?" said the doctor.

Charlie admitted, reluctantly, "He died in New York, sir."

"Died? And you came here all alone?"

"I did."

"Did your father get any of my letters?"

Charlie looked surprised.

"Never mind. Do you have any relatives here?"

"Here? My mother."

"No. Besides your mother."

"My father had a brother but he disappeared. My mother's parents are dead. The cholera epidemic in Illinois when I was five or six."

"Yes. I know of that. Your father's parents, what about them?"

"They did some kind of traveling lantern show. But that's all I know about 'em."

The doctor could not believe all that he was witnessing.

"How's my mother? Can I see her? I was hoping...to take her home. I have a lady in Albany who—"

"Home?"

CHAPTER 25

As the doctor led Charlie through the dour corridors of the asylum, he had no way of explaining really how the boy's mother was. How do you describe the emotional devastation to a woman watching the black children she'd taught be burned to death in their tiny schoolhouse when the good citizens of Cincinnati decided to torch Little Africa, their vicious appellation for the black enclave along the Ohio River? Or the psychological agony she'd absorbed as she tried to pull the screaming from the flames only to be dragged off herself by the very men who'd set the blaze? How do you explain the physical violence committed upon her body, and so also her mind? How do you tell all this to a boy of twelve, no matter how worldly he might appear? How do you explain the slow mechanical withdrawal of the mind under emotional duress, when you cannot fully explain it all yourself?

At the back of the hospital, on the upper floor past the wards where Charlie could hear a world of broken voices, there was a hallway with a row of small, individual cells for patients who were either too violent, and so a danger to others, or who were vulnerable to such violence. It was there Charlie would find his mother.

As the doctor unlatched the door, Charlie could feel his heart flutter and race. His mother was just moments away. All the longing and loss to be cleansed from his heart by her presence.

In the center of the room was a table with two chairs where his mother sat. A bed was against one wall and a basin on a stand, and there was a long slender window that was barred, and beyond the bars, the stirring of tree branches with light upon the leaves so they seemed like painted glass.

Rebecca Griffin was looking toward that window as Charlie entered the room from behind her.

"Mother," he said, in a voice that barely touched the air.

She did not move. He came around the table so she could see it was him.

"Mother."

She continued to stare straight ahead. Was it the bars she was looking at, or that tree with supple branches beyond, or was it something altogether else? She was paler than the boy remembered, frailer for one so young. Her hair had been cut short, and it hung about her head in an unruly fashion, and so unlike her even in the worst of times. But, it was she who had birthed him, and cared for him, and who'd helped him thrive in her affections. It was she hiding there in all that frozen stillness.

Charlie bent down and began to kiss her face over and over. He buried himself in the crease of her neck as he'd done as a child, and he could smell his mother there, and the memory of her smell went through him in a swell of emotions leaving no shadow within him untouched.

"Mother," he said again, pleading for her to see it was her boy who had crossed the nation carrying all that love with him just to be at her side. The doctor heard the boy's voice break upon the reefs of the woman's tragic inability to be present.

Looking up at the doctor, Charlie said, "Why doesn't she know I'm here?"

The doctor was trapped by an inability to answer, because there was no answer. "I'm sure," he said, "in her heart she knows you're her son, and you've come all this way."

Charlie looked to his mother, who had not moved a muscle in all these minutes together, and he shook his head from side to side. That was not an answer he could wrap his heart around, nor one that would take away the agony of being lost to someone, possibly forever.

He held her hands, he squeezed her hands hoping, then he had a thought. As desperation brings out such thoughts.

"I have something," he said to his mother, "you should remember."

Charlie went over to his haversack which he'd put down on the bed and from it took the Mansion of Happiness game.

"Remember this?" he said to his mother, holding up the box.

He took out the game and set the board down on the table. He gave his mother a marker and took one as his own.

"Remember telling me," he said, "why they used the spinner instead of dice. And how Daddy would only play if he used dice… You go first."

He slid the teetotum toward her and looked for any life in her expression. "All right," he said. Please Mother, he thought. Please. "All right…I'll spin for you." And he did.

"Six…okay…that's good." There was desperation in his voice, and a trace of hopelessness. "Move your piece, Mother." His throat was tight. "Why don't I help you?" He took her hand gently as if she were a child and set it on the marker. "Remember making me spell

105

out all the virtues and vices?" Her muscles were rigid but she offered no resistance and he guided her hand with the marker, square by square, counting along, "Three...four...five...six... water square... that's good...You get to move to space ten..."

He kept methodically pushing her hand along lightly, very lightly, and then he slipped loose of her and her hand continued moving square by square creeping its way along and he looked to the doctor in hopeful amazement as if a miracle were taking place. But the doctor just stood there in the doorway unmoved as Charlie counted, "Eight...nine...ten..." His mother's hand kept inching across the board.

"That's the square...stop...Mother..." But her hand just carried along as if guided by some invisible force till the marker was off the board and falling to the floor and then the boy's spirit just broke apart and he swept his hand across the board sending his marker and the teetotum, even the damn board itself, crashing against the wall.

CHAPTER 26

H<small>E RAN OUT OF THE ROOM</small>. In the hallway he put an arm against the wall, leaned into it, and wept. You could hear the sobbing down that corridor of cells. The doctor followed him out.

"It isn't fair," Charlie said. "It isn't fair at all."

The doctor came and stood behind him. Charlie kicked at the wall with his brogans until his leg wracked with pain.

"What did I do wrong?" said Charlie.

"Wrong...you?"

"You heard me," shouted Charlie. "What did I do wrong?"

"Nothing."

Charlie looked toward the open door to his mother's cell. That's what it was to the boy, a cell, not a room, certainly not a home, a prison cell wrapped in a life sentence and for no crime committed.

"There has to be," said Charlie. He grabbed the doctor by his coat. "Life just can't be that cruel."

The doctor took the boy by his hands but Charlie ripped loose of the grasp. He wondered what his father would say if he were here. He had the knack for playing fast and loose with the worst life had to offer. And Charlie could use some of that fast and loose right now to hide behind.

"Why don't we go down to my office?" said the doctor. "I have something for you."

Charlie hardly heard him, as he was intent on that stream of light coming from the open door to his mother's cell.

"I guess I can't take her and make a home."

"No. That would not be wise."

Charlie nodded in defeat. "I've got to go back in there now for a few minutes."

His voice was coming apart. He entered the room, his mother still in the same position with her arm extended to where she had last pushed the marker. Charlie picked up the board and the pieces of the game and he put them back in the box carefully, and then he slipped the box into the haversack and the haversack, he slung over his shoulder. He took a long time looking at his mother.

He reached for the extra chair and sided it by his mother and he sat and put an arm around her shoulders and talked to her as if she were there with him that very moment in the full blossom of her being.

"I'm going now, Mother…I will write you, and I'm sure the doctor will be kind enough to read you the letters, so you'll know where I am and what I'm doing and maybe later if there should be—"

He stopped. "If"—the word seemed to stretch on to the end of a world he could not get beyond.

He leaned over and kissed her on the cheek. He was afraid, as well as aware, that he might never see her again, and with that he pressed against her as if trying to absorb everything she ever was, or would be. He stood and brushed at her hair and he leaned over and whispered, "I'll love you enough for all of us."

• • •

The doctor opened a desk drawer, rummaged about, then handed Charlie a tintype in a cloth folder. It was a photograph of the boy's mother. She was sitting in a chair with a makeshift drape behind her. Her hair had been combed, her hands folded on her lap. She looked like she had no idea a picture was being taken.

"I wrote your father I had this done."

"Where you'd mail the letter to?"

"Kansas City, I believe."

They had been there for two months before they tripped it to New York. "He never said nuthin' about it," said Charlie.

The doctor understood why. "Where you going now?"

"I don't know, sir."

"Where are you staying?"

"Don't know that either."

"I can fix a room here till you make plans."

The sun was high and hot when Charlie left the hospital and went and sat at the edge of the canal to be alone and think. He let his legs dangle over the side. From far up the canal a carpet of black smoke hung about the rooftops. Something was on fire. He wondered if it had anything to do with the unrest in the city.

Charlie poked about his haversack, found the candy bag and got out a cheroot. He very carefully broke it in half and lit up. It was the first time he had a smoke all to himself.

He sat there thinking as he smoked, flicking ashes into the canal. Had all these sorrows come to pass because of the wrongs they'd done, his father and he? Was his mother's illness and father's death a kind of punishment for the scams and shames their souls had piled up, his father and he?

The game came to mind. You land on virtues, you go forward. You land on vices, you must go back and face a reckoning before moving on again. Maybe it was just a powerful bit of nonsense, but it had ensnared him with doubt.

He looked at himself there in the cloudy waters of the canal. You can tell yourself anything, except that something isn't wrong. He smoked and considered his predicament from fresh angles, his legs dangling there on the surface of the water like the legs of a hanged man dancing in the air below the gallows. At that notion, he stopped moving them right quick, thank you very much.

How does one escape their predicament?

He didn't have to find the answer. No, the answer had found him. It was as close as the collar of his coat and as tight around his neck as a noose. It was lying in wait and licking its fangs, and Charlemagne Ezekiel Griffin, better known as Charlie, was on the menu.

The money...He could take the money back to the church and ask for mercy. His father being murdered might sure give him a good hand to play. And besides...how did Handy and the other one come to know they had the money? Someone at the church had 'fessed it. If that didn't give him a pearl of an edge, well...Church people don't like any kinda bad word about them sneaking out of the parlor to the general public.

Of course, that wasn't the only choice. It was the lesser one, and he knew it. One that just skimmed along the border of aspiring to "our better angels."

He set the cigar down on the canal bank and got out the *Phelps*. There were a couple of maps his father had tucked up in the pages and using a straightened thumb to gauge miles he saw it was about the same length of finger from Cincinnati to New York as it was from Cincinnati to Kansas City and the abolitionists whose names had been forged in the letter.

He put the book in the haversack and took up his cheroot. He mulled over a course of action and considered what Missus Watters had said: *God has a plan.* What kind of plan could God have that would include a thievin' scapegrace such as himself? A pretty poor one, thank you very much. But takin' the money to Kansas and fulfilling a promise, even one made on bad faith, might prove to be a blessing. It might make something from the sorrowful mess that was his family—his mother left there to the asylum, his father left dead in the street, and himself left alone altogether.

It weren't much of a legacy, that was a fact. But the poem that showboater on the ferry had given him... *Everything that happened was a part of the boy.* He had a glimmer of how that might be right. But he sure wouldn't make a wager on it. And Missus Watters...Her goodness had made him feel utterly ashamed of his living, breathing self for the crime he'd committed. Was he considering the trek to Kansas because it was right, because he wanted to clear his family name, or because he was ashamed?

His father hadn't had much good to say about shame. That was a fact. He didn't take part in it, thought it a poison, even if swallowed in small doses. But he'd also said, beware of people who bore shame and used it as a course of action. Because shame can carry someone a long way, farther than food even, farther than all the cleverness in the world. Yeah...shame can make a dangerous man out of a simple fool.

THE UNDERTAKER'S FRIEND

CHAPTER 27

SOMETHING WAS SAID TO CHARLIE in a foreign language. He had no idea what it was, but getting kicked by a boot doesn't need translation. He came around to see three boys who looked like they were interested in thrashing up a little bad blood.

The one doing most of the talking was tall and lanky, with long arms and a pointy face. The other two flanked him. One had nasty pockmarks, the third walked with a crutch and was missing a leg.

The tall one kicked Charlie again. Just hard enough to keep his attention. Charlie guessed from the accent and the neighborhood, the kids were German.

"I don't know what you're saying…but don't kick me."

The boy tried to kick him anyway and Charlie swiped at the boy's leg.

"Who you are?" said the leader. "You don't live in neighborhood. You not German…no?"

"I'm here to see my mother," Charlie pointed to the hospital.

"Mother…asylum," said the one with the pocked face.

The kid missing the leg did his best impression of a crazy person with a legion of gymnastic expressions. Charlie saw it for the sad foolishness that it was. He could also feel considerable trouble coming on and angled himself so he could slip a hand into his haversack without it being readily observed.

The kid with the pockmarks swiped at the cheroot which was set at the edge of the canal path. Stuck it between his teeth and puffed away like a ratty little tough.

"You Protestant?" said the leader.

Charlie tried to stand.

The leader pushed down on Charlie's shoulder to stop him. "Empty pockets…Pope hater."

Charlie wasn't having it and forced his way upright. He was thinking, how do I get loose of these shits and fast.

It wasn't fast enough. He was struck across the back of the neck with the crutch and momentarily stunned.

They were on him fast after that. He was being bludgeoned with fists, kicked, battered across his back and shoulders with the crutch. He tried to burst his way past them, keeping low, but they gang tackled him there in the canal path.

People in the street took to watching the fight—onlookers from the bridge, from the roofs of the packetboats. The boy with the pockmarks kept shouting, "Pope hater…Pope hater…" and pointing at Charlie. You could hear that damn banshee up the street, and it wasn't long before the front door of the hospital swung open and there was the nurse who tended the front desk with hands on her hips, to see what in god's name the commotion was about.

Charlie had to get to his feet or be rendered unconscious. His face was cut, he was swallowing his own blood where his tongue had been slashed open. He got a tight grip on the pestle he'd picked up out of the canal path. He sidled and fought so he could get in a good lick against the leader who had a hand on Charlie's throat and was choking him. Charlie struck him with the pestle and there was a jet of blood from the bridge of the boy's nose. The boy screamed out and grabbed his face as if that would be enough to staunch the bleeding. Charlie got another shot in with the pestle, hitting the kid across the side of his mouth and you could hear a couple of teeth crack.

That loosed Charlie enough, and in the bloody panic, he snaked and kicked and twisted till he was upright again, but the kid missing the leg still had him by the ankles. The pockmarked boy tried to jump Charlie but he flattened that banshee from a blow with the pestle. The boy reeled back. Charlie dragged the third kid to the edge of the canal. He managed to kick his way free then he took the kid and shoved him over the side. He fell into the water, his voice crying out like a cat about to be drowned.

There's no telling how much worse things would have gotten had it not been for the nurse and doctor who rescued Charlie from a crowd that had at first been milling about and just enjoying the fight, but had become a mob that had grown antagonistic over one of their own being left bloodied and on his knees, and another, a crippled child, thrown into the canal.

There was violence breaking out all across Cincinnati. German businesses were being set on fire. A militia was organized to barricade and defend the streets leading into the Rhine district. It was a city drowning in the poisonous sentiments of racism and nativistic hatreds, and Charlie had been an easy scapegoat.

The doctor sat Charlie down in a small surgical room. He and the nurse tended the wounds about his face, the swelling under an eye, and the blood trickling out through his lips from a tear across the tongue. The doctor glanced out the window time and again. The crowd had thinned, but was not much less angry. Some pretty volatile stares were being thrown toward the hospital.

"Are they gonna come in here after me?"

"No," said the doctor. But to Charlie he didn't sound quite so sure.

"What are we going to do with you?" said the doctor.

"Don't have to do anything, sir. I'll be leaving for Kansas City quick enough."

"What? When did you decide this?"

"Sitting out there by the canal."

"Why?"

Charlie was tentative. "You can't speak of this to anyone. But… I've got to meet up with some abolitionists there."

The doctor and the nurse shared a look that spoke of total implausibility.

"Why in the world would a boy your age want to meet up with abolitionists?"

"I need to make amends, sir."

CHAPTER 28

THE DOCTOR SAW TO IT THAT CHARLIE WAS FED. He also wanted the boy to remain there awhile, not only because there were still some surly characters lurking about the streets where tensions ran high, particularly among those and who might seek retribution, but he also wanted Charlie to meet a couple who might be of some benefit to him in his travels, making the journey West simpler, and less dangerous.

Charlie sat at a long bench table in what was a commissary with cracked plaster and filthy paint. The windows were high up the decaying walls, and he wondered why until he realized this is where the patients ate. At least the ones capable of feeding themselves and maintaining some form of order. He kept a stoic distance, but very quickly became the center of attention. And not just stares or whispery chatter, one of the patients kept waving at him, another took to banging their spoon on the table to draw his attention until he had to be sssshhh'd.

He thought of his mother in her tiny cell, eating alone, being fed probably like a child. It ached to imagine the scene. He wondered if there would come a time he would not remember this day so well.

He didn't know if that were good or bad, but a feeling as dark as the heavens at midnight came over him.

The doctor returned with a couple he introduced as Cassius and Penrose Doral. They were brother and sister. Charlie gauged them to be about forty. She wore a staid brown dress and had a manly handshake and did most all the talking. Her brother Cassius wore a John Bull hat and sack coat. Charlie noted the flashy, embroidered suspenders. His father would have desired them, as he had a taste for flash. On Cassius they seemed out of place. The brother nodded a lot while his sister prattled on.

It turned out the Doral's represented a number of benevolent societies, and their job was to place orphans in homes. Charlie knew about these orphan trains. He'd seen them in passing. A platoon of helpless waifs and hard looking teenagers brought to a railroad station or dock and paraded in front of a potential mother and father. Are you interested in a little girl you can dress up like a shop window...Or a dirt faced boy for the one you lost...Maybe you need some help in your tailor shop, or hardware store, or sundry...Or a factory worker...Or farmhand?

Charlie made it clear he was going to Kansas. "If I need a home," he said, "I have one offered to me in Albany. A Missus Emmaline Watters. A fine woman...whose late husband ran the county almshouse there."

Penrose sat beside the boy and was quite commiserating. The doctor had confided his life story, and it near brought her to tears. "We're not here to convince you otherwise," she said. "The doctor tells us you have a bright mind and decided manner. We're going down the Ohio by steamer to Louisville. You can travel with us, and from there, take the train to Saint Louis, or continue by boat to Cairo. It will be yours to choose."

• • •

Penrose Doral was not a woman to be taken lightly. Those who ran afoul of her met with unadulterated wrath, and her fallen adversaries had taken to calling her the "Alligator Woman."

She led her brother and Charlie from the hospital. There were about a dozen angry malingerers at the canal bridge on Twelfth who she confronted right away with a harsh glare and harsher rhetoric. Penrose knew city officials, religious leaders, publishers of newspapers, including the German newspapers, and chiefs of police.

"If any one of you means to harm the boy," she said, "there will be hell to pay. And hell starts right here with me. So…who's first in line?"

The worst that happened—Charlie was hocked on by one of the men as he went past. Charlie turned and silently mouthed a few cheap epithets, hoping the man could read lips.

It was a hard dusk. There were plumelets of smoke across the city. The fires of xenophobia and rage. Crowds of immigrant Germans and nativists roamed the streets. You could see them sprinting along the boulevards, a cancerous mass of violence, destroying shops, looting, giving vent to the scorns of time.

Charlie thought he heard the far boom of a cannon, and Cassius told him that's exactly what it was. The German militia had set up a defensive perimeter on Vine Street, and were firing at nativists who meant to storm the neighborhood. A block from the ferry there were dead and wounded in the street. They had to hug the sides of buildings and sluice down alleyways to avoid being killed by gunfire.

The Doral's luggage was waiting for them at the ferry. Large carpetbags that Charlie offered to carry. They crossed the Ohio to Covington, Kentucky as the blues of evening settled over the river and their lives.

Charlie stood in the prow of the ferry, as he had done that day crossing from Brooklyn to the granite shores of Manhattan. Only this ferry was a pitifully small one, enough for a dozen souls, little more than a launch, with a hammered together boiler taking up most of the space, spewing out a cindered smoke as it chugged, chugged, chugged. Thank God the waves were thin and few along this stretch of river.

With the wind to his face, Charlie was leaving the home of his birth, with all its flaws, and embarking upon a great journey. He had a sense of elation, and a sense of dread. He held tightly in his pocket the Wedgewood piece with the slave in chains given to him in the basement of the church by a Christian black man.

"Hey, lad," said Cassius. "You look anxious."

"Excited to be on the way, is all, sir."

"A solid answer, lad. A solid answer."

They walked up Washington Street from the ferry and passed through a hub of customs offices and shippers, traders, importers. It was a deeply rutted road to walk and Charlie was kind enough to carry the Doral's bags. They stopped at a small brick building, the second floor being home to a law office. Charlie and Cassius waited while Penrose promised to be but a few minutes.

The two men stood beneath a streetlamp. Insects flew about the glass. Charlie noticed Penrose Doral looking down on him from the window. She smiled and waved, and Charlie waved back.

She came down the stairs a few minutes later with two black men trailing behind her. She handed her brother an envelope which he put in his coat pocket for safe keeping. Charlie noticed each black man was carrying a set of shackles.

"He's the one," said Penrose.

Charlie had no idea what she meant, but in a wicked moment

he learned. The two black men assaulted him. They were full grown, and no matter how Charlie fought and kicked with an insane feral desperation he could not loose himself. They were thick shouldered and strong, and they had Charlie down in the chewed up street, one of the men pressing a knee into the boy's chest, wrenching his arms up, driving out every ounce of air so he gasped in pain. They shackled one wrist and then another and they shackled one ankle and then another, and then they dragged the boy, weighted down in iron, to his feet. He stood there stunned dumb and stared at the chains.

"You are now the property of the Golden Hollow Plantation," said Penrose Doral, "and will be returned as in accordance with the law."

"You can't make me out a slave."

Penrose stepped so close to Charlie the shadow of her face covered the light from the streetlamp. "My dear young man, Cassius has a letter from a plantation in Arkansas describing a boy about your age who can pass for white sold to Golden Hollow in lieu of debt. Golden Hollow will in turn lease you out. You are smart, strong and healthy. You can read and write. You are a living, breathing banknote."

"The owner of the plantation isn't gonna believe it."

"No?" said Penrose.

"I'll tell him myself. I'll have him write a woman I know in Albany."

Penrose slapped Charlie hard across the face, so hard, in fact, the sound cut through the night air with shocking clarity. She caught the swelling under his eye from the street fight, and how it hurt. He winced with pain, his eye began to water, the eye socket throbbed.

"The owner of the plantation is deceased. It is being run by an executor who happens to be a business partner of ours and the attorney upstairs. Now…when we get on that boat, you will be a polite and quiet young man. Do you understand?"

He said nothing. He could not quell the fury at being taken, chained, beaten. She slapped him across the face even harder than last time, the swelling around his eye the target of her affection.

"Silence is insolence where I am concerned about being answered respectfully. Otherwise…I will have you lashed until your flesh turns to butter."

She put an ear to his lips. She was waiting.

"A simple 'yes, ma'am' will do, lad," said Cassius.

"Yes, ma'am," said Charlie. But inwardly he wished her and her brother a miserable death.

Charlie was imprisoned overnight in a storm cellar. He stretched out his arms. He could not see the chains in the dark, but he could feel their weight, hear the cold rattling to haunt his every moment. He was alone with God, his emotions, and his plight.

The first strands of dawn through the slatted boards woke him from an unsettled slumber. The sudden movement of a rusty latch, then a rush of light. Charlie, blind against the sun, joined two slaves in chains. Full grown men. The bounty of slave catchers and now the sole possession of the Doral's. Cassius marched the three to the river, wiping the sweat from his face with a fine linen handkerchief.

The wharf was lined with steamboats. Their destination was the steamer Megiddo. While they waited to board, Penrose Doral arrived with a dozen children for the orphan train in Louisville. Charlie and the other slaves who had been "sold down the river" had to stand aside in the mud for these white children to pass.

"Benevolent with one hand, bestial with the other. And that is the story of this river."

Charlie turned to see who it was talking like that. There was a gent amidst the waiting passengers, and among that crowd of the plain and polite, he certainly stood out. He wore a black frock coat and black silk tie and a topper made of black fur, worn shiny as satin from the elements. He had been remarking about the children being led up the plankway in single file, following Miss Penrose Doral like obedient baby ducks, in counterpoint to the chained animals posing as human beings being pushed aside to the muddy banks, of which Charlie now was one of their number.

And Charlie being the only white among the blacks stood out himself, and was the recipient of more than a few stares, including the man who had spoken. And he had eyes to stare with, dark and set back in blackish hollows framed by what appeared to be gnawed down cheekbones and a black cropped beard.

Charlie thought him a preacher or death itself. In fact he was neither, but the nearest thing to them. He was an undertaker.

He stepped forward from the crowd and waved to a crew of black deck hands carrying three coffins to the plankway. And this undertaker called the first mate over because he needed to know where on the deck the coffins were to be placed. Charlie overheard the conversation. The undertaker's name was Erastus Eels, and the dead were a family who had been exhumed and were being brought to a new gravesite in Jefferson, Indiana.

Erastus led that parade of coffins up the gangway following the first mate. He removed his topper and spoke aloud to passengers and deck hands. "Please make way for our glorious dead…Give them the time honored respect we all long for when God calls us home…But not too soon, we hope." He reached into the pocket of his frock coat and a moment later he was passing business cards out to any and all. "Erastus Eels at your service…Undertaker…President of the Friends of Charon Society…Gateman for that journey across the river Styx…Practitioner extraordinaire in the magical art of embalming…"

To one woman he said, "I'm sure you want to know you're in good hands once you've gone. That your loveliness is protected."

Grasping Cassius Doral by the shoulder, and slipping a card into his pocket, said, "And you sir…I'm sure you want to look your heavenly best. As you do now, when the angels come to take you to your just reward."

Charlie was right beside Cassius and found himself grinning. Erastus Eels…Dour Angel of Death one moment and smooth, light tongued pitchman the next. It eased the boy's mind, for some unexplainable reason, that such a grim countenance had a certain carnival hustler grandiosity to him. Erastus got a glimpse of this boy burdened down with chains, grinning at him—odd, to say the least.

The coffins were carried to the prow and set down in the open cargo bay alongside the wood for the boiler. The slaves being brought to auction in Louisville came next. Then Cassius Doral with Charlie and the two blacks followed.

The captain joined the first mate to look over the slaves' papers to make sure they were legal and in order. The passengers made their way up to the boiler deck and their cabins. Penrose Doral stood at the top of the stairs. Charlie saw she was watching him, and watching him hard.

She knew, what he knew. That if he was going to cause a ruckus and try to get free, now would be the time. Since every passenger, deck hand, and slave, had taken their turn looking over this chained up boy who could pass for white with flying colors.

Cassius was wiping beads of sweat along his forehead with that scented handkerchief, when he handed over the papers to the captain.

"Those papers are a fraud, sir."

The captain looked up. Charlie had said it plenty loud enough for anyone to hear. Cassius tried to hold himself stoic.

"The papers are a fraud. They were written up last night by an attorney on Washington Street."

Penrose was already coming quickly down the stairs.

"My mother is in the Cincinnati Hospital and Asylum. Ask the doctor there. He knew my father and my mother. I am no fugitive slave—"

Everyone along the deck was watching now.

The Captain questioned Cassius. "What about this?"

"The boy is a despicable liar."

The captain turned to find this woman fast approaching. "And you are?"

"Miss Penrose Doral, this is my brother. We represent the Presbyterian Benevolent Society. The orphans on board are under our council."

"I'm not lying, sir. Just ask at the hospital."

"The boy's mother cannot speak," said Penrose. "She has lost her mind, and it's obvious why." She put her sights on Charlie. "Having a colored child. Even one who can pass."

"Just ask at the hospital," Charlie shouted. "The doctor knows I'm telling the truth. He wrote my father." Charlie looked about at the people staring. "Anyone… Please…I'm telling the truth."

"Please review the paperwork," said Penrose.

Which the captain did. He was slow, careful, judicious. "The paperwork isn't right."

"I told you it was a fraud," said Charlie.

The captain held out the Arkansas letter. "It isn't notarized, ma'am."

"You are correct," she said.

"I told you," said Charlie.

"But in Arkansas," she said "letters such as these, by law, do not need to be notarized."

She turned her icy stare to Charlie. He saw the captain was wavering. Unsure of who to believe, who seemed the most fitting.

"You can see the boy is violent," said Cassius.

In a last ditch effort to save himself, encumbered as he was with chains, Charlie managed to get a hand partly in his pocket and scrounged up that cameo.

He held it out, he held it up for anyone to see. "Does anyone know what this is? Please…please. I'm being wronged here. I—"

Penrose grabbed the piece out of his hands and flung it away. Charlie watched it carom across the deck and disappear. And with it, went his chance.

CHAPTER 30

CHARLIE WAS MADE TO GO SIT with the other blacks and within spitting distance of the coffins. They were partly covered by a tarp, but Charlie could see strips of weathered rot from the seeping earth they'd been buried in.

Cassius said nothing as Charlie was herded along with the others, and Penrose, bless her dear black heart, gave Charlie a look that made the painful weight of those chains seem like a holiday.

Passengers crowded the promenade along the hurricane deck as the Megiddo made way. There were steamers moving up and down the river, a traffic of boats burdened to the water line with bales of cotton stacked as high as the pilot house, and the sunlight on that water shining gorgeous and all those banner clouds stretching white to heaven. But all Charlie saw were the chains. He moved his wrist testing out one thought—gettin' free.

A slave beside him whispered, "Da capt'n know you ain't color'd. All dat was just fer show. Prob'lee right now is cutt'n hisself in fo' a piece wit dat white witch."

When they made North Bend, you could hear the whistle of steamers along the line, and then the Megiddo joined in chorus, and Charlie suddenly crossed paths with a memory. President Harrison's tomb was on the bluff above the river at North Bend, and tradition had it, that whenever a steamer went past the tomb it gave out with a call in tribute.

Charlie had been there once with his mother. It was when the trees were all rust and gold and she was still well. They'd sat on the stone steps just beneath the resting place.

"I think I'm going away," his mother had said.

"Why?"

"I don't know. I just feel I am."

Nothing more was said. Huddled up there on the Megiddo, Charlie wondered, did she have a premonition of her illness?

That day he'd feared he'd lose her, and they walked hand in hand after that, the fallen leaves high about their ankles for fleeting moments as the wind blew.

Was it from that day on he'd had this presence of aloneness within him, and why he'd so easily become a mark and fallen in with his father's larceny, over his mother's pleading? He wondered, huddled up there on the deck, was that day on the bluff another moment like the ones in the poem, that became part of the child? Like this moment, here and now, with all these chained souls?

Charlie bent and tried to clear the roofline of the upper deck and see where they'd walked that day, his mother and he, but the bluff was still flush with green.

He looked at the river now. At the current. How far the shore. The cover of trees along the banks. A black close by, watching him, whispered, "You'd sink with all dat iron."

Charlie glanced at him. Had his desperation so shown through?

"I seen it," said the black. "Water gobble ya up."

Figuring he knew of what he spoke, Charlie nodded.

The medallion. Charlie wasn't far from the railing where that beastly woman had chucked it. He stood some and slinked his way among the blacks to see if maybe it had gone overboard.

"Sit your ass down, nigger," ordered the deck boss.

There were crates and tarped goods all over the deck, the piece could be anywhere, including in the Ohio.

It took being ordered for a second time before Charlie realized the mate meant him.

Charlie obeyed so as not to arouse any ill will or ill-advised suspicions. He took to listening to the slaves, while he studied his surroundings. Any bit of information might help, escape being the order of the day.

The deck passengers contented themselves with each other, already marking out their poor but precious slips of territory where they could eat and sleep. Soliciting help there would be tricky. This crowd aspired to the upper deck, and who among their number might be a risk taker.

The upper deck crew went about their business. The waiters, valets, chambermaids, and cabin boys were either black freedmen or leased out slaves. What could be used to persuade them? If they hadn't taken their own lightning run at freedom, why take the risk for someone else?

The deck crew was something else altogether. They carried wood for the boilers, wrestled with heavy crates, shoveled manure from the deck where they had herded up the livestock. Many were slaves, the rest, Irish. Word was, among the Irish, were plenty of thieves and roustabouts. A perfect crowd for bucking the law. He searched through their foul and violent number for who might be a most likely candidate to solicit for an escape attempt, taking into consideration he could get his throat cut in the process.

"Arkansas…I doubt you even know where Arkansas is."

Charlie turned to see who it was that had spoken. There in the shadows with a strip of moonlight across a terse stare—the undertaker.

"I got a general impression where it is," said Charlie. "I lived in Kansas City with my father for a couple of months."

"Where were you born?"

"Cincinnati."

"Your mother in the asylum there like the woman said?"

"Yeah."

"And your father?"

"Dead…in New York."

"The Dorals are a pretty sharp pair."

"Sharp…not so pretty."

"They give you that swollen eye and those cuts?"

"Street fight. They added to it."

"What's your name? Your birth name?"

Charlie hesitated.

"It's not a trick question, son."

"Charlemagne Ezekiel Griffin."

"Charlemagne, well—"

"Charlie. They call me—"

"A touch regal for those chains, don't you think? Of course, a number of that vaunted class did end their whimsy in irons."

The undertaker sidled over to the railing. The full moon on him now. The dark of the river behind him. He got out a black pipe and a pouch of tobacco and tapped the pipe on the deck rail to clear it, then took to filling a bowl for a smoke.

"When I was coming on board," said the undertaker, "I saw you grinning away. And I thought to myself…A boy in that predicament, chained down as he is, standing there grinning…He's either God's own personal optimist or an unadorned idiot completely unaware of his plight." He struck a match on the rail bar. A comet line of phosphor upon the night. There, then gone. "Which are you, Charlemagne…God's own…or idiot?"

CHAPTER 31

"I WAS GRINNING 'CAUSE I WONDERED, were you a real undertaker?"

"As compared to what?"

"To a gamer...confidence man. The way you were pitchin'... puttin' out your cards."

"Well...well. How do you come to measure such things, Charlemagne?"

"Charlie...I was trained in the arts, as they say."

"Really now."

"Thimblerig, three card Monte. Playing the shill from the audience. Guess the right card or rousin' a crowd."

Erastus' eyebrows rose in a most unflattering way.

"I could be a real asset to someone like you," said Charlie.

"I'm sure." Erastus drew from his pipe, the smoke taken by the breeze along the river. He just stared at the boy. And Charlie waited. "Professional" silence is what his father used to call it. Some of the deck passengers were getting a little festive with liquor being passed about. One had a banjo and took to playing.

"Charlemagne, you know how this boat got its name... the Megiddo?"

The boy moved a bit and his chains dragged up a less than merry little tune. "I go by Charlie," he said, "and no sir, I don't."

Erastus stepped around him and a few of the slaves sleeping there on the deck, so he could check on those coffins. "Megiddo is a town out Palestine way. Where the Christ was born. And Megiddo sits up on a high bluff and has this commanding view of a vast plain." He made a sweeping gesture with the arm holding the pipe. "Vast as all of Jefferson County. And it guards a pass that connects Egypt and the empires of the North. It was so strategic a place that when Napoleon visited it...you know who Napoleon is?"

The boy searched his memory. The name was in there somewhere. He went to scratch his head, to loose the cobwebs, but the iron cuffs hurt too much, so the hell with it. He sat hunched like a fox a little longer, then it came to him. "He was a French emperor or something. Got whipped bad in a big battle. Then got shoved off to a dungeon or something?"

"Close enough," said Erastus. "Well, this Napoleon said he could maneuver the greatest army in the world over that plain. Now this town was also writ about in the Bible. You know our Bible?"

"My mother gave a whack at it from time to time, but I was a poor audience."

Charlie watched Erastus check to make sure the coffin nails hadn't been loosed. "In the Bible they talk about Megiddo, but it's called Armageddon in the book. The place where the final conflict between good and evil is to take place."

Once Erastus was sure no one had trespassed on the dead for whatever bauble they might be carrying, he swept the tarp back over those weathered shells. "Well," he said, "the owner of this boat is a Southern man. A slaver. And naming this boat like he did he's making a point." Erastus used that pipe in one hand as a yardstick pointer. "One side of the river is good, the other evil. You can guess from his point of view which is which. And the boat…is the town in that high bluff guarding the pass."

Erastus started away. "Good night, Charlemagne."

"Charlie…They call me Charlie. And, sir—"

Erastus stopped, and Charlie, in a soft voice, so as not to be overheard by spying ears, said, "You think you could find a place for me beyond these chains?"

"Solomon couldn't help you right this minute. See, there's a rumor on the hurricane deck you're heading to Cheapside."

"I don't know what that is, sir."

"Cheapside is the biggest slave market in the state. So, if you're gonna escape, you better get to it."

● ● ●

There was no clawing through the chains, no miracle to jimmy a lock, going over the side was useless, too much tide to cross to reach land. Not even Jesus could walk that far on water. Charlie remained vigilant through the witching hours, searching for a snag along the river—a fallen tree, parts of a boat wreck, cargo swept overboard - anything he could cling to as a raft.

His hope for escape grew grimmer by the hour and what was left but this brood of drunken deck passengers wandering about in the dark and pissing over the railing where he sat, accompanied by a banjo and Jew's harp no less, and singing…*The mas'r is proud of the old breadbore, for it brings him plenty of tin…The crew is darkies and the cargo corn, and the sentry comes tumblin' in…There is plenty on board for the darkies to eat, and there's somethin' to drink and smoke… Der's the banjo, da bones, and the tambourine, der's the song and the comic joke.*

Whoever wrote that damn song, Charlie thought, hadn't spent much time on a steamer decked out in about forty pounds of chain.

Come morning he was still a slave and in chains when they docked at Saint Louis...and still a slave and in chains when Penrose Doral marched off to the train depot in all her benevolence with a platoon of orphans.

Even desperation had failed him, and he was left alongside the two captured blacks and Cassius, by the wagon that would carry them to Cheapside and their ultimate fate.

CHAPTER 32

"How would you like to live in a good hotel?"

Charlie had been sitting on a broken down cratebox in the sun by the wharf and he looked up to see who was talking, and were they talking to him.

A young man in a light colored linen suit with slickly combed butter color hair, and clean, clean hands was smiling down at him from all that sunshine.

"How would you like to live in a good hotel?"

Charlie shaded his eyes to see better. "I don't have any reason to say no to that...so far..."

The young man laughed at the somewhat impertinent answer, especially under the circumstances. He could not have been thirty and his expression, a portrait of childlike wonder, which Charlie could not figure out at all.

"Daddy," said the young man. "This is the boy I was telling you about."

A few feet away was an elderly gentleman in a similarly colored linen suit with cloud white hair and finely barbered goatee. He was resting a bit on a cane.

"You're right, Beckley," he said. "That damn child is near about as white as you and me."

Beckley pointed to the two blacks with Charlie, squatting there in the sun and silent as stones. "Put the boy next to a couple of niggers dark as those two and he'd be whiter than winter. What's your name again?"

"Charlie...Charlie Griffin."

"Charlie...That won't do. Charles. It's got a better money feel to it."

Charlie glanced at Cassius who was over by the plankway in conversation with the Megiddo captain. "I don't know if Mr. Doral would allow me talking to you gentlemen."

"He knows we're gonna bid for you at the auction."

"Sir?"

"We have plans for you, Charles. We're promoters," Beckley said.

"You can read and write?" said the old man.

"Yes, sir."

"Talks well, doesn't he?" said Beckley. "And he'll look fine in a suit."

Beckley Paul and his father, Luther, were promoters. And Beckley had come up with a proposal that was brilliant in its simplicity. They were going to create a charitable organization that was to be named the American Mission Society. Its purpose was to raise money to establish and run small schools for black students in poor communities. And in the spirit of equality, the Society would be run by a freedman. The Pauls had a couple of candidates in mind who were first class sharpers. One in particular had been branded on his forehead by a former "mas'ra" for thinking too much. He made a fine presentation, could speak well, and spin out quite a tale when called upon.

Charlie—Charles—was to be the centerpiece of this venture. The Pauls would clean him up, dress him up, and start him up parading from one Northern city to another—Chicago, Cleveland, Buffalo, New York, Boston—anywhere one could find abolitionists with deep pockets and bleeding hearts. They would rent a meeting hall or local church, and Charlie would tell his story. And if not exactly his story, a story that Beckley and Luther fleshed out with details that would make *Uncle Tom's Cabin* pale by comparison.

They would also take photographs of Charles. Calotypes actually, so they could print endless paper copies. These they would sell for, say, twenty-five cents apiece to also fund the Society.

"Just think," said Beckley, "your own photograph of a black child, signed to you personally." And Luther, who was a fanatic when it came to creative detail, came up with the idea of draping Charles in an American flag for some of the pictures, and in others, the flag would be the backdrop, instead of a blank canvas tarp.

Of course, the true brilliance of the plan was the fact that Beckley was using a boy who basically passed for white. You see, he had long since realized that most white people, even the most ardent abolitionist, were uncomfortable around members of the Negro race. They wanted them to partake of freedom and enjoy personal dignity, but they didn't want to actually socialize with them. They wanted to offer a helping hand, but at a polite distance.

A child who basically looked white would make it a lot easier to arouse their sympathy. They could look at Charles, talk to him, touch him. He could be one of their own precious children. That was the cynical originality of the plan that made it reek of success.

The Pauls had not only made a fortune in the past biting the hand that fed them, they had devoured it right up to the elbow.

Charles saw this confidence scheme as a perfect means of escape. Once he'd shed those irons and was in a northern city, he'd be gone quicker than Br'er Rabbit.

To think he'd been dying of distress an hour ago, and now… Give a fella just a dash of hope and he's off to the races. And he did shill up to the Pauls, pouring on the attitude with "Thank you, sir" and "Yes, sir, that's right smart," and "I can sure do that for you, sir."

And then he had a thought that absolutely felled him. Luther and Beckley Paul were his father and him. Older, better dressed, and more well heeled, certainly, but they were part of the same rank corruption, dragging decent souls along on their larcenous ride. And the joy Charlie saw in them over their plan to shellac the public reminded him of a life badly lived. If he were alone, Charlie would shed some dirty tears over it. Instead he did all the appropriate "Mas'ra" business while silently he redoubled his determination to see the journey to its completed promise.

CHAPTER 33

CHARLIE KNEW NOTHING about the slave auctions, and his mind could not register fast enough or clearly enough all the travesties he saw. It was a block long mob scene of blacks and buyers. The blacks all lined up in rows or standing on benches with their arms at their sides, so potential buyers at the back of the crowd could see well enough when the bidding started.

There were stalls past the courthouse where buyers would go to inspect their potential chattel. The buyer there to fondle and grope, force mouths open to inspect teeth, make the black walk, run in place, do exaggerated movements to prove they were not handicapped or lame. They would prod and squeeze muscles to determine youth, or make them bare their backs to see if they'd been whipped for being a troublemaking nigger. Many of the young women were stripped naked, some of the men also, the ones they really thought to be bucks.

Charlie had never witnessed human beings naked like that, stared upon as beasts in the pure sunlight, and he averted his eyes. The Dorals led him past a whipping post on the courthouse lawn, there to remind the slave comportment was mandatory.

When it was his time to be viewed, Charlie, being light skinned, young, and well spoken, drew a particular crowd of buyers.

The Pauls were there, as well as a number of well-to-dos who wanted a light skinned house nigger who knew how to read and write. Lewis Robards had sent a roadman down from his Short Street office where he had an upstairs of mulatto fancy girls. Charlie might be a natural to stud out. There's always a market for light skins. Then there's another type of buyer altogether, who prized having a handsome young valet to satisfy their private needs.

All Charlie's possible masters had one thing in common. They wanted to see him naked. He was ordered to be off with his clothes. He had no way to contend with such business. They had removed his shackles, and he could have run, but to where? He was hemmed in by a congress of plantation owners and businessmen and there were at least half a dozen auction block workers, all black and full grown, who looked well versed at handling insurrection.

He was ordered again under threat.

He slipped off his haversack and set it on the ground. Then he did the same with the coat. The coat with the money sewn into the lining. All that money...right there. And no one had any idea. Money to escape from the world with, if one so desired.

"Be quick about it, boy."

He looked for a place in his mind to hide, but there was none. He lifted a leg and removed one shoe and then did the same for the other. He unbuttoned his shirt. He was a living piece of forsaken immobility with the terrible spinning of the world going on around him. He felt the sting of the auctioneer's crop on the back of his legs.

"Quicker, boy."

He removed his shirt and let it drop to the grass. He undid his trousers. He shed the last of his clothing and stood there to the great satisfaction of the buyers, the prurient eyes of the plantation owner and businessman, the salacious stares of the Dorals and the Pauls. There was a cold pleasure in the power to have someone naked and helpless before you. He could feel that without even looking. What tests some of God's creations must withstand from their own.

There were hard veins in those stares and claws that fastened around your heart until there was painful utter shame at your plight. And he knew for the first time, truly the first time, what it must be like to be any of those black souls on the auction block. To be at the mercy of the auction block. A power more violent, more intrusive, more almighty than any weapon created.

To know the auction block was to know where the family was torn apart, where children are taken from you, your pride stolen, your hope broken, your sense of being and purpose stripped and blackened. And he knew it now, as they knew it before him.

He was prized young manhood that would fit any number of tasks. He was prodded and touched and talked about like he did not even exist—less than gossip or a quick joke or "how's the weather?" The auctioneer used that crop to make him face one way and then the other. To turn and bend over, to get down on his haunches and then spring upright. They remarked on his pure skin, and no scars, the firm muscle.

He was in a footrace with those few minutes, trying to escape what he could not outrun. He kept his line of vision upon one tree on the courthouse lawn. The sunlight streaming down through the branches like God's own mercy. He thought of the tree outside his mother's cell. A cell now shared, hundreds of miles apart. He thought of playing Mansion of Happiness on the train with Missus Watters. Maybe this day, this hour, this moment is where you had landed on vices and had to move backward before you started forward again. He thought of the poem. Would all this taking place in the courthouse square become part of the child?

He seethed with the need to cry, but refused. Who said hatred is a slow fire? He'd heard his father claim the world is full of charlatans and madmen, but no one seems to notice. He was a trembling witness to that fact. Would all that become part of the child in the poem?

"Dark are the walls we build to stand higher than the next man. And yet these same walls keep us further from heaven."

Someone in the crowd had said that aloud. Someone the crowd was now railing against. Impossible to see who it was. An errant preacher…A proselytizer for the god of the darkies…A traitor to the sovereign state of Kentucky.

"Do I hear a hundred…I have a hundred…Do I hear two hundred…I have two hundred…Do I hear two hundred and fifty…?"

The auctioneer was in full throat.

There were a handful of bidders until the auctioneer reached "I have six hundred…I have six hundred…Do I hear six hundred and fifty…?"

When they topped eight hundred it was down to two bidders. One was the Pauls, the other a well known agent representing clients who preferred to remain private. The Pauls knew this type of bidder might well tend to the salacious, which meant the bid could be more emotional, reckless.

"I have eight hundred…Do I hear eight hundred and fifty…?"

The Pauls hesitated. Charlie was dressed by then. He held his haversack and coat against his chest, which was hollowing out with each successive call from the auctioneer. When the Pauls finally bid, Charlie felt a momentary release from panic.

"I have eight hundred fifty…Do I hear nine…Do I hear nine…?"

The Pauls watched the agent bid without hesitation.

"I have nine…Do I hear nine fifty…?"

Again the Pauls talked among themselves. Uncertain, glancing from Charlie to the agent, whispering to each other. Charlie wanted to scream out, "Bid, you sorry basta—"

But he knew. He knew already. He had witnessed these instances of uncertainty in the expression of the people his father had tried to hustle. The Pauls were not prepared to bid that high against the unknown. That demands another level of daring, or foolishness. They needed to see the actual bidder. To evaluate his intent, how he dressed, acted, did his expression give away need or desperation? Yes, Charlie could read The Pauls like a preacher could read the Bible. With his eyes closed.

The auctioneer pressed.

"I have nine hundred…Do I hear nine hundred and fifty…?"

The Pauls failed to bid.

"Sold," said the auctioneer. And he pointed toward the agent.

CHAPTER 34

CHARLIE WAS HAULED OFF like livestock by one of the blacks who worked for the auctioneers to where the agent was preparing Charlie's bill of sale.

"Sir, who was I sold—"

"Take him to my waiting pen," said the agent, handing a set of papers to the black.

The black obeyed. Charlie tried to ask again, but the black shoved him forward with a meaty hand square between the boy's shoulders. They passed the Dorals who were waiting for their payment and Charlie hocked on the ground right in front of them. The black grabbed the boy by his scroungy collar, apologizing to the Dorals, and shook him. "Just 'cause ya look like a white boy, don't mean ya can ac' like a white boy."

Charlie clung to his haversack and coat as he was veered and herded and prodded along no better than some sheep. There were holding pens down on Limestone in an empty lot by the McGowan Jail. The roadway was lined with wagons and well appointed carriages and Charlie was dragged toward, of all things…a hearse. And framed within that glass housing, three stacked coffins Charlie recognized.

Sitting curbside and smoking a pipe was Erastus Eels himself. He was reading the *Lexington Observer*, a disinterested portrait of a gentleman as ever was. The black handed him Charlie's bill of sale.

"It was you…?"

Erastus folded the newspaper. He had a rangy length about him as he stood, and a look of hardened satisfaction. "You are now the property of Erastus Eels… Undertaker."

A look of abject fear of the unknown seemed to dissolve quite a bit in the boy's expression.

"Let's hope neither of us lives to regret this," said Erastus. "Now…climb aboard that cemetery roamer. We got challenges tonight, Charlemagne. And things could get mighty indecorous."

As the boy climbed up on the box seat, he reminded Erastus, "Charlie, sir…They call me Charlie."

Erastus reined those horses into the road and put the whip to them good. They were traveling out of Lexington and toward the afternoon sun. And putting quick miles under the wheels too, thought Charlie.

"I want to thank you, sir. I don't know if I said it before. I was so excited—"

"I wonder what the Pauls would think if they found out they'd been shucked from having their boy."

"I know how I felt."

"I'm sure you did."

"What have you got in store for me…if I might ask?"

Erastus put on his best formal stare. A look that said he was all too familiar with defiance and destruction. "If you jumped from this wagon, right now, just jumped into the road and took off back yonder into the trees, I probably couldn't catch you, could I?"

Charlie looked back over the hub of that cemetery wagon. A country road like endless country roads making the way from whence they'd come. Hillocks swept with trees, immense spances of wild grass and soft ravines, a lone farmhouse in the shadows of afternoon. Charlie wondered about what to answer. Considered the truth a better option than a lie, particularly under the circumstances.

"I could probably get away. I run fast. Of course, you might have a gun and take it to heart to shoot me."

Erastus opened his frock coat. Tucked down in his trousers a single action Colt that had some real wear on it. He tapped the gun gently. "I carried this pretty thing with me during the Mexican War."

"I thought you were an undertaker?"

Erastus let out a grim laugh. "In case you haven't heard, in war everyone is an undertaker."

They continued on, Charlie taking sidelong glances from time to time at his new master. Lots of wondering going on in that boy's head.

"You know what I like best to read in newspapers?" said Erastus?

"I'm afraid I don't, Mister Eels."

"The special notices...Public sales. Someone's got a deal on foreign liquors, for instance...or paintings to sell...A country residence with all kinds of nooks... Spanish Jacks...I particularly love ads for Spanish Jacks...And wild game, too...Or a new cathartic pill. They always give me a boost to read. Promising vitality to your loins when they're too tuckered out for swordplay."

Erastus threw his head back and hooted. "They don't write the ad quite that way. But they should. By the way," he said, changing the subject, "do you know how to use a gun?"

Charlie got a little wide eyed. Just for a hitch. "Excuse me?"

"Pistol…shotgun…rifle?"

"Yes, sir. I'm not a crackerjack shot. Fair with a pistol. Can hit a can if it's not far. Not much with a rifle. And a shotgun—"

"You know what special notice caught my eye today in the Lexington paper, while I was waiting on you?"

"I'm afraid I don't, sir. See, I was too busy being auctioned off at the time up the street, to notice."

Erastus let out a crackling mean laugh. "Sense of humor, boy, in a slave is a good thing. It'll make the decades of suffering just roll by."

"I'm happy to hear it."

"Well, in the paper, there was an ad from a shop on Main Street. Selling new toppers with corrugated brims. They promised beautiful style and finish. Now, if I'd a had time, I'd a strolled over to Main Street and seen how one of those new toppers set on my altogether unregal head. That's what I love about the special notices. It seems like everyone in America is selling one thing or another. What are you selling, Charlemagne?"

"Sir, they call me—"

"Don't sir me. Call me Erastus. Call me Mister Eels. Call me Charon himself. But answer the damn question, what are you selling?"

CHAPTER 35

THERE WAS A DREADFUL BITE in his tone and that shook the boy up considerably.

"Well? What are you selling?"

"I'm selling nuthin'."

"You think you can pull a thimblerig on me?"

"No. I wouldn't even—"

"Half of what you say sounds like a lie, and the other half couldn't be anything but a lie. Charlemagne, you're one of those people who's on the move even when they're sittin' still."

"My name is…forget it. Mister Eels, sir, Erastus… I'm just trying to stay alive."

"How original. Let me catch my breath before I faint."

They were silent after that. Just the two in their own worlds and the slow humdrum clopping of the horses on a hardened road.

As the day wore on, every now and then a wagon or rider drifted past, each and all raising a hat or nodding deferentially at the dead they were carrying.

They came upon a covered bridge near about dusk. The terrain around it lush with thicket and trees. Erastus brought the hearse to a halt. He took out his pipe and lit a bowl and sat looking over the pleasant quietude.

"What are you looking at?"

"The scenery," he said. He glanced back down the road. It was long and straight until it disappeared in the waning light. He ordered Charlie to come with him.

Charlie jumped to the ground and joined Erastus as he surveyed the bridge and the shallow creek it crossed over. He followed the rough edge of the brush along the roadway.

Erastus went and opened the back of the hearse. Charlie saw there were a collection of shotguns and rifles wedged alongside a coffin. Erastus grabbed hold of a stock and passed the double aught to Charlie. "You'll be using this."

What in the world could be going on in that man's mind, thought Charlie, hoisting the shotgun up on his shoulder while Erastus picked through a pile of canvas and cloth scraps in the back of the hearse. He hauled out piece after piece, testing each to find one that fit around the boy's head, and when he did, he tossed it to Charlie. "Tear strips along the edge so you can cover your face below the eyes and tie it off."

The boy leaned the shotgun against the wheel and did as told, cutting the strips, and when he put the cloth to his face so he could try and tie it off, his head jerked back.

"What's that smell?" said Charlie.

Erastus had been hunting up a scrap that would work for him. Charlie held up the rag. "It stinks god awful."

"It's probably got a little of the fluid on it I use to embalm the corpses. And sometimes…well…when you wipe down a body, you pick up traces of that human rot."

Charlie felt a little bile launch up into his throat. He tossed the cloth back in the hearse. "Maybe I could find one that—"

"Sure. But follow me first."

Erastus walked down the road a ways. He pointed to a patch of vine strangled thorny bushes by a clump of grey stones.

"You see those rocks there?"

"Yeah."

"That'll be your station. Just off the road. Back in the brush. Where you can't be seen. When I yell to you to fire off your weapon, you put a shot straight into the air. One shot. Understand?"

"One shot. In the air. When you call to me."

Erastus walked back to that cemetery wagon, smoking his pipe, contemplating the contours of the landscape around the bridge. He reached into the back of the hearse and out came this strange looking coat that went to his ankles. He slipped on it.

"What is that thing?" said Charlie.

"It's a Mackintosh. From England. Made of what they call vulcanized rubber. Doctors use them during autopsies and dissections. Cause you can wash the blood right off a them."

Charlie blinked, stared dumb struck.

"Now aren't you glad you asked?"

• • •

Charlie took up his position in the brush. The night soaked up any trace of him. Erastus had hidden the hearse in a clump of trees beyond the bridge and far enough from the road you'd need a dousing rod to locate it. Erastus himself was this side of the bridge where the creek ran wild over grey stones.

Charlie had no idea who or what they were waiting on. The few times a wagon passed he thought, this might be it. He was wrong.

He had lonely time to think. He could have taken off and been free, fast as you can snap your fingers, but he didn't. He felt this sense of debt to the undertaker that manhood demanded he play out.

Soon after, on the wind, Charlie heard strained singing and then the heavy echo of hooves crossing that covered bridge.

"Weep no more my lady, ohhh, weep no more today...we will sing one song for the old Kentucky home..."

The songster could hardly keep in the saddle and not thirty paces from where Charlie hid, the rider reeled out and landed hard in the road. He gave his poor steed hell for the ungracious way he'd been dumped. He even kicked the poor mount. But did that quiet his singing, it did not.

Charlie thought, this can't be who we're waiting for.

"They hunt no more for the possum and the coon...on the meadow, the hill and the shore..." The drunkard staggered 'round his mount. *"The time has come when the darkies have to part..."*

It took him a couple of tries to set a boot into that stirrup so he could hoist up and dump his plump fanny into the saddle, and off he went.

"The head must bow and the back will have to bend... Wherever the darkie may go..."

When it got all quiet again except for the sound of night critters moving about the darkness, Erastus called out, "Enjoying yourself there, Charlemagne?"

Charlie winced. "Having a grand old time, Mister Erastus. Out here in the middle of nowhere with a hearse full of dead folks and waiting on who knows what. Who could ask for better?"

"Good...'Cause I believe our party's coming."

Charlie pushed some brush aside. There was a speck of light making its way along, far down the road. From the way it glowed, it looked to be a lantern hung from a wagon most probably.

Charlie waited till those hooves and wheels were right up on him, and he poked his masked face forward. It was a lantern all right and who should be up there on the box seat, illuminated in all that kerosene glow, but the Dorals.

CHAPTER 36

WHEN THE DORALS NEARED THE BRIDGE, Erastus stepped out into the road, his face covered, the vulcanized coat glowing from the lantern like something dark and wet from the sea. He was bearing a shotgun. He fired off a shell into the weeds. There was a gasp, but it wasn't from Penrose.

"Pull up those horses," Erastus shouted, and the brother obeyed.

Charlie had made his way out from the brush. Erastus had hold of the leads. "Get down off that wagon."

Penrose stood. "Do you have any idea who I am?"

"Why...you're an all too precious lady who's going to bleed all over that wagon if you don't grace me with your presence. Now get down into the road and bring your wealth."

"I have a gun here," she said. "And it's aimed right at you."

Erastus shouted, "It's time now."

Charlie fired off the shotgun. The blast wreaking havoc on his ears.

Well, this put the fear of God in Cassius and he stepped down from the box seat, arms above his head all droopy at the wrists, his

156

shoulders stooped. He looked like a damn weeping willow.

Penrose was consumed with rage and wouldn't yield to threats, so Erastus fired off another round and blew the lantern all to hell. An explosion of sparks and glass across the night. Bits of fire everywhere. Penrose slapped at small sparks of fire on her evening coat.

The horses spooked and reared and Charlie saw it was all Erastus could do to control them and so Charlie came hauling it up the road.

"Get down now," shouted Erastus, "or you'll be deader than Cleopatra."

Penrose climbed down carefully, holding her dress, and cursing like an unholy sailor.

"Go to the side of the road and turn around."

The Dorals did as they were told. The brother pleading in a colicky kind of way. Erastus stood behind them and swiped at the air as if contending with a rank odor. "One of you is going to need a change of undergarments."

Penrose Doral could not tell Erastus in enough descriptive ways what a vile, swamp minded creature he was.

"Dump your wallet and purse back here in the road."

Charlie was calming the horses while Erastus went through the Doral's belongings. He told Charlie to loose the team and chase them away.

"You're gonna leave us to walk?" shouted Penrose.

There wasn't much among the Dorals' belongings. Certainly not the price of two slaves and Charlie Griffin.

"Thin pickings," said Erastus, "for such fine citizens."

"We don't believe in carrying paper money. We deal in bank drafts, you pathetic fool."

"Your arrogance humbles me to no end."

Charlie had the team loose and he hurrahed them till they were stampeding it over those bridge planks.

"Well," said Penrose, "are you done with us?"

Erastus pressed the shotgun against the back of Cassius' head. "Before we part ways, I'd like to satisfy my curiosity and see if you might have a money belt tucked down in your bloomers."

Cassius wafted his arm as his way of saying he would do as told. It was either take off the coat or undo the galluses. He was so clumsy with fright, he got one gallus loose and the coat half off and he was a befuddled mess. But it didn't matter. Erastus groped him around the waist, and sure enough ——

Erastus tore the money belt loose.

"We'll see you in jail for this," said Penrose.

"Yeah…but which one of us will be in the cell?"

He knelt and got a good look at the packets. They had body to them. He tossed the money belt to Charlie.

Cassius said, "You're not going to kill us, are you?"

Erastus stood. Charlie watched him. He did not want the Dorals killed. Erastus was fingering the shotgun. It got so quiet all you could hear was the creek, the water bubbling over the rocks, making its way through the night to the Ohio, the river of freedom.

"Say something, mister," said Cassius.

His voice was pitiable.

"Strip," said Erastus. "Both of you."

"What?" said Penrose.

"Everything. You're on the auction block tonight. And you're gonna walk out of here like you crawled out from the womb."

The begging that came out of Cassius Doral went right down into your soul.

"No," said Charlie. "Don't do it."

Erastus turned to the boy.

"Don't make them. That's just—"

The boy was being blindly honest. He wanted to spare them a painful degradation he knew too well. It was enough to have to exist with the memory of it oneself, without having to relive it through some cursed revenge.

"Please," he said. "Just let them go."

Penrose turned. She'd recognized the voice and when she saw this masked youth in the moonless road, even dark as it was, wearing that ragboy coat and the hideous railroad cap, "It's you," she said. Her voice filled with venom. She was in a complete state of indignation and rage. "I'll have you jailed for this and not in some reformatory either."

Now she turned her poisonous stare upon Erastus. "And you... I'll bet you're the one on the boat. That god ugly scarecrow of an under—"

Erastus grabbed her by the face and shoved her from the road. The ground there gave way to a swale of undergrowth where she tumbled down, a grey looking figure to disappear in the gloom, leaving behind a trail of curses marking her way. And her brother, he didn't have to be told, or shoved. He just jumped, like the prancy little coward that he was.

Erastus took off running and Charlie followed. The heavy clopping of their boots as they crossed the bridge.

Erastus stopped somewhere down the road, a little strung out for breath, and pulled off the canvas covering his face.

"She knows it's you, Charlemagne. She can make a lot of trouble in this section of country."

"Maybe you'll see your way clear to let me head to Kansas."

Charlie handed Erastus the money belt. Erastus slung it over his shoulder and studied the boy standing there deep in the privacy of his own reasons.

"You not wanting me to strip 'em. Charlemagne, you might be a little too Christian for your own good."

"I'll try to be better next time, Mister Eels."

CHAPTER 37

OUT OF A PLAIN AND ORDINARY SILENCE, came this awkward but extraordinary statement, "My father stole a lot of money from a church."

They had been traveling the night on that hearse for a good long while, past lone farmhouses and wayside townships spotted up in the darkness with a few hearth fires. On both sides of the box seat were kerosene headlamps. So, the road was always a few spare yards of light and the shadows of the horses ahead of them. Slow and ghostly and beautiful in its own way. A kind of solitude for the imagination, and it caught Erastus unaware to hear the boy come out with this.

He had been smoking his pipe which he now removed from his mouth, and said, "Did I hear you right?"

"Yes, sir."

"Stole...from a church."

"Schemed actually."

"From...?"

"Henry Ward Beecher."

"The abolitionist?"

"And evangelist. He runs a church in Brooklyn… Plymouth Congregational."

"Beecher…His sister—"

"Wrote *Uncle Tom's Cabin*."

"Your old man was shooting pretty high."

"Well, he did have a sense of himself, yes."

"How did he steal it?"

"Well, like I said. It wasn't stealing. It was more of a confidence game."

"Well, that makes all the blessed difference in the world."

"I know your meaning, Mister Eels."

"You think you can see your way clear to entertain me with the story? I mean, if you have the time."

Well, Charlie had already reckoned he'd let it all come out with Erastus. So he told him the whole tale there on the road, spinning out one truth after another, having no idea that Erastus Eels was taking them to the Kentucky town of Shippingport on the Ohio River, where the undertaker had every intention of pulling off a little political mischief of his own.

When the boy was done, Erastus just sat there staring like he was rooted to the box seat, but he wasn't staring at the boy so much, as he was that frayed piece of cloth disguising itself as a coat. As a matter of fact, he pointed his pipe right at it a number of times.

"That's right," said Charlie.

The undertaker threw his head back and hooted out so loud it scared the bejesus out of the horses and their drowsy heads reared up.

"Is it that funny?" said Charlie.

"I was thinkin' about the Dorals. All the effort for nine hundred dollars of mine they no longer have. And if they only knew—"

He pointed his pipe again at the coat. "I'm inclined to write them. Later, of course." He started imagining the letter. "Dear Penrose and Cassius…Hope this letter finds you in miserable health… thought I'd pen you prejudiced degenerates to antagonize you further…And if what I tell you don't make you scream the teeth right out of your head…then I'm no judge of character…Signed yours truly and all that…Erastus Eels and his knight in training one Charlemagne Ezekiel Griffin.

"How did you come to decide to tell *me* this, Charlemagne?"

"Charlie, not Charla…" Ah, what was the use, Charlie thought. "My father used to say, 'the first man you trust, may be the last man you tell.'"

"I hate statements that have the ring of bitter truth to them. But you told me anyway."

"I discovered I don't exactly think like my father in such matters. And that thought has left me awfully concerned and feeling quite contrary."

Erastus smoked his pipe and considered. The horses pulling slowly. The wind rustling up all kinds of sounds and shadows that made you listen and look. "Thoughts have a nasty habit of doing that," said Erastus. "First, you have one thought you just start to get comfortable with and here comes another contradicting the first, and then a third pops up out of nowhere like a bandit, disagreeing with the second and the first, and pretty soon you're breeding thoughts all over the place 'til the inside of your head is overrun with 'em. It's the stuff that begets drunkards, villains, and philosophers, that's for sure."

"I know you're making a joke, but it's true anyways."

"But how did you come to tell…me…*me*. How did you decide?"

Charlie bit his lip. He knew, yet felt unsure to say. The fear of seeming foolish seemed to be a constant. "Back at the bridge when I asked you not to strip them. You didn't. You didn't have to do as I asked. I expected you wouldn't. But you did."

. . .

It was not the light upon his eyelids that awoke him, but the fact the hearse was not moving. He sat up on the box seat where he had been sleeping and looked about. He was covered with the vulcanized coat.

They were camped in a small clearing. The horses had been loosed and were grazing. Smoke from a small fire where a pot of coffee brewed drifted into the bluish light. Charlie stepped down into the wet grass. There was as yet a chill in the air and he draped the coat around him. Erastus, being well over six feet tall, the hemline scored along the ground.

They were somewhere on the shores of what must have been the Ohio. The banks on both sides hidden by river birch and pawpaws. He found Erastus down by the water where the soil had eroded, and the tree roots were exposed to the sun, and had blackened from years of dry mud. Erastus was sipping from a chipped coffee mug.

"Thanks for the coat," said Charlie. He noted the campfires back in the trees stretching far downriver. "Where are we?"

"Shippingport. Across the river is Clarksville, Indiana. A lot has happened along this stretch of river. Slave catchers." He was pointing at the fires. "Lot of bones under all that water of the ones that didn't make it."

Charlie was staring upstream. A ferry was crossing those muddy waters to Clarksville.

"Do you know who Lewis and Clark were?" said Erastus.

"I can't say I do."

"President Jefferson commissioned them back in eighteen aught three to explore the country bought in the Louisiana Purchase. That exploration started right here when Lewis sent his friend Clark a letter asking him to be second in command."

Erastus sipped his coffee and looked Charlie over. Charlie was still intent on that ferry. A boy in an oversized coat. Going forth on the chance that all hopes are created equal and righteous effort will be rewarded. A boy who had already stockpiled enough irony for a lifetime, but didn't even know it.

"You know anybody in Kansas?"

"My father knew a couple of gamers, but they were road people."

"In Missouri?"

"No."

"Know anyone who can guide you to this James Montgomery in Kansas?"

"No."

"How will you do it? What's your plan?"

"Plan? I guess...I'll start walkin' and as I go I'll start askin'."

"You know what border ruffians are?"

"Slavers that travel in packs and roust up free staters."

"They're all over Missouri. Along with highwaymen, ragtag thieves, blood villains, and every type of abettor you can conjure up."

Erastus finished his coffee. Down the river were men with a pack of hunting dogs on long leads. They were scouring the brush.

"How would you like to learn about embalming?"

"Learn about it...Why?"

"It's a timely profession. With all the new scientific advancements. Plenty of opportunity on the horizon for a go-getter. Some say it's the coming rage."

"But you have to be around dead bodies all the time?"

"It makes them a lot more compliant about being embalmed."

Just the thought of all those corpses had Charlie gettin' squirrely all over.

"I think I'll shy away from that career if you don't mind."

Erastus tossed away the last of his coffee. "Is there a surprise in store for you."

He had spoken offhandedly.

Charlie said, "What?"

"Forget it."

Erastus started back toward the hearse. "I know someone down in Cairo. He might be able to set you in the right direction. If the ruffians haven't finished him off yet."

In the clearing, the damp air was touched with the scent of wood smoke. You could hear the dogs in the distance howling away. Someone was on the run. Their existence hanging in the decision of a few seconds, or a change in the wind. Can they swim well, will their legs hold out, will fear overcome their cunning?

"Erastus...why did you buy me off the block? You didn't need to. I can see that now."

Erastus was alongside the cemetery wagon, with his imposing, hollowed look, a scorched purpose to the eye. He took something from his black frockcoat pocket and said, "Catch."

He tossed it to the boy. Charlie knew right off what that black and white bauble was before he even caught it. Sure enough. The medallion the Doral woman had thrown away in contempt.

"I saw it carom across the deck," said Erastus. "One of the coffins kept it from kicking into the river."

It was like a piece of his past had been given back to him. And Charlie held it in both hands as if it were such. Even his father was

166

there in that bit of jasperware, in the crummy boardinghouse room the night before his death.

"How can I thank you?" said Charlie.

"You'll get your fill of thanking me before this night is over."

CHAPTER 38

THEY WERE LED BY A SILENT CRONE of a black woman on a mule. It was a long day's ride and by nightfall they were on a dirt road far back from the river. In the distance a few lights among the darker shapes of the trees. The faint impression of two shotgun cottages where a dozen blacks sat soundless watching their approach. A white man appeared in the pooling light of a doorway as the hearse pulled up. The white man waved to Erastus, who nodded and then told Charlie to get down from the wagon seat.

The white man was named Abraham, and he wore the clothes of a well to do. Erastus introduced Mister Abraham to one Charlemagne Griffin, his friend and youthful associate.

Charlie had no idea why they were here. Only that as of this moment the blacks on the porch were being herded into the cottages until there were but two young black men remaining. One of them seemed to be named Jupiter and Erastus asked him, "Are the graves dug yet?"

Jupiter pointed to a path among the trees.

"Charlemagne will stay here and help. Jupe, just tell him what to do."

Jupiter said to the young black man beside him, "Merc, get a hammer for 'dis boy."

Erastus told Charlie, "I've got to go off with Mister Abraham. If things go bad, head to the ferry landing. I'll catch up with you, if I can."

"What's all this—"

Erastus didn't answer. Charlie watched him walk to the hearse and get his pistol from the box seat. Tucking it into his trousers, he followed Mister Abraham along a walking path that traced up past the cottages.

The one called Merc handed Charlie a claw hammer.

"What do I do with it?"

"It's for res'rectin' da dead."

Charlie had no idea what the hell they meant, and didn't want to ask.

The first thing that had to be done was lug those coffins from the hearse and then labor them down into the woods where Jupiter had pointed.

Making their way in the dark, the smell of summer pine and jasmine in the air, then setting a coffin down beside one large hole, then going to retrieve the next, Charlie got the whole history of these two cousins named Jupiter and Mercury.

It seems their master, who had since passed away and willed them their freedom, had thought up the notion to name all the slaves born on his farm after the planets. And when he ran out of the planets, he went to work on the constellations. He said once he ran through the constellations, he would start to name the babies after the capitol for each of the slave states. It was, he'd said, his way of showing private ownership of the universe.

Mister Abraham had leased the cousins this land, and they were free to hire out or work any profitable trade they cared to. Charlie asked, if they were free, why didn't they cross the river?

"We got family," said Jupiter, speaking for both cousins, "and we got good business here." Charlie suspected there was more to it than that from the tone of the answer. But he didn't notice Merc wink at his cousin.

"Hey, Charleemain," said Jupe. "You okay wit' dead folks?"

Merc was already busy loosing nails from a coffin lid.

"What does that mean?" said Charlie.

"It mean like it say."

Merc pointed his hammer, and told Charlie, "We got ta get da lid op'n, boy."

Charlie looked at a coffin, looked at the hole. "I don't understand."

"Jupe," Merc said, "should we tell him?"

"Naaa," said Jupe.

"Tell me what?"

"Tell him, Jupe. It best."

"If you feel so. Charleemain, we got to take dem bodies from da box and toss 'em into dat hole."

Charlie looked from the coffin to the hole. Why was there just one hole? It sure wasn't big enough for three coffins. Charlie felt his stomach begin to move on a course all its own, and in a most uncomfortable manner. Charlie, not wanting to seem like the coward, began to use that hammer claw and pry up the nails. But he was feeling a pale sweat creep along the edges of his forehead. And he knew what that usually led to.

Every time a rusty nail grated out from those pine boards, Charlie got gamier and gamier. And when the cousins pulled free the coffin lid and Charlie saw into that box a decaying mess that had once been an older gentleman. Holy bejeezus. The corpse looked like some kind of desiccated hermit in a suit. With a mouth permanently wide open like he was about to shout out, and his eyes in this half fluttery, sort of open, but not really look, like he'd just woke up from a nap. Charlie began to gag, his chest constricting and expanding like a poorboy bellows.

"Now, Charleemain," said Merc, "dis is impo'tant. We got to lift da body and toss in da hole."

"And when ya lift da body," said Jupe, "what been dead a long while, sometime dey come apart."

"Like a chicken dat been boil't too long," added Merc. "And a wing or a leg jest drops off."

Just imagining that had Charlie scrambling from the hole, and there he was bent over, hands clasped to his knees and puking up a bucket's worth of his insides.

"Dat no man of da world," said Merc to his cousin.

Ohhh…the cousins took to commiserating over the boy's plight like they were genuinely concerned.

"You just keep pukin', boy. We'll lift da body."

A few moments later there was a thud and Merc said, "Holy heaven…da head fell off."

Charlie did not want to have *anything* to do with this.

"Hey, Charlee-main, we got sumthin' for you."

Nothing to do whatsoever.

"Here…catch."

Merc tossed something at Charlie. It could have been the head, it was about the right size. It was coming right at him and Charlie put out a hand to block it. It wasn't the head, but a pillow that had been in the coffin. The cousins laughed till they were apocalyptic hoisting the next body out of the coffin and tossing it like a doll into the hole, and there was Charlie gagging till his eyes looked about to blow clear from his skull.

CHAPTER 39

CHARLIE MANAGED TO RIGHT HIMSELF and eventually help the cousins get those corpses into the hole, then covering it over with dirt. He took out a cheroot, and with a knife he borrowed from Jupe, cut it cleanly into thirds. The three ceremoniously sat there in the cool dark of the woods, with Charlie bearing the cousins' humor as they regaled on how he showed no real aptitude for dealing with the dead, but was a pure talent when it came to puking up his guts. Charlie had a fair amount to say on the subject, none of which was for polite company.

When Erastus returned with Mister Abraham, they were not alone. Following in their shadow was a black man and woman and what turned out to be their son of nine years.

They were being hunted hard by the slave catchers and Erastus was there to take them across the river. The man, Charlie was to learn, beat his owner to death with a metal hame for being intent on splitting up his family to pay down debt, breaking a longstanding agreement with the now hunted slave.

They made their preparations, getting each of the three into a coffin with a jug of water. They were deathly afraid, but not as afraid as they were desperate. Each prayed as the coffin was nailed shut.

Erastus took Charlie aside as the coffins were loaded into the hearse. He held out his hand. "Do you know what this is?"

Erastus was palming a deringer.

"Yeah," said Charlie, "I've seen 'em. It's a Philadelphia."

"If things run afoul at the river, I don't know if I can protect you all. So, you're to cut and run. Also…you can go on the ferry like you don't know me. I'll still take you down to Cairo. Unless I end up drinkin' mud."

Charlie took the single shot pistol, and Erastus had a belt pouch of ammunition which he slipped into the boy's haversack.

They journeyed at night so it stayed cool as possible inside the coffins. Erastus would call out from time to time to let them know every little thing was all right. They reached the river by dawn. "We're here now," he said. "Not a word."

There were slave catchers walking the length of the wharves. A rough looking lot of yahoos with wild dogs on long leads. There was an unpitying self-holiness about them. A run in with these boys you'd scarce forget till the day of your death.

Erastus had climbed down and was in conversation with the riverboat captain showing his transit papers and arranging for deck-hands to load the coffins on board.

Charlie went to sitting off alone on a dock pylon to watch the slave catchers harassing blacks waiting for boats, rousting them for information about runaways, intimidating them wherever possible. Their dogs being kept just enough in check so their bared teeth were a lunge away from all that black flesh.

The coffins had been carried from that cemetery wagon and were stacked up by the plankway, and out of civility they were covered by a tarp. The dogs, though still a ways down the wharf, had already begun to strain at their leads.

Charlie could not help but imagine what it would be like nailed inside one of those pine boxes, helpless, waiting, imprisoned by fear—the unknown just inches away, and the heat of the day slowly creeping across that wood casement.

And what if they discovered you there? he thought. What if they decide proper retribution would be to drown you in the river? So the very waters of freedom you struggled toward would seep through the seams between board slats, and you'd slowly sink down into the blind depths of a muddy, barbarous death.

He could not fathom how his mind had taken him to this place, like some dark hand clutching him by the coat to drag him with unremitting force until he saw and felt that he himself was in the box. He could walk away, he had been given that freedom to walk away—had it handed to him like a blessing—but that was not true freedom. That freedom came with its own chains that he did not understand.

Charlie looked to Erastus who, though in conversation still with the captain, had taken note of the dogs clawing at the earth as they pressed toward the stacked and tarped crates. And when the snapping beasts got close enough, one of the slave catchers pulled back the tarp to see that it was coffins.

The animals rose up on their hind legs and were scraping at the wood and Erastus, now in fear for them all, politely presented himself as the undertaker in charge of the bodies, and would the gentleman kindly pull their animals back and show the dead a just respect.

But those slave catchers were another matter altogether. They were hard text who looked to scatter your brains just as surely speak to you. You'd have to flatter yourself to think that civility would rule the day. Erastus reached a point where Charlie saw him undo his coat button, so he could more easily get to his weapon.

Something inside the boy, be it a longstanding rabblement or unspecified rage, brought him to his feet. He was feeling a pain beyond the laws of pure hurt playing out in his life, and before he could even begin to capture what it meant, had him striding right for the slave catchers. By now they were around the coffins, suspicious as much as curious, when Charlie shoved one of them hard in the back. The man turned cursing to see he had been rammed by nothing short of a kid.

"What the hell do ya' think you doin, boy?"

"My father is in one of those coffins, and I won't have you desecratin' them. Now you and that dog git."

The man was enraged up one side and down the other at being ordered by no less than a child. The men with him made sport of his being tongue lashed by a boy.

But the man saw something in that youth's face. Erastus saw it, too. Erastus recognized it. Genuine anger, over the loss of some precious dignity.

Then, Charlie pulled out the deringer and he aimed it, and he heard himself from far, far away saying, "If you and your friends don't move on, I'll shoot that dog."

TAR BABY

CHAPTER 40

A DOORWAY OF LIGHT stretched across the atrium of the Cincinnati hospital. The nurse at the front desk looked up from her reports. The sun reflecting hard upon her gold rimmed glasses. A hulking presence of a man entered and stood before her in a waistcoat and tie. He had a generous smile.

"Can I help you?"

"Yes...I'm here to see a doctor." He handed her a letter and pointed to the name it was signed by. "Sorry... I'm not good at pronouncing certain type foreign names."

"Yes," said the nurse, scanning the signature. "And you are?"

"William Tule."

"And what may I say is this about?"

"The letter, of course. You have a member of the Griffin family here. Rebecca Griffin. Wife of the late Zacharia Griffin. Mother of Charles Griffin. Charlie...a boy about twelve."

"Yes," she said. "The boy was here just two days ago."

"Really," said Tule. "That's the best news I've heard since leavin' Brooklyn."

"Brooklyn...New York?"

"Is there another?"

The doctor led William Tule to the commissary where they sat at one of the long bench tables. It was quiet, the men were alone but for a black who was swishing a mop back and forth across the floor. Each man had a steaming mug of coffee.

Tule sipped and waited as the doctor reviewed the letter.

"I sent this," the doctor said. "How did you come by it?"

"I was hired by the vestry of the Plymouth Congregational Church of Brooklyn." From a waistcoat pocket, Tule pulled out a business card and presented it to the doctor.

William Tule
Political Aide—Investigator
Twelfth Ward
Brooklyn, New York

"You came all this way...why?"

"A confidence game. The robbery of four thousand dollars. Committed by Zacharia Griffin. You have in your hands the letter taken from his body after he was killed by the authorities."

"When did this happen?"

"A few weeks back."

"The boy. I knew there was something, but—"

"The church is run by Henry Ward Beecher. Brother of Harriet Beecher Stowe...*Uncle Tom's Cabin*. Beecher is a well known evangelist. Zacharia Griffin had solicited him to raise money for certain 'political' causes. Which Beecher did. But it was all a confidence game. And his son was an active participant. Actually pretended to be a cripple."

"Charlie…Charlie Griffin?"

"We believe the boy is carrying the money."

"Impossible. We had to feed him. He had nowhere to stay."

"He is a professional gamer. He escaped from a reformatory in New York. His father served time in Sing Sing Prison. The boy presented himself as a cripple. Can I talk to his mother regarding the boy's whereabouts?"

"She is incapable of answering. And Charlie…I liked that boy."

"The best thieves and liars are often the most pleasant of people." He set the cup down. "Is there anything more you can tell me? No matter how insignificant?"

• • •

Handy was waiting at the Twelfth Street Bridge smoking the dregs of a poor boy cigar he found in the gutter. He was staring at the charred bones of a keelboat that sat foundered in the canal. He was putting in his time waiting on Billy Tule. He hated Cincinnati. He hated anywhere this close to the river because the river was just a spit from the Kingdom of Slavery. And somewhere in that bountiful province, his thumbs were buried.

When he finally saw Billy Tule exiting the hospital with his hands plugged down in his pockets, he knew. Tule joined him on the bridge.

Handy pointed to the boat. "Riots."

"When they're not killing niggers, they're killing each other."

"Bad news?"

"It ain't Christmas."

There's a kind of darkness certain people can move right through and not be seen. They are so good at this they leave no mark upon the moment. It is as if they do not exist, and the only trace of them is the violence that comes later.

• • •

Penrose Doral awoke like some night creature, her eyes wide as coins. She thought at first it was her brother turning over in his sleep that had startled her, but she reached out and he wasn't there. A hand then grabbed her by the hair and another clamped over her mouth. "Screaming will lead to your death. Do you understand?"

She could see nothing. There was only this huge pad of flesh that reeked of pipe tobacco pressed to her lips. She nodded that she understood.

The hand released and then a bandana was quickly wound around her head to cover her eyes. "You'll sit there and listen and answer. Do you understand?"

"I understand…Where's my brother?"

"Speak," said Tule.

"I'm here," said Cassius.

"Where?"

"On the floor."

"The floor—"

Tule took Penrose's hand. "I want you to feel something." He guided it to the blade of a knife in Handy's possession. Her fingers recoiled but Tule forced them to run the length of its steeled edge.

She said, "What is it you want?"

"The boy."

"What boy?"

"The one you took across the river."

"I've taken many boys across the river."

He shook her. "Charlie Griffin."

"Griffin," she said. Her wily little mind went to work. Who were these men, really? What did they want, and more importantly, were they a threat? Tule had demanded to know about the boy, and Penrose who was an expert in dealing with the powers of moral darkness, did not succumb to answering right away. But when she did, she spoke not like someone vanquished. "Cassius," she said. "I don't believe we need fear these gentlemen."

• • •

"Well," said Tule, "there's no shade where that bitch is concerned."

Handy was looking across the Ohio and into the benign light of a Kentucky morning. A poor brother of the chains who'd got himself loosed and was now expected to journey back into the terrible mouth of bottomless black.

Tule was sitting on a dock crate smoking his pipe and looking over the — *SPECIAL NOTICE* — the Dorals had published in the *Louisville Weekly*. It was wedged between an ad for *Hurley's Sarsaparilla* and *THE BLISS OF MARRIAGE*. It read:

$500 REWARD
Runaway from subscriber on the 9th of this month after an act of ROBBERY. NEGRO BOY who PASSES for WHITE. Goes by the name of CHARLIE GRIFFIN. Said boy is about thirteen years old, tallish, slender, greenish eyes. Was last seen wearing dark road coat and railroad cap, brogans, carrying a haversack. Thought to be making his way to Missouri. May well be in the company of ERASTUS EELS, Undertaker. $500 Reward whether taken in state or out of state.
                              Penrose and Cassius Doral
                              Cincinnati, Ohio

Tule had been going on about the damn advertisement and what a threat it was, adding strangers to the hunt, and the Dorals refusing to remove the special notice from the papers but offering to pay them the reward and a bonus if they would exact her particular notion of comeuppance.

But all Handy could see or hear was Missus Watters back in her Albany bedroom, framed by moonlight as he approached her with a knife.

"You know what this is?" she'd said.

"I knows what it tain't."

She had been holding out a golden crucifix she wore on a chain around her neck.

"They want you to be a beast," she'd said, "use you like a beast, make you live like a beast. But that doesn't mean you have to return in kind by acting the beast."

She was plying him with superstitions. That's what he believed. Just like the masters did and the ministers with their determined purpose. God to him was nothing more than the ultimate bandit they want you to bet your immense and weary hopes on, and here she was giving it. Christ will cure the sickness of every beast. She was black as him and should have known better. The monstrous crime was not slitting all their throats and feeding them to the pigs.

"The arms of God are forever open," she said, "waiting for everyone since the day they were born to just ask for forgiveness."

He could feel his face flush with unbearable rage. "Dat jus' da fear talkin'."

"No," she said, "I am not afraid."

Even as he said she was afraid he saw she was not. There was a wealth of fearless dignity in her that made him hate her even more than the man who'd despoiled him.

He was almost upon her when she said, "You will have to go where you are most afraid to go, if you do this."

He stood before her with the knife. She did not back away or cower.

"And you will be destroyed in the process," she said.

He grabbed her by the hair.

"God spare your eternal soul."

He drove the knife clear through her throat and scored the very cord of her spine. He could hear blade on bone. She would have fallen to the ground, but the strength behind the thrust kept her standing. When he pulled the knife from her flesh there was a threading sound and she just crumpled to the floor dead. He knelt alongside where the blood shot from a severed artery. He was like something mortally wounded striking out at cruel futility, when he stabbed her again. Then, he grabbed the gold crucifix from her hand. He felt he must have it, he did not know why, and the very need was like a degrading poison.

The sunlight glinting off the Ohio, Tule came up alongside Handy. The long heat was settling in. "Hey...I've been talking to you."

Handy just kept staring straight ahead.

"What's the matter?"

"Dat po'sin cuntree."

Tule looked across the river to Kentucky. "You're with me?"

"Dat don' change nuthin'."

"You got papers. I signed 'em. We'll be all right."

Handy was sweating from the back of his neck right down into his trousers. "Still got deze, boss." He raised his thumbless hands. "Mark'd."

"You also got that, ain't you?"

Tule flicked with a thumb the gold crucifix Handy now wore on a horsehair rope around his neck. Handy knew he'd meant it as a crack.

Tule started for the boat. "We'll get that boy…If you don't go nigger on me."

CHAPTER 41

THERE WAS NOTHING TO BE SEEN of Cairo under all that fog. Nary a rooftop or a treetop. Charlie and Mister Eels were deck passengers on another packetboat and even from where they'd camped up front with the cartage they could barely make out the prow. It was slow and treacherous going as the captain didn't want to pull a "Glendy Burke," get snagged and sunk, and have his name cursed by every boatman who made their way down the river.

Erastus knew a gent who lived at the Cairo Hotel and went by the name of Butler Phillips. Erastus explained to the boy this character knew the ways and means of the anti-slavery movement across Missouri and could guide Charlie, if he had a mind to, through the shoals of violence and retribution that were overtaking the state.

"I wonder where they are now?" said Charlie.

Erastus knew who the boy meant. Somewhere back in Indiana, three former slaves released from their coffins were getting a taste of a new world struggling to be born.

Steamboats lined the Cairo shore. They looked like ghost ships in all that grey slop, the deckhands minions of some dark netherworld waiting on the sun to burn hell out of all that mist.

Cairo was at the confluence of the Ohio and Mississippi Rivers, on a slight peninsula, and if not walled in by levees it would be nothing but a swamped rat hole. It wasn't much more as it was.

"A hotbed of disease," said Erastus, "an ugly sepulcher, a grave uncheered by any gleam of promise. A place without one single quality, in earth or air or water, to commend it. Such is this dismal Cairo." He drew some on his pipe. "Charles Dickens said that. You know who Charles Dickens is?"

"I can't say as I do."

"English writer. *Oliver Twist*. You ever read that?"

"That was crackerjack. My mother read it to me. I read it after. She used to call my father that sometimes when she got sore…Oliver Twist."

"Dickens signed a copy of the book for me when I was working bellhop at the Cairo Hotel. I wasn't much more than your age then. He was traveling the country and stayed there. The Cairo even had numbers on the guest rooms back then. And that was saying something."

They walked together up from the river like old partners in crime. Cairo had been home to Erastus Eels once upon a time. From newsboy to bellhop to soldier in the Mex War. Then after getting all that gunpowder out from under his nails, he took up a year of instruction at Shurtleff College, then on to the practical realm of undertaker and secret abolitionist.

He pointed out for Charlie the crawlspaces he'd slept in during summer and cellars he'd confiscated during winter to cheat the cold. And the people who now only lived in the pages of his memory, the miscreants and misfits and mean hearted and the ones who lived with purpose and could always throw a little compassion his way. He hoped now God was doing the same for them.

There was a storefront that about said it all when it came to describing Cairo.

— FAMILY WHISKEY — TAR AND FEATHERS —
COWHIDES — BOWIE KNIVES — and —SLOW POISON

Whatever the Cairo Hotel had once been, it was now a portrait of hard times. The grand porch was missing roof shingles and looked like the broken down mouth of an old man. Such a downfall saddened Erastus, and Charlie could read the severity of discomfort on the undertaker's face. Down the length of the porch guests and longtime residents took up on wicker sofas, or plank chairs, reading their newspapers, trading gossip, drifting in thought. A bellhop attended to their meager requests.

It was when they were partway up the walk and just clearing the edges of the fog that the bellhop took notice of them. Erastus waved and called out, "Manor."

The black bellhop looked shocked to see him and came bounding down the steps two at a time. Out of breath and anxious, he grabbed hold of Erastus. He was a freedman and not much older than Charlie.

"You got to get out of here, Mister Eels."

"What are you talking about?"

He pulled Erastus back toward the fog and out of sight of the porch, as one of the old time residents stood to get a better look.

"Have you seen the paper?"

"No."

Manor looked Charlie over closely. "Damn, if you ain't white." Manor pushed Erastus toward the street. "They after you, Mister Eels."

"Who?"

"It's in the papers."

Manor looked around, glancing up and down the street quick as a fox, making sure no one they knew was witness to this. "You know the old windmill by the pond where you and Mister Butler would go to drink and talk it up?"

"Where is Butler?"

"In Missouri. You git straight down to that windmill and don't be gettin' seen by anyone, please. And I'll bring you the newspaper."

Manor took off back into the fog. "Do as I tell you, now."

• • •

Out toward the Mississippi levee, the town thinned out. It was lowland there, all swampy and forested, with patches that had been farmland. They waited by a broken down windmill built to grind grain. The farmhouse was a skeleton of boards, the millstone stolen, the brakewheel and tail useless and rusting. But the wheel blades still made that slow, creaky grating as the air turned them. Charlie sat there watching. The windmill was about thirty feet high, and with that fog, all he could see was when the blades made their lowest descent scything through the damp morning mist. There, then gone, then there again. That the wheel itself had survived gave Charlie the strangest sensation.

"How bad do you think it is?" said Charlie.

Erastus had been smoking his pipe and creating a back and forth path in the high weeds. "I don't like to think about how bad a thing is, until I know exactly how bad it truly is."

"You mean, you prefer keeping the wolves at the door."

"Precisely."

"Well…Here come the wolves now."

Someone was making their way through the brush at a sprint. Then out of that runny mist, a short of breath apparition, and in a bellhop outfit no less.

Erastus took his time looking over the - SPECIAL NOTICE— that had been posted in the newspaper. His expression quietly going from grim to grave.

While he did, Manor made a close examination of Charlie's face. "I never have seen any colored person as white as you."

"That's 'cause I'm not colored," said Charlie. "It was a lie."

"Nuthin' to be ashamed of. I got some white blood in me. Not as bad as you, but lyin' don't help."

Erastus passed Charlie the paper.

"You're facing a man's fate," said Erastus. "You might as well read it for yourself."

Erastus turned to Manor. "Where's Butler? Do you know?"

"Rode up to Cape Girardeau."

Manor leaned over Charlie's shoulder and pointed to the notice. "See what they say…Charles Griffin…*Colored*."

"Do you know any freedman with a skiff that we can trust to take Charlie across the Mississippi? I'll pay him well."

"Yeah…but only after dark."

Manor got out a pencil and another copy of the Special Notice he'd torn from the newspaper. He forced the pencil into Charlie's hand.

"What's this for?"

"Your name," said Manor. He gave Charlie his back, swung the notice over a shoulder and held it there. He jerked a thumb at it. "Go on and sign. This ways in case they hang you or shoot you, they can't claim I was a liar about knowing you."

CHAPTER 42

THEY WAITED UNTIL NIGHTFALL in the trees up along the levee where the steamer Richmond lay mired in silt, its hull adorning the muddy shoreline. The mist had lifted along the river but not so the lowlands north of the city. The shoreline there a perfect shroud to wait in. When the skiff arrived, the boatmen had agreed to flash his lantern three times so they would know it was him, and where the boat would make the beach.

As they waited, Charlie looked over the Special Notice as if someone he did not know had lifted his name and part of his life story and run off with it. Imagine trying to explain that to an upright judge—another aside of his late father's.

He experienced a moment of wordless admiration looking at the paper, even knowing that was reckless and foolish. He folded up the newspaper and slipped it into his haversack.

He looked over at Erastus. He was leaning back against part of the Richmond's bulwark that the seasonal floods had carried up to the tree line. Erastus was writing on the back of one of his business cards. Charlie wondered what would come of their friendship.

Would they ever meet again? He felt this profound sense of loss that no measure of faith could erase.

"It's terrible," said Charlie.

Erastus looked up from his writing.

"You just start gettin' comfortable with someone and the next thing—"

"I'd take you up to Cape Girardeau myself, Charlemagne. But I have people and actions here I committed to."

"I didn't mean…You think Butler will be easy to find?"

"There's anti-slavers all the way up the river to Cape Girardeau. The newspaper there will know how to find him. I'll telegraph there, and leave word to be on the watch for you."

"I'll see if the boatman knows where I can get a horse. I ride pretty well."

Erastus could see the boy was a little unnerved. "You don't have to do this. Someone your age…No one would fault you—"

"I would."

Charlie forced a smile. He took to watching the river as a means, thought Erastus, of hiding a moment from the eyes of another.

"I'm sorry for the trouble I brought down on you on the road that night," said Charlie.

"You brought me a lot more than that."

Charlie wasn't quite sure how Erastus meant that. But the tone in his voice hinted at something more personal, affectionate even.

"I don't know what happened at the ferry," said Charlie. "The words just seemed to come out of my mouth. Like I was making them up."

"You weren't making them up. And they didn't just come out of your mouth."

"No?"

"They were living in there, and just waiting."

"I don't understand."

Erastus took a few steps to the shore. Something seemed to have captured his interest.

"Erastus? I don't understand. What do you mean they were just waitin'…For what?"

"The light," said Erastus. And he pointed.

From out on the river a light glowed momentarily then went suddenly black. A moment later the light reappeared, a long streak of it reflecting off the black waters. Then the light went dark again and there was only the river.

Charlie came alongside Erastus and said, "Is it…?"

Again the light appeared like a tiny golden eye buoying in the dark only to go black again.

They made their way from the fogged in trees to the beach. They could hear the oars of the boatman slinging water. Their time together was growing short.

Erastus took his business card and slipped it into Charlie's haversack. "When you get to Girardeau, you wire me in Cincinnati and Louisville. Tell me where you're going. I'll wire you back at those places. This way we…stay in contact."

Erastus took a small packet of bills and offered them to Charlie. "We don't want you going into that coat of yours. So…this will pay the boatman, and buy you a horse and saddle, and keep you in food and an occasional cheroot."

Charlie refused. He wanted to make his own way, but Erastus told him, "This is the Doral's money. And I think it righteously satisfying that you spend it well."

"If it's the Doral's money—"

They could see the skiff now. Like the pale white crescent of a moon rising on a timely seiche of water. The boatman must have been able to see them, as he shouted out, "You Mister Eels?"

"I am that," shouted Erastus.

"Dat boy my party?"

"This is Mister Charlemagne."

"Da boy got to come out in da water some."

It was time. The boatman stood up in the skiff. A powerful tor-soed gent of a freedman.

"You tell Jupe and Merc," said Charlie, "that I'll be carrying che-roots for 'em next time."

"And I'm sure those two scoundrels will have some devilment worked up for you."

The boatman shouted again. "Come on now. Don't want ta get suck'd up in da sand."

"Foolish as it is," said Erastus, "I'm gonna try and fit a lifetime of advice into a few moments. So…What do you know about the blue jay?"

"The bird?"

"The bird."

"I know a good deal. I know the damn thing is the King of Mischief."

"If you know that, you have man himself pretty well figured out."

Erastus took a step toward Charlie as if to embrace the boy before his leaving, but Charlie put out a hand to shake, as if it were some authentic form of shared friendship and manhood. Erastus took the boy's hand in both of his and shook it tenderly.

Charlie waded out into the tide, and the boatman put forth a hand and lifted him into the skiff as if he weighed nothing at all.

Charlie watched as the skiff swung about, and so they crossed the Mississippi in the dead of night under the steady hand of the oarsman. The Cairo shoreline behind him darkened until all that remained was a loomwork of trees and silent ground mist like the eternal driftings of smoke.

And it came to Charlie during that lonely passage how he had failed Erastus. That he had not expressed in words how thankful he was to him for saving his life, and how much he owed the undertaker for his timely intercessions and guidance. And that by trying to be a man and shaking his hand instead of embracing him, Charlie had, in fact, failed to be a man. Salvation comes in many colors, with many faces, along many roads. And this was a scar, Charlie believed, he would carry until rectified.

"Dat's gunfire, I believe," said the boatman.

"What...Where?"

The boatman pointed. Just south of the monolithic outline of the sunken Richmond were small daggers of light in the mist.

"Looks like some creature is on da run."

CHAPTER 43

THE BOY DIDN'T KNOW a journey could have so many beginnings and so many ends. Although his father had warned him of this with his own brand of contemptuous humor, with as many towns as they'd had to flee or quietly disappear from. "It's like in the Bible," Zacharia had said. "The good book is one long parade of beginnings and ends with a slew of bloodshed and begatting tossed in between to keep the reader oca'pied."

This did not ease the boy's heart any. The boatman guided Charlie to an enclave of freedmen who lived at the edge of a swamp near the headwaters of Lake Saint Mark. The hovels were a ragged affair, the folks there poorly clothed and barefoot.

A liveryman had a few mounts to sell. One turned out to be a Spanish Jack, of all things, Erastus' favorite. Charlie thought it a good omen. The liveryman explained how those horses were brought over by the Conquistadors coming from Cuba. They were smart horses, alert and agile. Quick learners, survivors. This one was about thirteen hands high and a good fit for Charlie. The liveryman even had a Grimsley saddle, an enlisted man's saddle, to offer. It was well past worn to hell, the rawhide covering the tree flayed, but even that was better than no saddle at all.

Charlie showed the liveryman the medallion and asked about Butler Phillips. The freedmen knew him. "Dat bast'd means to set da worl' on fire, if he gets da chance…God bless 'im."

When Charlie paid with the treasure Erastus had given him, his heart ached at the sight of it. It was as if Erastus were right there, a look of immense importance to his features.

"The horse got a name?" said Charlie.

"A course it got a name. The chil'n calls him… Stranger. 'Cause he jus' sho'd up one day."

The liveryman then smiled, and Charlie understood what he meant. It was like the story of how the wallet just showed up in the pickpocket's hand.

• • •

Charlie made his way up the Mississippi Valley with the river to the east and the Saint Francois Mountains with their red granite and elephant rock to the west. Charlie listened quietly to the thoughts and stories of the people he passed or rode alongside.

This was originally Creole country, settled by French trappers who'd come down from Canada. But the country had since been "vandalized by immigrants" and the Indians driven out or "civilized." It was now the province of cold hard fact and the rampant greed of progress, of which slaves were one. Political convictions could break out into absolute lawlessness with barely a word. And since the people there made no secret of their opinions, there was always a hint of vengeance in the air.

Under the guise of being shy, Charlie maintained a wary silence.

If the people he came in contact with were black, he would eventually show them the medallion to make sure it was safe to talk, and this is how he learned about trouble spots and snares that a youth traveling alone should be aware of. From the whites he inquired little, listened a lot, and maintained a simple lie, that he was going to Cape Girardeau to find work.

Along the way he did pick up bits and pieces of talk about Butler Phillips. Mostly from slavers, the businessmen and farmer breed, who were never short of bold proclamations and haughty threats. He even overheard a rumor at a campsite of waggoneers that an administration of justice by a political faction of ruffians was going to be brought down on Mister Phillips, and he shouldn't expect to be alive come Independence Day.

"Charlie, most men spend it all in the talking stage." That's what Zacharia would explain to his son, with the caveat, "But even in a paradise of cowards, it only takes one."

By the third day, storm clouds were moving in from the east. Grey evil looking formations like the advance smoke of an army. The day grew cool and the high grass and trees yawed then straightened in violent abandon.

From his haversack, Charlie removed a canvas tarp his father had cut into a kind of slicker the boy could put on by slipping his head through a hole in the center. His father had shown him how to coat the canvas with beeswax as sailors did, so the water would bead up like shiny little jewels then just drain off the canvas, and so he would remain dry.

He rode for miles in the rain. A slanting, driving, sheeting downpour. The sky was unsettled and wild and the earth seemed to exist with a force beyond recompense. To the west, the Ozarks were black as the smoke from a terrible fire.

And he was alone. There in the wilderness. A speck in the passage of history and time. In a world beyond his recognition. And he was scared. The landscape was an awing vision of natural violence. The world had grown more daunting suddenly, the journey more dreaded, his task seemed like nothing more than the reckless judgment of a child. And he had no one who he could lean his hidden imperfection on. He was diminished in spirit, his resolve foundering, and he began to cry. All his courage and promise were tears running down his cheeks to mix with the rain that dripped to the earth to turn into the mud under Stranger's hooves.

When the lightning came, he veered from the road. The sky crackled and there was a rolling explosion in the heavens above. The earth, for a moment, was immersed in light. Stranger's head reared and the boy leaned in and though still crying, found it within himself to calm the mount with timely strokes.

He rode among the trees until he discovered a thicket so dense the pine needles that covered the ground there were hardly even damp. He climbed down from that paltry saddle and took hold of the animal and wept into its muzzle where only the earth and Stranger would be the wiser.

He felt like a coward, he felt he was betraying everyone with his cowardice. His father's memory, however tainted, his mother's imprisonment. The list went on. He had to remember why he'd come. Why he'd taken this task on in the first place. He relived every moment, like in the poem, every moment, every person becomes a part of you. He had to remember what others had vested in him and so find ways to turn that into the strength he didn't have to keep on.

He was shivering right down into the guts of the earth. He felt as if the emotions coming from his heart had been written on weary paper, and the words had a precious sad story to tell. But there was a reason, and within that, smaller more personal reasons, and each reason was a person as important as the next. And all those reasons spoke and became you.

Yet he wanted to escape. To make this a dream you can't remember much past the following morning. But how do you escape what is true, when you know what is true?

He thought of the original act against Ward Beecher that brought him here. He'd committed, in his own way, a sin. He thought of Benchley and his father and their plan to exploit him as a black to make money. And he thought of himself and his father and their plan to exploit Beecher and the Gloucaster's.

If what he'd done wasn't a sin, it was something just as bad because it had come from the heart.

He wiped at his tears and thought to himself, "You dumb troublemaker."

CHAPTER 44

SOMETIMES THE BEST LIFE CAN OFFER is you cry yourself out. Charlie sat with his back against a tree, his legs all pulled up, his arms wrapped around them, all bundled under that canvas slicker. Stranger was left to work the pickings in that clearing and seemed quite content.

The rain still fell hard, but the kindness of the high and dense treetops kept them dry. His darkness of soul was lifting some when he heard the sudden report of gunfire. He leaned out from the trees to listen. It wasn't coming from the road but farther back in the woods. A rapid cadence of what might be pistol shots, but under the blanket of all that rain who could be sure.

He stood and tied off Stranger's reins and started off into the woods pushing aside the dense undergrowth, shouldering his way along. It was gunfire all right and coming from one place now. A singular shot to be countered by a razerous volley.

The sky was still black with rain. Through the trees Charlie could begin to make out thin ribbons of meadow with a stream cutting right through the center of it. He slunk down at the edge of the tree line and saw in the deep green lush grass a mount lay dead, and kneeling behind it a lone man with a revolver. Smoke from his weapon hanging in the rain soaked air.

Across the stream where the ground gently fell away, were a half dozen riders with rifle and pistol firing at him. There wasn't much to make of the riders in all that dark grey menace, but one of their number must have given a command as the man began to fan out.

The one behind his dead horse saw they were getting ready to charge and began to reload his weapon with an air of desperation.

The riders shot forward against that grim sky howling like grizzled banshees, their horses leaping the stream or crashing across it. Lethal with their gunfire the man huddling behind his horse was momentarily wracked with pain and stood, his arms disjointed, trying to grab his chest.

As they trampled down upon the fallen body they circled and emptied their weapons on him. And then one of their number, a gent in a long blue coat and white broad brimmed hat, with what might have been a plume of bird feathers, knelt over the body. To Charlie, he looked to be pinning something to the man's chest. He then mounted, doffing his hat at the corpse, and the riders took off filling the air with a vitriol of hurrahs.

Charlie remained hidden until after those riders bled away in the hard rain and the meadow was silent and beautiful. He sprinted from the trees hunched down, his elbows hiked out, and only slowed with trepidation as he approached the death site.

The man lay back against his horse. He was well dressed, with a grey mustache and graying hair, and he was one blown to hell soul, with a puckered hole in his cheek, black with blood where the bullet had gone clear through. And it was raining down on his open eyes.

Charlie thought of Erastus suddenly, and the night in the fog along the river, the flashes of light, that had to be gunfire. Was he alive? If he was there should be a wire… at the telegraph office.

He had never been this close to the moment of death. The man's finger still gripped the trigger of his weapon, his face was still taut with expression, and the rain streaking down that face could as well have been sweat. Charlie forced himself to look at this cold blooded atrocity, as much to know, as to try and understand, what can come of this world.

There was also something pinned to his chest. Charlie knelt down. It looked like currency. The writing a reddish color, and within a nine sided star, the word — DIX — and beneath that — NEW ORLEANS.

The money was attached to the coat lapel by a stickpin which Charlie removed with great unease. He turned the bill over in his hands. Printed on the reverse side, in one corner was the number — 10 — and in the other corner, an — X — while across the middle — CITIZENS BANK OF LOUISIANA. There was also an engraved picture of a steamer in troubled waters. He laid the paper money back on the lapel and pinned it as it had been. He did this with extreme care, as if somehow he might rouse the dead.

• • •

There was haze across the river valley, but Charlie could begin to make out the rooftops of Cape Girardeau along the steely glint of the Mississippi. A sense of excitement began to overtake the boy, and he leaned into Stranger's neck and said, "We've come through some dark days, ain't we?"

Charlie inquired his way to the telegraph office. In the past, the lines had been subjected to delays between the Cape and Nashville and Louisville, but all that had been remedied by a gutta-percha line run across the river. If Erastus was in good health, and God willing he was, there should be word from him.

It was a busy and contentious office that Charlie Griffin entered on that day. Boys his age were picking up and delivering wires for the shippers and traders along the docks. It had been quiet on the road, but this flood of noise left him disoriented, and his heart raced like when he'd just entered a carnival or fair. He found his way to a young man who stared at him from behind an iron cage.

"Is this where I come to find out if there's a wire here for me?"

The fellow had a ratchet face with long muttonchops and he gave Charlie a most unforgiving stare. "Well…where else would you go? You have a name, boy?"

"Yes, sir. It's Char—"

He stopped right there. He knew if Erastus was alive and had any kick in him, he would give Charlie a good goading.

"Could you see if there's a wire for Charlemagne Griffin?"

The clerk took on an expression of complete and utter disdain. "That's a whole lot of name for such an unimpressive fellow."

"I can spell it better than I can wear it."

The clerk went and looked through an iron rack filled with wires under the letter G. But there was nothing. Then he fingered through a second rack, and the outcome was no better. Charlie began to have his doubts and became fidgety. It wasn't until the clerk was well into the third rack that he pulled an envelope, which he then slid through the cage opening. "For Charlemagne Griffin…*himself.*"

"Do I owe you money or anything for the wire?"

"The person what sends it, pays for it. Don't you know anything?"

"I know there's worse things than being ignorant. And you're one of them."

Charlie went outside and found himself a bit of sidewalk to splash down on and read his very first wire. He stared at the envelope. This was like some earned stripe on the march to adulthood, getting a wire. He opened the envelope with care, and inside it was a kind of letter.

Charlemagne —
Hope this wire finds you well and kicking. Interesting night after your departure. Look forward to telling you all about it. Wire me in Cincinnati.
— Erastus Eels, Undertaker

CHAPTER 45

THERE WERE ABOUT HALF A DOZEN newspapers in Cape Girardeau, and all but one were slaver — The Expositor — and it was always under a steady assault of either taunt or threat. A man looked up from his desk and cigar and copy to be proofed and saw what might amount to a teenager standing across the railings and waiting for him.

"What are you here for, boy? Job? Handout? Got neither. Good day."

"I'm looking for Butler Phillips."

The man's eyebrows tweaked over the rim of his glasses. He just stared at Charlie. He was hamfisted and bald, and he reached for his cigar and got this odd smirk on his face. He took a puff and glanced over at one of the reporters at a nearby desk who had overheard the conversation. "Butler Phillips," he said pointing his cigar.

One man's smirk turned into another man's smile altogether.

"Well, son, how would you prefer him? Standing up...or stretched out?"

Charlie thought the remark odd. "Which comes sooner?"

The two men nodded to each other. Good answer they thought. The one with the cigar stood and had Charlie follow him to the front door. He reeked of tobacco and booze and unwashed pants. He pulled the door open and pointed across the street with his stogie. "See that crowd?"

It would be hard to miss. There were at least a hundred and fifty people listening to a fella's oratory, and he was kicking up quite a demonstrative cloud of words about the rights of slavers.

"You just go out there and bear witness for a while. Butler will be along."

The reporter stood and walked past both of them.

"I might as well get out there now and cover it."

"Sir," said Charlie. "I never met Mister Butler. How will I know him?"

"Son...I'll bet a silver dollar to a dime you'll know when it's him."

"Sir?"

"And by the way. When the fighting starts, or if a gun gets drawn. Beeline it the hell out of there."

Charlie took up a bit of sidewalk away from the crowd. He'd heard all this kind of talk before. The government was going to lay down their hour of vengeance unless the states righters and slavers put their will to the test. The speaker warned there would be war, that it had already begun in bloody Kansas. It was down to a coin flip. Heads—the good old days. Tails—free niggers everywhere. There was a lot of head shaking and hand wringing from the speaker about the terrible fate of executed kinsmen. From Charlie's meager perspective life was becoming one long series of threats, where only the faces changed.

He noticed blacks in the entrances to alleys, or under the shadow of storefront roofs, where doors stood ajar, as silent witness to their own degradation. Freedmen or not, all bearing the downside of caution, until a justly incensed democracy became the threat the speaker railed about.

This was the world that Charlie's father told him to fear. Not the one of pickpockets and larceny, but of legal mendacity and the will to power. Nothing spoken that day was veiled. It was all said out in the open, like the bullet hole in the dead man's face.

Heads began to turn, and there was a smattering of laughter. Charlie looked up the street to where the crowd's attention was now firmly fixed. Even the speaker himself stumbled a bit when looking upon this sight. A two wheeled cart pulled by a pair of sorry mules approached at a slow gait. The cart had been framed in on three sides with picket fencing to make it resemble a ridiculous chariot. The mules were wearing ill fitted crowns, and there was a gent standing in the cart bracing the leads. And of all things, he was dressed in some kind of roman soldier costume.

Charlie had seen the likes of it once, worn by an actor in a play at a theater his father had taken him with tickets, by the way, paid for by a successful, though larcenous, run of Vingt et Un.

The driver of that cart wore a canvas tunic and strips of lead sheeting looped together by rope through small holes cut in the metal surface to resemble armor. He had on a cockeyed helmet, hammered together from wood scraps and painted gold. It was shamelessly funny, Charlie thought, unless you were an actual Roman.

The cart pulled up to the edge of the crowd. The driver had a brazen grin and thorny blackish eyes, trim mustache that peaked at the edges, and an imperial that grew down from just beneath his lower lip.

He was a young man. A couple of years short of thirty, Charlie guessed. He stepped from the cart, patting his trusty mules. He was wearing what looked like military boots and a holstered Colt. Charlie noticed up close that even when the man was smiling, he wasn't. Charlie could also make a pretty fair guess that this had to be Butler Phillips.

Phillips put up his hand and stepped among the crowd. The speaker was cursing out this Butler Phillips for being a nigger lovin' heathen and there were insults and barbs tossed at Phillips and catcalls, and there was some applause too, as there were free staters on the street and abolitionists.

And then this Butler raised his hands to speak. His tone was loosely sarcastic and wry, and wry.

"Americans, Missourians, slavers. Lend me your goodwill a moment...'Cause a moment is about all I'll get...I come to bury slavery, not to praise it."

The state of vexation throughout the crowd began to rise dramatically.

"As the engine of capitalism, slavery has become sadly wanting. Free white immigrants work just as hard and for even more paltry wages...Machines will replace us all in short order, and who will be the *mastas* then?"

Someone in the crowd threw a punch at Butler and got in a good lick. Butler pulled off the helmet and hit his attacker across the face with it. Then all Butler had left was a handful of junky wood.

Wiping the blood from his mouth, Butler pressed on. "We know slavers are greedy and ambitious to a fault...And Brutus and Caesar, just school yard children who need a lot more sterner stuff to be in league with the likes of you."

Then he pointed and pointed and pointed, and he was jumped, and he was down. He came back at his oppressors with a vengeance, kicking and spitting and landing blows. Some of these fools hit

Butler squarely in that lead sheeting, and did they live to regret it. He went through the crowd, making a clanging noise like a living chime. And he wasn't fighting alone now.

Charlie found himself a barrel in front of a shop to stand on and better watch the action. There was a wicked joy to it and he could hear Butler yelling from somewhere under that mob, "I speak now of what I know. You keep your slaves for sex…Just ask your women who…who…" He was there for a moment before he disappeared, only to surface again… "Who could name your illegitimate children by the dozen…And that is why states like Georgia and Mississippi are nothing more than legalized brothels."

CHAPTER 46

THEY STITCHED BUTLER UP over in the newspaper office. He'd been knifed across the forearm, and someone had used a rock to make a sweet dent in the back of his skull. Besides the doctor, editor, and reporter, there was a young black named Eadon who seemed to be Butler's right hand man and comrade at arms.

"Eadon," he said, "go down to Water Street, and make sure no one is executing bad manners and burning our businesses down."

Butler took the stitching in good humor and went about changing his clothes right there in the office with the windows open to the public, stripped down to his drawers—passersby staring in disgust, some cussing him out, women aghast, children scampering past then making a timely swing for another look. Did he give a damn? Not likely. Bad manners were like vintage wine to him, and him talking all the while, and Charlie watching silently from a corner by the door, taking in every comment and sainted insult.

The whole business on the street with the chariot had been a ruse for an article the paper was to publish about the vile mores and sexual mistreatment of slaves. They had done a takeoff of a speech from a play Charlie had never heard of and would use it as the headline, which would include the "ensuing riot" in the hopes the article would get picked up by the national press. Thanks to the telegraph, such shameless reportage was becoming the vogue, and a new means of spreading the word.

Butler Phillips meant to cause hell, and if he could do it with a little style and wit, all the better. Especially as a soul who enjoyed marks of extraordinary adulation. He finally turned his attention to this silent creature just inside the doorway with a railroad cap all twisted up in his hands and a haversack like Butler himself used to carry slung over his shoulder.

"What are you? Boy...Statue?"

"No, sir...I...I'm here to find you."

"Well. I look to be found." He turned to the others. "I hope this isn't some assassin in disguise. You an assassin in disguise, boy? You mean to see me dead like most of my dearest fellow citizens?"

Butler had dressed. He wore well made breeches and a short brocade vest, and those military boots, with the Colt hitched at the waist. He was all pressed and clean and neat as Sunday.

"I'm Charlie Griffin."

Butler slapped his hands together. "You mean... Charlemagne Griffin, boy. Hey...this is the one I was tellin' you about. You made it. Erastus wrote me about you. A page long letter. And that says something. Come with me."

Charlie followed Butler out.

"Let's get something to eat, and talk."

"My horse is over there, can—"

"Sure. We'll feed him too."

As Charlie ran across the street to get Stranger, he turned back to see Butler checking his revolver and eying the street on the chance someone might execute a little untempered hostility.

• • •

It turned out Butler owned a number of properties on Water Street just down from the Howell and Reynolds steam powered mill. There was a livery, a two story office building for wholesalers, a boarding-house where Butler resided on the top floor, and an eating establishment called Jesse's. Jesse being Eadon's mother.

The family ran the place and Butler gave them quiet partnership, as they were freedmen and had been in the state since before the hardening of the laws. Jesse claimed to be from Mississippi, and her cooking deep Southern, so Jesse's was one of the few places in the Cape where abolitionist and slaver let each other be.

The buildings had been done in the "German Vernacular" style, which is why Butler had bought them. There had been a run of German immigrants over the last decade and "German Vernacular" meant lots of brick, arched windows, and stone foundations. Their strong suit being they were tough to "accidentally" be torched.

They'd put Stranger up at the livery and no sooner had they sat down and ordered, when Charlie leaned over and whispered to Butler, "I saw a murder coming here, sir."

If there ever was a shocked look on a fellow, Charlie thought, this was it.

"Son, if that comment doesn't get a conversation off to a gallop, only God knows what will."

Charlie proceeded to tell the story as he'd witnessed it in the rain, trying to remain as calm and accurate as possible, with Butler raising a hand every now and then and paddling at the air for Charlie to smooth it down. The story culminated in that strange bill pinned to the dead man's chest.

Butler, upon hearing this, went into his billfold and set a bit of paper currency on the table. It was an exact replica of the one Charlie had been trying his best to explain.

"'Dix' is French for ten. It's paper currency from a New Orleans' bank. Sound money. Pinning it to the victim is a way of Dixie Jack's, that's what they call him, telling the world he was behind the slaying. But, of course, Dixie Jack isn't fond of leavin' witnesses."

CHAPTER 47

"I'll get you to James Montgomery," said Butler.

Charlie was walking with Butler up Water Street. Charlie saw how people took note of the man, and it made the boy feel sure somehow.

"You know where he is?"

"I know where he'll be. Fourth of July. There's a big political rally up north. Free staters going to Kansas to fight the ruffians."

The Fourth of July was only two weeks away.

"That is, if I'm still alive," said Butler.

He saw the boy was bitterly wounded at the comment.

"Don't take it to heart, Charlemagne. My talkin' like that is my way of wishing myself luck."

"I missed being born on the Fourth of July by two minutes," Charlie said. "That's what my mother told me."

"Too bad she didn't lie and let you be born on the Fourth."

"That's just what my father said."

"And he was a born liar, I bet."

"He lied like some men breathe."

The shadow of a horse and rider had been slowly advancing up the sidewalk and across the shopfronts they'd passed, and now it flanked them, moving at the same pace, blocking out the sun.

The rider being backlit as he was, it took a moment for Charlie to make out features. But it was him. With the long blue frock coat and white hat and those plume feathers. Only this close, Charlie could make out grey stars sewn on, like epaulets, to the coat's shoulders.

"One of your many followers?" said Dixie Jack.

Butler's glance never left Dixie Jack. "Just a young adventurer who is indulging in my boring stories."

Butler took Charlie by the shoulder and guided him so the boy would be walking on Butler's far side.

"You didn't have to do that. My aim is good."

"As in accuracy...or intent?"

"I heard you made some political news today."

"My hope is that you read about it in some of our finest papers."

"You could be fined or jailed for such an act. Possibly worse."

"I thought to be a reporter once. But it demands such a lonely and rigorous dedication of purpose. A balance I believe neither of us possesses."

"Never mind the low pay," said Dixie Jack.

"If anyone knows about low pay it is the slave."

"Tell that to the workers up north. Any way...you strike me more the actor type."

"Shallow...conceited," said Butler, smiling.

"Ensconced in thoughts of private glory."

"I showed that today."

"You're due a comeuppance, Mister Phillips."

"A little comeuppance won't stand in the way of progress, Mister Shepherd."

Dixie Jack spoke past Butler to Charlie. "Be careful there, son. This man is easy to listen to. And his passion has sent many an innocent to the grave."

Dixie Jack rode on at his leisure.

"He's the one I saw," said Charlie. "Pinning the money to the man's coat."

"He's a handsome fellow, isn't he?"

Dixie Jack was that. He was proud and vain and young and fair, with warm milky eyes, and he carried himself like someone who could walk out of a senseless fray unscathed.

"He means to see you dead," said Charlie.

"Dixie Jack and I are both the rich, corrupt sons of rich, corrupt fathers who, in turn, are the sons of other rich, corrupt fathers, all the way back to the founding fathers. What else can men of our class do but kill each other over their personal sense of primacy?"

They walked on after that, with Butler taking out a packet of Rizla and tobacco, and he rolled himself a cigarette, making small talk, as if the last few minutes had never happened.

"You know, don't you?" said Charlie.

Butler put the cigarette between his lips and he spread out both arms.

"About the coat. Erastus told you. Why I have to meet this James Montgomery?"

Butler answered the boy with a benign silence.

"I will get there, said Charlie. "I decided that back on the road. I know…I'm not fearless or remarkable in any way. I know I'm not old enough. But I won't let you down. I won't become a burden. And if I do, you can cut."

CHAPTER 48

PLANS WERE MADE FOR THEIR DEPARTURE. It was decided Charlie would stay with Eadon as Butler believed there might be "errant" gunshots thrown at his window after dark.

Eadon had an office where he handled all the accounts for the Water Street properties and a couple of rooms where he lived in a small brick building alongside the livery.

Butler suggested, in no uncertain terms, that Charlie immediately indulge in one of civilization's time honored traditions and have himself a bath, so no one in Cape Girardeau mistook him for the sewers of Paris. Butler then handed Eadon some paper currency, including a Dix, which he held up for Charlie to see. Eadon was to use the money on clothes for the road. Breeches and shirts, socks and drawers. "Everything except a coat," said Butler. "Charlemagne seems to have a special attachment for that coat. And we do our best to indulge special attachments."

Eadon was uneasy for most of the night. Through a network of house slaves came rumors that trouble was being bred. Keeping the back door open and the room dark, Eadon could look across the roadway to Butler's apartment on the top floor of the boarding-house. He had Charlie come over to see for himself. Every kerosene lamp had been lit, and the windows of Butler's apartment looked to be on fire in a show of pure defiance.

Eadon had a shotgun cradled across his lap. "He's a crazy man," whispered Eadon. "But you saw that already." Eadon mumbled to himself, cursing. "You can't know this man. He's told half a dozen different stories about his life and when people confront him on it he just laughs in their face. No one has any idea where he gets his money, and he's got a wagon load. Sometimes he disappears for a week or more at a time. Comes back all raggedy and exhausted. Never a where'd he go or what he'd done. Where a normal, sane person goes left, he goes right."

Charlie sat down beside Eadon. He had a cheroot he'd cut in half. The two smoked and kept guard like a pair of midnight centurions.

"You think the rumors will hold up?" said Charlie.

"I hope not. But the people talking got long ears."

"You have a lot of books on your desk. Readin' books." Charlie had been sitting at Eadon' desk earlier and that's where he was pointing.

"Studyin' to be a lawyer."

A couple of men drifted into view on the other side of Water Street. Two sets of eyes from the dark followed their movements. There didn't seem to be anything prophetic there. They just sounded like a couple of gents in the aftermath of bar time.

"We're going to Fulton first thing when we leave here," said Eadon.

"What's in Fulton?"

"Trial of a colored woman. And there's gonna be blood."

"What do you mean?"

"She got indicted for killing her owner. He'd been raping her for years. She has a younger sister hidden out in the woods. A real sharpshooter. Swears she'll kill the first slaver she sees if they convict her sister. You know what rape is?"

"Can't say as I do."

"You know what sex is? Sexual intercourse?"

"No…but I'd damn well like to learn."

They shared a cracking good laugh, which they had to muzzle, and they went to keeping a sharp eye on the street which proceeded to go mournfully quiet, and it was that quiet which filled them with distress.

The cheroots had long since burned out and cooled in a hammered lead ashtray. Charlie tried not to fall asleep but he found himself dozing and resented his body for failing him. He awoke to find Eadon was not there. Had it been a few moments, minutes? He saw the lights were out in one of Butler's rooms. He called in a whisper, "Eadon?"

He was out back urinating and whispered back, "What?"

When he returned Charlie was standing by the window and pointing. One of the rooms. The light was gone—

The opaque shadows of horsemen came streaming out of the alley beside the boardinghouse at a full gallop and firing their weapons. The windows across the front of Butler's apartment were shattered. A kerosene lamp shot out, the drapes caught fire and the heat sucked them up so that they furled across the window like a torched flag. There were cries and shouting from all quarters along the street. Eadon stood in the alley with the shotgun braced up on his shoulder when Charlie saw they had taken Butler. He was tied to a saddle, hatless and tottering and barely conscious.

Charlie shouted, as Eadon fired off a round, "They have Butler."
A rider was blown back out of his saddle and right into the legs of
an oncoming mount. The horse buckled and caromed over into the
sidewalk, breaking its neck. Both men lay dead in the rutted wagon
marks of Water Street, with the light from the burning rooms bearing down on them.

Eadon had run to the livery and swung the doors open on their
huge rusty hinges and was saddling a mount with Charlie just a few
paces behind him. The boy was shaken and out of breath.

"They have him," said Eadon.

"What are you going to do?"

"I'm going after him. You stay here."

Taking Butler away alive gave Eadon a pretty sure guess where
Dixie Jack was going. Blacks under the reign of slavers knew from all
those white whisperings the ruffians gathered in their secret castes in
the marshland just south of La Croix Creek. When Eadon reached
where the Bloomfield Road had cleared Cape Girardeau, he could
see down through the long stretch of evening faint traces of dust
where the moonlight shored up on that windless highway. And he
knew he had been right.

He heard a rider fast approaching and swung about with his
shotgun to find it was Charlie on his Spanish Jack. Eadon made a
jerky gesture with his arm. "You go on back. Tell my folks what's
happened."

Charlie refused. He was adamant in the face of every pleading or
threat Eadon made. With no recourse, Eadon rode up alongside the
boy and punched him from the saddle. Lying there in the road, Eadon
would have taken Stranger and left the boy afoot and bleeding from
his nose and mouth, but Charlie would not unhand the leads. Eadon
cursed the faithful little bastard and took off into the dark after Butler.

Beyond the creek, the marshland became a murky 'spanse of cypress and tupelo trees. A corduroy road had been laid out with planking so workmen could fell the trees to be used for railroad ties. The road was in a state of disrepair and unfit for wagons, but horses could make a slow go of it.

Eadon knelt with his fingers to the wood trying to feel for the vibration of hooves, when Charlie appeared on Stranger. The blood had since dried around his nose and mouth.

"Damn," said Eadon. "I didn't want to have to hit you."

Charlie was looking into all that gloom. "They go in there?"

"Yeah," said Eadon. He went to his horse where he kept more ammunition in a saddlepack. "They could have killed him back at the Cape. They have something in mind." Eadon handed Charlie the reins of his horse. "You wait till dawn. If I'm not back…Well, if I'm not back—"

Eadon took off on foot, a shadow in the summer's night leaving barely a sound to mark him.

The boy dismounted and led the horses to the side of the road. He squatted there on his heels and wiped the sweat from his face on the sleeve of his new shirt.

He was not wearing his coat. It was the first time since he'd put it on, he was without it. He had taken it and the haversack off during the wait and set it on Eadon's desk. He'd have to rectify that in the future. If there was a future.

Eadon did not come. Charlie thought of the Gloucasters and Missus Watters and God. He felt unworthy of asking God to see them safe, that somehow by doing so he would poison their chances, when came the approach of a lone rider.

Charlie could hear the hooves on the planking. He put his hand out, his fingers, like Eadon had done. The sound of the hooves painstakingly slow but so smooth and steady, no one would have guessed that the joinery between the timbers was shot to hell as it was.

The horses sensed the approach and their necks arched and they neighed. Charlie stood. A mask of man and mount towered before him.

"I was certain there was another one out here somewhere when the nigger came on foot. But I didn't expect a child. You remember me, don't you, boy?"

"I do, sir."

"Remember what I told you today, when I was speaking with Mister Phillips?"

"Yes, sir."

"What did I tell you?"

"You said Mister Phillips is easy to listen to, and his passions have sent many an innocent to the grave."

CHAPTER 49

ERASTUS EELS HAD NOT BEEN HARD TO TRACK from Cheapside. A man traveling with three coffins and a boy of twelve leaves quite a trail of manifests along the river. And having that Special Notice gave Tule an opportunity to pursue the matter of Eels' whereabouts with an appropriate diligence.

He and Handy had made a small camp west of Louisville in a stand of trees off the main road. They had discovered that Eels crossed by ferry to Clarksville with his coffins and then proceeded on to Cairo. He'd left as a business address, the Cairo Hotel.

There was one question that plagued and vexed Billy Tule to no end. Erastus Eels crossed from Cincinnati to Kentucky with three caskets for reburial. And then he had crossed back from Kentucky with three caskets for reburial in Indiana. It made maddeningly little sense.

"It all dere, boss. All dere. In dem coffins."

Handy then went on and told the tale of a nigger he'd heard about who went and had himself put in a crate and then had his black ass mailed from some slave state to an abolitionist in Philadelphia.

When Tule saw the simple brilliance in the plan, he was delighted. "Eels was carrying empty coffins. Weighted down probably. But comin' back, he had a couple of niggers packed away...We're gonna make something of this if that's his game. There's profit here for us." Tule sat back with his pipe, joyously counting the money in his head for putting the bust on Eels. He told Handy, pointing his pipe right at him with almost familial pride, "You're one slick nigger figuring that out."

Handy smiled, but took the statement as nothing. He knew how stupid Tule was, not having any idea of what means there was of getting niggers across the river. "Boss," said Handy. "A nigga' cut off 'is own head if'n it gits him 'cross da r'vir."

They went to sitting back and enjoying a little whiskey and plotting out how they were about two days from putting their talons on the boy, when they were come upon by four men. Like scavengers from a dream the four made no sound stepping out of the dark pine wood. Three stood before them with their heavy calibre weapons drawn. As to the fourth, they would never have known of his existence except for him tapping his shotgun against the side of a rock.

Tule knew he and Handy were nothing more than fodder there in the light of the flames, and any trouble Handy or he might commence would be finished upon them.

"What you say, gents?" said Tule. "We got coffee and whiskey. Rest your bones, if you care to."

The men made little work of such talk. They knew it for what it was. Bull from a frightened man. One of the men, wearing a filthy shirt made from a burlap bag said, "What you think there, Asa?"

Asa, the one with the shotgun was a black, and as wizened looking as Methuselah.

Asa stepped forward and slipped the shotgun barrel under Handy's chin and edged it toward him so he could get a long, lean look on that face. The two blacks stared at each other. They were hard cases bred on poison. Men who had been pulled down into the pit, whose every dream had been slaughtered, their souls looted at the whim of white pleasure. And you wouldn't want to try and survive in the footed shapes of their stares.

"Mister Jeffrey," said Asa. "This nigger is a run'way."

"No," said Tule. "He's got papers."

"Asa says he a runaway. He a runaway."

"Show 'em your papers," said Tule.

Handy went to reach for his shirt pocket, but the shotgun against his chin advised him otherwise.

"I kin smell a run'way from miles."

These weren't slave catchers, but the droppings of a grisly brotherhood that hunted the wilds for blacks to sell. And it didn't matter if they were runaways, or freedmen, or owned. If they were loose, they were had. These roughnecks sold their haul on the black market, so to speak, for short money, to overseers and farmers who didn't indulge in formal paperwork, and who whipped a day's work out of their niggers until they died chained and shackled to their posts. It didn't matter how troubled or violent these anonymous creatures were, because they all ended up buried in the notations of a dusty ledger.

Mister Jeffrey came over and squatted down in front of Handy. He scratched at his chest through the stinkin' burlap shirt, lookin' at him right and lookin' at him left.

"Yeah," he said, "runaway. And missin' those thumbs. You one mean nigga' problee. And the knives too. Asa, got to relieve him of those blades. He won't need 'em no more. We got a farmer what need a forty foot well to be dug and the ground just keeps cavin' in. Lost one buck already."

Mister Jeffrey rubbed his unshaven face. He took off a hat that wasn't hardly fit for a scarecrow and let it swing in the hand that wasn't busy holding his revolver.

Without looking at Tule, he said, "I do believe I'm going to take this nigga' off your hands."

Tule kept his wits calm about him. Handy was looking to him to see if they were going to make a fight of it. Tule understood the plain and simple futility of that. "Gentlemen," said Tule, "this nigger always did ask considerably too many questions."

Handy realized Tule had abandoned him and lunged for Jeffrey, trying to swat away the barrel of the shotgun before he was taken. But he wasn't quite fast enough. Mister Jeffrey had anticipated him posing some kind of threat and had flung his hat in Handy's face, compromising his vision for just what it took to bring the barrel of his gun down squarely on the brim of Handy's skull. You could hear the air go out of him, and his face hit the ground flat and hard, and before he could right himself they were on him with shackle and chain.

Handy saw that he was a prisoner again of the chains, that he could not tear loose the locks through force of will, that he was humbled, taken, made to heel at the order of another man, that every step he took would be accompanied by the jingling scorn of shackle iron.

Death would have been simpler, madness so much the better. His agony went beyond rage. He looked up at the sky, the stars, and wept uncontrollably, worse than an inept child shamed. Fugitive sounds came out of his chest as he cried, and cried out, that Tule could hear well after Mister Jeffrey and his raggletag band disappeared in the distance, a quivering echo of a drowned man, faint as it was, but just enough for Billy Tule to follow as he began the hunt to get his nigger back.

CHAPTER 50

"I DON'T BELIEVE IN BRINGING DOWN violent prophecy on children," said Dixie Jack. "But I am reminded that in ancient Greece some of the most dangerous soldiers were children."

He edged his mount forward. Charlie sat astride Stranger, silent and afraid. "Ride back to town and tell Butler's abolitionist friends and his "colored" followers we'll be returning him in the morning to the courthouse. Humbled some, but well enough for us to put on a spectacle of our own for the newspapers. Leave his servant's horse here." Charlie handed Dixie Jack the reins.

As he started away, Charlie was warned, "Boy…don't become a source of vexation."

When Charlie returned, Water Street was alive with light. The fire brigade had saved the boardinghouse except for the top floor. The two dead men in the street were being loaded into a wagon, and the felled mount had been harnessed and was being dragged to an empty lot where the carcass would be burned.

Charlie discovered his coat was gone. He looked everywhere. His hands were shaking, her became vilely ill. All these miles, all this effort. The lapse of a few moments—

"What's wrong?"

Charlie turned to find Eadon's mother standing there.

"My coat," said Charlie in desperation. "I lost it. It was—"

The woman pointed to a small room where a cot had been set up for Charlie to sleep. He raced past her. There it was on the bed beside his haversack.

"I saw it on the desk," said the woman, and—"

He clutched the coat to him. He put it on immediately.

"What's wrong, son?"

His mouth opened but he could not manage a thought.

Come morning a crowd gathered around the auction block. Abolitionist and slaver, freedmen and slave. Dixie Jack's people had been out in full force, putting forth the word. There was a strong smell of comeuppance in the air. Every newspaper in town had been advised to have a reporter on site.

The sky bore no clouds that day, it's only imperfection, a trail of paling smoke from the fallen roof timbers of the boarding house. A pack of boys came sprinting up German Road shouting, "They're here. They're here."

And so they were. Dixie Jack and his ruffians leading the very same cart Butler had ridden in the day before. And there he was again. But this time, Butler Phillips was roped to the frame to keep from falling, his hands were tied behind his back, and he was naked.

Charlie watched from the side of the road as the cart passed. Butler had been beaten, there was a gash across his forehead. He looked unsteady, but defiant. The children of slavers gathered up road mud and dung and flung it at him. For many of the women the sight was too vulgar. Some, Charlie saw, took plain delight in the humiliation, and there were others who seemed to take a prurient joy beyond the act itself. Where was the law? This was the law. The unspoken law.

Some of the citizenry tried to stop the degradation but were driven from the road by mounted ruffians.

Eadon followed behind the cart on horseback. He too had been put to the fist, one eye was swollen shut. His mother fought through the crowd to be at her son's side. She clung to his legs, only to be dragged away and thrown to the road.

The cart was brought to a halt at the auction block. Butler was untethered from the frame and walked with hands bound, up that flight of stairs by Dixie Jack and two men carrying open cans of what Charlie knew to be pine tar.

The calls from the crowd were harrowing—the vitriol, the condemnations, the complete disregard for dignity. People weren't being dragged through the gutter, be it abolitionist or slaver, it was a foot-race to get there first.

If they expected Butler Phillips to be brought down by his humiliation, they were sadly ignorant. He was, if nothing else, a devout adversary. And Charlie, that morning, saw something he had not seen in a man. The ability to stand before your haters and be unapologetic, to suffer with dignity, without disguise or concealment. He only knew this existed in books, or Bible stories. He had never seen anything close to this in his father, and he realized too, there, that day, that this was the life of a slave, under the heavy saddle of men's will.

As the men with Dixie Jack began to smear tar across Butler's back and shoulders, as they slopped it on his chest, Dixie Jack turned to the crowd below and Charlie saw that he was carrying a book in each hand.

"Mister Phillips here," he said, "sought to enlighten us yesterday. So I felt to return the favor."

There was applause from the crowd and the condemnations of the enraged.

"Free stater," said Dixie Jack, standing before Butler. "Well, he's about in the freest state he'll ever be."

If that didn't bring the rousing to a new pitch. Slavers pressed all about the bottom of the auction block to get a verbal lick in. And from among them, a banjo began to strum up a lively dig of accompaniment.

Dixie Jack put up his hands with those books in them to quiet the voices. "I didn't bring Mister Phillips here in that 'state' to prove we are the better men. Not with heart or with gun."

He raised each hand with a book in it. "These are our most dangerous foes. Because these books mean to sway a nation and the world against us." He held one forth. "*Uncle Tom's Cabin.*" He held the other hand forth. "Thoreau's *Civil Disobedience.* These writers aim to poison the populace against us. They already regard us as whiskey drinkin' tobacco guzzlin' white trash rednecks who never had a thought or ever read a paper, who can hardly 'writ' their own name."

The people there cursed Thoreau and they cursed Harriet Beecher and there was a smattering of protests and a fight broke out over by the road.

"What we need," said Dixie Jack, "is a *slaver* Harriet Beecher Stowe. And a *slaver* Henry David. Men and women who can fire up the torch using the pages of a book.

"That's why I asked all you newspaper men here. You boys need to write about today, and how today is not a call to arms, but a call for minds. And now I'm going to put an exclamation point to the idea and give you something more to write about. So the national press might find it interesting and exciting enough to put in their papers. Just like Mister Phillips was trying to do here yesterday with that carnival show."

He turned to Butler Phillips, who was now fairly striped with tar, and Dixie Jack opened one of the books and started to tear out pages, and the pages he'd torn out he shredded between his fingers into smaller strips, and these strips he pressed to the tar. Then he did the same with pages from the other book, and his men, there on the auction block, saw fit to lend a hand.

It was a new brand of tar and feathering. And did this incite the crowd with joy? A man there stripped to God's beginnings, who looked as if he had been caught in a storm of snowy paperflakes. "The new American 'Tar Baby,'" said Dixie Jack, with the bold sweep of an arm. "This is an abolitionist book fit to read."

"And we're not done yet." He motioned to his men for Eadon to be brought forth, and he was pushed and prodded up the auction block stairs. "I believe," said Dixie Jack, "it's time to auction off our Tar Baby. And who better to do so?" He draped an arm over Eadon's shoulders, as if they were old pards. "Who would know more about the workings of the auction block, than one of our own 'fair haired' colored boys?"

The banjo music rose in biting riffs, and the shrill whistling from across the open lawn put any sporting event to shame.

Charlie slinked his way through the crowd to the foot of the stairs. He saw the look on Eadon's face. The shame at being there, the shame at what he was being ordered to do. Charlie made a dash to get past the ruffians guarding the stairs, but he was grabbed and flung to the ground. He had no idea what he would have done if he'd gotten up those stairs. But he'd wanted them to know, even if he was only the crumbs of a man, he was with them.

CHAPTER 51

"WE'RE GONNA START THE BIDDING AT A DIX," said Dixie Jack. "And see how low it goes before anyone bids on the Tar Baby here."

Eadon was to play field hand and fool in this petty drama of what everyone silently understood was an act of sexual humiliation. A white man being socially castrated before the sanctity of the mob and not a sheriff to bear witness. A tale of plain speaking domination at the hands of your political enemy, and helpless to exact your will. The ultimate cruelty—a white man being auctioned off by a nigger. It was also meant as a cautionary nightmare to the free staters and abolitionists, and a subtle dig at their fears about what might happen if "the darkies ever ruled the daylight."

Butler knew all this. He also understood anyone in the crowd who was on his side of the political ledger should remain silent and just let this pathetic attempt at distinction play out. Raise the ire of the ruffians and you could expect their violent presence one evening, then there goes your well being and your belongings and so be it.

Butler shouted out, "What is happening here is nothing. Don't put yourself at risk from this undistinguished trash—"

He was put to the floor of the auction block by the blunt force of a gun barrel.

What the boy witnessed in all its miserable degradation enraged him. The unsettled business of his father's murder came rushing back—the terror, and the heartbreak. And seeing the trespass against this man, who would not yield to the boot, who kept shouting to the crowd of their barbarity, like some rough and jeering guardsman. Seeing him hit again, Charlie's throat closed, and he shook his head violently for them to stop. And then he remembered the pistol Erastus had given him in his haversack.

Eadon was ordered to begin the bidding and when he did not, Dixie Jack slapped his face. The black's eyes flinched, and he was slapped again. He clenched his teeth and the muscles along the sides of his mouth trembled. He was ashamed to be part of this, ashamed that he could be compromised into being a part of this, ashamed he just did not spit in Dixie Jack's face and be done with his life. He was slapped again, and his eyes welled up with tears, for the degrading of his friend was the degrading of himself.

"The bidding will start with a Dix," said Eadon. "Do I have a Dix…A Dix…"

Charlie had reached into the haversack and had hold of the pistol…If he could just get past the ruffians in one dash. Even if he made it just partway up the stairs. It was a scheme that had a beginning but no end. What if he were intercepted on the way and his act brought even further harm to Butler Phillips? But look at him there. Bloody, tarred, those bits of book pages looking like foolish scales——

"I'll bid a Dix."

Charlie turned to see Eadon's mother there holding up a Dix in her black and weathered hand. People in the crowd watched in cold passing. Even the banjo was down to one shrilly note as Eadon finished up the auction. "A Dix going once…A Dix going twice… Sold…To Jesse Thompson of Water Street."

There was a smattering of applause from some of those in attendance which did not sit well with Dixie Jack and his compatriots.

"Why don't you bring that money up here to me, Miss Jesse."

He made the woman climb the stairs to him. As she passed around Charlie, she handed him her shawl. "Take dis to Mister Butler so's he can cover hisself."

"Yes, ma'am."

Charlie dashed up the stairs, thought better of it, stopped, and turned back. He put out a hand to help the woman, but she scolded him with the crone wagging of a finger to get on with it.

She was face to face with Dixie Jack, while her son and Charlie covered Butler with the shawl and helped him down the stairs. Butler managed to tell Dixie Jack, "I hope to keep our next meeting down to a brief sentence or two."

When it was just he and the old woman, Dixie Jack said, "You're a pretty hard case for an old lady."

"Plenty of credit to go 'round for makin' me dat way."

"Too bad your son's not the man you are."

He'd made sure Eadon heard that.

"The Bible on all a us ain't writ yet, Mister Shepherd."

"True. But for some it comes sooner than later."

"Sooner or later don't count much in heaven, Mister Shepherd. Onliest place sooner or later count, is in hell."

ANGELFIRE

CHAPTER 52

HE SAT ON A STOOL in the kitchen of the restaurant. On a table beside him was a bottle of whiskey and the glass from which he drank. He had covered his genitals with a cloth while Jesse and two other aged black women went about the slow and difficult task of removing the strips of paper and then the tar.

Charlie sat across the table from Butler, his arms flat on the planed wood, his chin resting on his crossed hands. He watched in silence as the women dabbed the tarry patches with seed oil and then their knotty fingers went to work, wetting the tar with turpentine, kneading it as if it were dough. They carefully, almost delicately, began to peel away that gluey pine, doing their utmost to tear away as little flesh as possible in the process, sending entreaties to God under their breath at every failure.

Butler bore it all. Not a complaint or a curse, as his body became an endless map of abrasions and bleeding strips where the skin had been blistered away.

He drank and talked with the ladies, enticing them to idle kitchen gossip, and whatever painful suffering he went through was concealed somewhere in that cold, telling stare where truth, honor, and self respect lay in wait for the moment of avengement.

"You're watchin' pretty hard there, Charlemagne."

Charlie nodded.

"What ya' thinkin'? Care to let me have a look?"

Charlie shook his head no.

"Well. What say you ladies about Charlemagne here?"

The women spoke with little more than eye movements, a half gesture, a breath.

"Boy is a thinkin' machine," said Butler.

"Butler, sir," said Charlie, "Could I buy a Dix from you?"

Butler spread out his arms. "At present, no pockets. After though. Do me a favor. Go find Eadon. Tell him the three of us are leaving here today for Fulton. He'll understand."

This brought a rise from the women. One whispered, "Angel-fire." And the others nodded in agreement, and one of them half whispered, "...And the arms of the wicked shall be broken."

Charlie got up to go find Eadon. Jesse took him aside at the back door to the alley. She wiped the tar from her hands on a filthy rag, and from somewhere hidden in that dress her fingers appeared holding paper currency. One of those was a Dix, which she pressed into Charlie's hand. "Mister Butler will see me good for it."

"Thank you, ma'am."

She didn't let go of him yet. "I saw you today at the auction block steps. You start thinkin' and actin' like a man. They'll do to you like a man."

• • •

Eadon was in his office, at his desk, crying, when Charlie showed up. Eadon saw Charlie there in the doorway just staring and ordered

Charlie out. When Charlie did not obey, Eadon flung a book at him.

Charlie ducked it all right, then said, "Butler wants you to get everything ready. The three of us are traveling to Fulton this afternoon. Wherever that is."

"It's up near Jefferson City."

"Don't know where Jefferson City is."

Eadon wiped at the tears. Embarrassed. "I failed him. I shamed him, and I failed him. And in shaming him and failing him, I shamed myself."

The book had ended up in the dirt, just outside the alley door. Charlie went and picked it up.

"I should have gone after Dixie Jack. Like a man I should have refused to auction. I should not have allowed myself to be slapped. I should have, at least, spit in his face."

Charlie wiped the book clean with his coat sleeve and set it back down on the desk.

Eadon said, "I know what they're saying, the people out there. I can imagine."

Charlie understood all too well. The origin of the tears from the root of the soul. The sense of oblivion where there is a desperate need for certitude. He could not have explained it, not in words. Explaining it was beyond him. But he had experienced it, he had lived it. Charlie went and sat in an old chair with ratted cushions. He slumped down and stretched out his legs and folded his hands.

"How old are you?" said Eadon.

"I'll be thirteen in two weeks."

"Then, you have no idea what I'm talkin' about."

"You're not much older than me. Twenty, maybe." said Charlie.

"Twenty is forever compared to you."

Eadon sat there like a gloomy soul driven to the brink by the venomous play of hatreds around him and unable to contest it.

"I know things," said Charlie. "I've done things you can't compare to. More shameful than today by miles. That's why I'm come here to ask Mister Phillips to help me. To amend a grievance."

"What are you talkin' about?"

"I took money. With my father. In a swindle. We pulled a 'sharper,' tricking good white folks and good well-to-do colored folks out of their money. Decent people. Like your mother and you."

And so he told Eadon the whole story. He even let him feel the coat where the money was hid away. And not just to ease the youth's shame for not doing something that was beyond his manifest in the first place, or that his suffering was spilled in vain, but for his own peace as well, as it was forever there, the shame. It would be so, until he rid himself of that coat and the burden he carried inside it, and he waited on that solitary hour as the world waits on the sunlight.

Later that afternoon, they ventured forth on the Perryville Road. Dressed for hard days, with an extra mount to carry supplies, ammunition, and weapons.

Butler wore a loose fitting linen shirt with banded collar. His wounds were salved and dressed, and the loose fitting shirt left the open sores less painful. He wore a light straw panama hat to brace his eyes against the sun as he steadily scanned the country behind him with field glasses.

Dixie Jack knew Butler would be heading north, not only for the abolitionist rally on the Fourth in Pikes County, but to the Fulton Courthouse, where the trial of the black slave who had murdered her master for repeatedly raping her would be underway.

Eadon called out to Butler, "Rumor has it the abolitionists asked you to meet up with this Angelfire and bring her with you to the rally."

Charlie had heard that word "Angelfire" in the kitchen. The old women speaking under their breath with a kind of prayerful shining caused him to ask what this—Angelfire—was.

"Sister of the woman on trial," said Eadon. "A runaway slave. Swears she'll start killing slavers if they convict and hang her sister. They say she shot down two slave catchers sent to hunt her out."

Butler was scanning the country behind him. With the failing day, it had become the land of a thousand shadows.

"Is it true?" said Charlie. "The rumor?"

"A rumor can't be true," said Butler. "It's only true when it happens. And for both your sakes, it's just a rumor."

Back there in the ashen twilight, where the road slithered through the high grass, he could make out dim figures in a hazy dust. He thumbed the focus on his field glasses. A world of detail quietly registered a small flock of men, three, maybe four, coming on with a hard grace, kicking their mounts violently in the flanks.

Butler had been wearing the field glasses on a lanyard around his neck. He let the glasses now rest against his chest. Charlie noted the conflicted look on the man's face.

"Is it bad?" said Charlie.

Butler glanced at the boy.

"Somethin's back there, isn't it, sir?"

"Gents," he said. "You need to follow my orders religiously 'cause in short order I am going to execute a lesson in the perishability of the flesh."

CHAPTER 53

BUTLER PROCEEDED ON, but at an easy gait so their pursuers would not realize Butler was aware of them. It was only a matter of time before they were to be overtaken. But Butler kept on, with Charlie and Eadon watching each other, wondering, looking back into the cooling shadows and banded light. Butler said not a word until he reached a place that warranted his stopping.

There was a forest of slash pine on one side of the road that rose to a bluff. The dry grass was high there and home to feral hogs. It would be a dangerous misery to try and herd a rider through that. Butler dismounted and went to the packhorse. From a saddlebag he took out a map which he then went and handed to Eadon.

"About ten miles from here, the road breaks off, and one part tracks to the northeast and Pike County. You take Charlemagne here and the packhorse. About three miles south of Bowling Green is the First Congregational Church. It is a freedman church. Everybody up there knows the church. That's where Montgomery and the abolitionists will meet up for the Fourth of July."

Butler forced the map into the hands of a shocked and reluctant young man.

"You said we're all going to Fulton."

"The boy needs to get to Pike County. I'm entrusting him to you."

Eadon held up the map angrily. "You knew you were going to do this all along."

"I had an idea."

"But you said nothing."

"I will deal with these gents here. I will go to Fulton as I'm expected. I will bring the girl if she's damn well alive by then. And...I will meet up with you both at the church. Not very profound, just planned simplicity."

"I'm a better shot than you are," said Eadon. "How many times have you told me that? With a rifle—"

"But I'm more deadly, son."

"I won't go. After what they played at the auction block."

"Don't let some notion of dignity cloud your judgment in a dog fight."

"Fine thought comin' from you."

"The boy has to get to Pike County and Montgomery. And with you taking him, it'll be—"

"He knows about the coat," said Charlie.

Butler turned his attention to the boy. Charlie was leaning across the saddle, railroad cap in hand, twisting it nervously. "I told Eadon this morning when you asked me to go look for him. I thought it... right."

"Then you can understand," Butler saw Eadon was troubled.

"It's not you both they're after. You take the road into Pike, no one will follow. It'll be clear sailing. You can daydream most of the—"

"That's what I resent," said Eadon.

Butler put a hand on Eadon's leg. "Son, there'll be plenty of days for the worst of it."

"He's going with you to Fulton," said Charlie. "And so am I."

Butler looked between the two of them, trying to conceive of what was taking place.

"Dixie Jack knows," said Charlie.

"Knows what?"

"I told him," said Charlie, "I knew it was him who felled that gentleman in the woods near New Madrid."

"I don't understand."

"The Dix."

"What?"

"The Dix that Eadon's mother gave me."

"Boy...what did you do?"

He told Butler, with the swift currency of one being chased, how he went looking for Dixie Jack and found him outside a tavern with a fleet of ruffians. The proud cock, showing off, dazzling in his own vanity, and how Charlie waited across the street to see what direction he walked and then Charlie sprinted ahead and slipped into a dry goods store and waited in the shaded doorway.

He had written on the Dix and had it folded between two fingers when Dixie Jack passed by, rambling on with one venerated anecdote about himself after another. Charlie zipped out of the doorway and bumped right into the slaver.

"It's as easy to put something into a man's pocket as it is to pick it," Charlie told Butler.

And when Dixie Jack saw who it was that had crashed right into him, he took on a look of pure scorn. "Gentlemen," he'd said to those with him, "this is one of Butler Phillips' most loyal followers.

You're turning into the proverbial bad penny, boy."

And with that, Charlie was shoved aside.

Butler had no way to contend with the proclamation he had just been presented with.

"What did you write on the Dix?"

"Said I knew he'd murdered that fella near New Madrid. And I signed it."

There was precious little time to think.

"Do you realize what you've done?"

"Yes, sir. I do."

Butler looked back down the road. He was grave and silent, and then he shook his head over some private thought. As he started over to the packhorse, he said, "Eadon, get out the Hawken."

Eadon leapt from the saddle. "Doin' it..."

Butler removed two French revolving rifles from their scabbards and a box of ammunition. He pointed with one of the rifles. "Eadon, you go up that bluff. Find a spot where you can command the road. This is where I'll confront them. Don't fire until I engage them. Don't let any of them cut and run. No witnesses. Charlie..."

The boy slipped back on his cap. "Yes, sir."

"You take all the horses, and you go up the road a few hundred yards. Nice easy trot so they don't get suspicious. Veer off the road and back into the woods. You wait there. And son...we can't lose the horses."

Butler passed Charlie the reins. He grasped the boy's hand in a pronounced, paternal gesture.

Eadon had already scaled the bluff and was running along the tree line. Charlie started away on the Perryville Road, pulling three mounts behind him. Butler went and sat on the stump of a fallen tree that lay in decay just off the roadside. He set his second rifle down there, and the ammunition, and so he waited. When he heard the heavy cadence of hooves he took off his hat, set that too aside. He could see just over the rim of the brittle grass, and when he had his first sight of them he ventured forth into a burning dusk and opened fire.

One of the horses was shot out from under its rider and it crumpled to the earth in a ravaged cry. The rider was thrown with outflung arms into the roadway.

Charlie had made it to the edge of the forest when he picked up the first volley of gunfire. It was a slow and labyrinthine passage through the trees with dimming light. Then Charlie heard the echo of that big bore Hawken.

The riders veered from the road. Two of the ruffians were wounded, one was on foot. They were trying to flee, their horses plowing through the high grass. Before them, tusked and ferocious hogs scattered in a wild melee of grunts and squeals. The shooting grew more intense, the voices desperate to the pit of the soul. A bloody tale was being played out along the Perryville Road.

The running gun battle grew closer where Charlie waited with the slatted light. They were in the forest somewhere. A man called out that he had been hit in the chest and was dying. The pitched cries of a huge tusked hog attacking one of the riders. There was another round from that Hawken, a rolling thunder of a shot. The horses grew frightened, their long necks jerked and they sidled in confusion, so Charlie wound the reins around his wrist. Better to be pulled from the saddle and dragged across creation than lose the horses.

The mounts railed more violently now at the threat of something turning apart the brush. From the weight of the sound Charlie suspected it might be a boar, but it was a ruffian thrashing his way into a clearing between the trees like some harried game.

Shot and staggering in the half dark, a hand to his blood stained chest, he spotted Charlie and the horses. He was carrying a huge Walker pistol. "I need one of those mounts, fella…" He aimed the gun with an unsettled hand. "You hear. I need one of those damned mounts…Bring one here."

Charlie made neither a move, nor said a word. His whole being was concentrated on those reins tied around his wrist. The rough was a thin shell and Charlie could not make out his features in the half dark, but when he spoke, it was clear he was choking on his own blood.

Charlie heard Butler and Eadon shouting to each other. They were not far off now and the rough heard them too and he aimed the Walker with both of his faltering hands. Charlie closed his eyes and bent down low in the saddle with the mounts turning back and in on themselves.

Whether the shot went wild or had been meant as a warning, it didn't matter. The ruffian took a step closer, demanding, threatening, another wavery step, his words half consumed in his throat.

And when he got close enough Charlie could see, he was not a man. He was a boy, maybe fifteen, sixteen years old, clean faced and lost. And just as frightened as Charlie, and desperate, knowing life was sweeping away, when he saw Butler Phillips striding toward him, one of the revolving rifles in each hand.

He came upon the boy like some ravened force. The boy was crumpling to the ground in exhaustion and defeat and he put up a hand as if to hide behind it, pleading, "Please don't. Mercy—"

Butler shot him in the side of the head. Just like that, the boy was driven to the earth. He would be fifteen, sixteen, thought Charlie, for all eternity. And Butler, Charlie saw too, was calmness personified.

CHAPTER 54

YOU CAN SLEEP GOD'S OWN SLEEP and it doesn't matter, the upright and the blind are the same, casting about dumbly in that shoreless void. The wizened old Methuselah dozed, sitting with his back against his saddle, always keeping guard for Mister Jeffrey.

A sound like the rush of air awoke him. A voice whispering in his ear said, "What you just heard was me slitting your throat."

That old black man went to shout out, but the words died where his windpipe had been severed. Billy Tule slayed the others where they slept, firing headlong into their bodies with two revolvers. All except for Mister Jeffrey, who sat there recoiled against his saddle with not an ounce of arrogance left in him.

"Cast your weapons aside," said Tule, "and lend me them chain keys."

Mister Jeffrey did as ordered, fumbling with his breeches in the process. Handy was on all fours and clung to Billy Tule's boots like a thankful beggar. Mister Jeffrey tossed the keys over to where Handy was still on hands and knees at Tule's feet. He couldn't grab for them fast enough to free himself.

"The knives," said Tule. "Where are they?"

Handy had already loosed his wrists and was crawling over to one of the dead whose arm lay smoldering in the last embers of the campfire. Handy removed his weapons and slid the sheaths back into the grooves they'd worn inside his belt. He sat back and unloosed the shackles then let out a savage cry.

He stood and turned his black stare to Mister Jeffrey. There was only one cure for what ailed the former slave. He slung the chains of his humiliation at Mister Jeffrey, who wiped at the blood where the wrist lock had cut his face.

Mister Jeffrey spoke now to Billy Tule. He was on the downside of any courage he'd had. "I didn't see you dead."

"No," said Tule. "And I won't see you dead either."

He put an arm out to tell Handy to remain where he was. "But your business isn't with me, is it?"

Handy slid the knives from their sheaths. He looked like something cured in madness and with a cloven rock for a heart.

"Stand up," said Tule.

The man stood. His filthy shirt hanging out of his pants, barefoot, socks a patchwork of holes.

"You know how to run, Br'er Rabbit?"

Mister Jeffrey understood all too well. There wasn't five cents worth of pity in his future.

"Can I get my boots?"

"You don't need boots," said Tule. "You need wings."

Mister Jeffrey reached down inside himself for a flinty breath, shouted out a foul oath, and took off at a run. He leapt the charry dregs of the fire and the body stretched out beside it, with shirt sleeve and flesh afire, and was gone into the black and sleeping country.

They could hear the undoing of branches as he cut a desperate man's path through the underbrush hoping for escape into the darker reaches. Handy waiting until Tule gave him leave to hunt the white man down, holding the black until his blood couldn't bear it any longer. And then, with the sweep of his arm, Tule said, "Run him down, boy."

• • •

There was a drinking bar with an old upright in a backwash of streets past the Cairo Hotel where the blacks lived. It was an all right enough place when the weather was good, but had a leaky roof covered by a tarp, and when it got cold the place was a wind rattled, wretched affair.

Blacks came there to drink and listen to music. There was always a singer or two, and some of them reworked the old ditties by spiking up the language and making them all brash and unrepentant, as if to give the sly impression there was a new world order tucked away in their hip pockets.

Manor was sitting at a broken down table with another fella who was buying the drinks. "I swear to you," said Manor, "that colored boy was as white as the president of the United States."

"I know," said the black with Manor, "I seen 'im."

This caught Manor off guard, and he looked about. "What you mean? Seen him? When?"

"Gonna shoz ya sumthin," said the black.

From his coat pocket, the black took out a small ill weathered family Bible. He opened the front cover and there, inscribed in ink, the names: Rosemary and Zacharia Griffin. And beneath that: Son—Charlemagne Ezekiel Griffin, July 3, 1842.

"The boy's family Bible?"

The black nodded.

"How'd ya get it?"

"Boy'z ma'am."

Manor finally felt comfortable and pointed. "What happened to your thumbs?"

"What ya s'pose?"

Manor nodded. "Yeah…take it all, don't they?"

Handy nodded.

"Boy'z ma'am sick. As' me cum fin' him. Mista Eels cum here. Heard ya' knowz."

Handy took out the letter from the doctor at the hospital and gave it to Manor to read. He held the paper closer to the lantern. Scanned the writing with quick black fingers.

"Boy'z pap dead," said Handy. "Her wha' freed me."

Handy said nothing more. He kept all that deadly venom locked behind an emotionless expression and waited to see if the trap sprung shut.

By the time the body of the young bellhop was discovered in a roadside latrine, Billy Tule and his unholy ally were stepping off the boat in Cape Girardeau. It took about as long as them walking up to Water Street and standing in the shadow of the boardinghouse and burned shell of the restaurant to learn of Butler Phillips and his murder of three ruffians from the lone survivor of the gunfight. And that with him were two youths, one who might well fit the description of Charlie Griffin.

They rode north on the Perryville Road in the company of slavers. Billy Tule had presented himself and his intrepid tracker as soldiers for the cause. That vagabond patrol was making for the town of Fulton where Dixie Jack promised a thornfest of retribution.

CHAPTER 55

THE ROAD IS HOME TO LIARS. Because you're not there to remain attached to a place, a life, or an identity. Those are just human trappings, temporary trading posts in your life. The road is an invitation to do away with your very existence in a matter of miles. It is a never ending series of destinations that offers rewards, as long as you have the audacity to accept such a treasure, and not fall prey to human predictability.

Charlie had committed so many of his father's sayings to memory, such as people did with passages of the Bible. He knew those sayings better than he'd known the man himself. The words being more him, than him. And Charlie was constantly trying to think how to use these for his benefit.

They were vigilant and wary as they traveled north. Where there were pockets of slavers, they rode mostly at night. From freedmen they learned Dixie Jack had telegraphed ruffians he knew across Jefferson County and that Butler Phillips was making for Fulton and not likely alone, as the killings on the Perryville Road attested.

They were up in Saint Francois County when the packhorse

came up lame. There was a sutler depot at the base of Iron Mountain and the road up to the mines. It was a rough compound of businesses and shacks and taverns, and there were plenty of traders, road trash, drunken miners and transients on their way to a dream. You could see the fires from the smelters up on Iron Mountain from the settlement, like God's own forge. Butler had them enter these uncertain dens alone, and they would stay alone until farther on down the road.

Charlie wandered about the settlement while Butler bought a new packhorse. Eadon was busy talking up freedmen who'd just come by wagon from Fulton to work the mines. And did they have a story to tell about the black girl who had murdered the two slave catchers. There's nothing like a shared killing men could silently toast.

Outside a sutler's warehouse, the wagon of a Mennonite family and all their possessions was being sold off. It seems the family had died of brain fever, and the husband's last request was that profits from the sale were to go to the Evangelical Seminary at Marthasville.

Their possessions were laid out on a pine chest: tintypes, a mirror and brush, a cameo, a shaving mug, plain dishes. Meager by the meagerest standard. There was even the husband's diploma from the seminary. But it was the tintypes that captivated Charlie, and the one of the husband and his wife and son, who was close to Charlie in age and size, brought back on the bleak strains of longing and loss. There was not a picture of him and his parents anywhere in the world to prove they had been together in time. The closest to that was the family Bible he had forced his father to carry in his carpetbag. And what become of that? An omen of helplessness swept over the boy.

He looked at the dead man's clothes, and the clothes of the dead man's son. The drab Mennonite pants and drab Mennonite vest and the dour Mennonite hat. And he thought of his father telling him, "The road is home to liars."

• • •

That dusk, three riders journeyed forth with only the fires from the smelters on Iron Mountain to guide them. Hellish flames reaching to the heavens, and there in the darkness of the highway, a Mennonite father and his Mennonite son in their drab black Mennonite pants and vests and their dour Mennonite hats with a freedman cook alongside them.

In the days that followed on the road, these newfound religious souls were greeted with the doff of a hat or a word of fellowship, often just plain kindness passing between strangers, but there was also the air of polite indifference from a wagon of travelers, or at a campsite, the folksy stare that contained the shadow of religious hatred.

As they traveled deeper into the state of the nation, social constraint gave way to raw power. Not only were blacks beaten down or humiliated, but whites had their wagons searched, their privacies upturned, and riders who might be the hunted Butler Phillips were violently rousted. It was pastoral to a world devouring itself with terrifying earnestness.

They crossed the Missouri near Mokane, on a backwash ferry suited for riders and carts. It was a grey morning, humid, a thin drizzle, though not enough to cause the rain to drip from the brim of your hat.

On board were a couple of slave catchers with a black in chains. He looked to have gotten the worst of a pretty rough fight. The slave catchers began to talk about Butler Phillips. They actually used his name. That people heard he'd been seen riding north to Fulton. That he was in the company of "a nigger named Eadon" and at least one other person. That they thought they'd been cornered in a cabin south of Jefferson City, and they shot it out with the fella, but the corpse turned out not to be him.

One of the slave catchers was staring across the ferry at Butler and Charlie. There wasn't but maybe twenty feet that separated them.

"He's got the evil eye on us," Charlie whispered.

"Hey…you people Mennonites?"

Butler looked across the ferry and nodded.

"They say Mennonites won't fight. Won't go to war. Won't save their country."

He waited for an answer. What the three together knew about Mennonites wasn't enough to fill a thumbprint. So Butler said, "We try to be the best sons and daughters of Jesus Christ that we can."

The slave catcher had a dark and inky stare. "Mennonites are shit," he said.

Upon leaving the ferry they were cursed out and spat upon. "Better of bein' a nigger," said one of the slave catchers as they disembarked. And once Eadon thought it safe enough he called out to his fellowship of Mennonites, "Well…the lie, it seems, is working wonders."

They rode up country through landscapes that looked to have been exquisitely nourished by God, and that is where they came upon the hanging.

They were just outside of Fulton on a wagon road. It wasn't actually a hanging, it was more a lynching. There were about a dozen hard looking men on horseback at the base of a tree that was long since dead. Its bark chipped away, its trunk and branches black as char and bone. The dead man was white, and he'd been stripped down to his drawers. His boots and pants and gun lay neatly in the grass. A sign had been posted on his drawers. It read: SLAVER.

From the talk Charlie could pick up, they were abolitionist haters and slavers all. And they looked to mete out some pretty harsh business on anyone who ran afoul of their present state of mind.

They were taking the body down as Charlie and the others rode past. One of the men tasked with the job shouted, "What are you damn Mennonites staring at?"

"Forgive us," said Butler, raising his hat in a conciliatory manner. "It's just such a shocking sight. Our prayers to you, good sirs."

They rode on. With Charlie at the rear towing the packhorse, stealing glances back, and feeling a certain sense of relief with each passing minute, until the presence of dread had him call out, "I believe a handful of men are coming this way."

Butler eased about in his saddle. It surely was true, and if the speed of their approach was any indication of intent, their intention was not good. He cursed quietly, and then said, "Lead us not into temptation...unless I start firing."

CHAPTER 56

THEY WERE QUICKLY OVERTAKEN. One of the riders yelled, "Hold up there."

And Butler did. He then turned his horse about. "What can we do for you gentlemen?"

The one who'd had yelled to them as they brought down the body, did the talking. He was about Butler's age, with one milky eye that looked like the sun does when it is obscured behind a deep mist. The man leaned his face out at an angle to favor the good eye, which gave this otherwise ordinary looking man a troubling countenance. To Charlie, he could imagine that face delighting in strange torments.

"You a Mennonite?"

"We're Mennonites."

"I mean true Mennonites."

"Mennonites…yes."

The man pointed at the two scabbards in Butler's saddle. "I thought Mennonites didn't believe in killing or fighting. I noticed the scabbards as you rode past." He crept his mount closer, studying

the weapons with that good eye. "Those are some pretty fancy orna-
ments. Revolving rifles. Not your everyday hunting up a little stew
weapon. What's a Mennonite doing with an arsenal like that?"

"Well," said Butler, "...I...wasn't born a Mennonite. I...turned
one...when I accepted Jesus Christ as my savior...Before that...I
repaired and sold weapons... I...have a buyer for these guns in Fulton."

"Pardon me," said the man, "but that story doesn't swallow too
well."

Charlie saw that the other men were wary, but they did not seem
to have the incited fervor this one was carrying around.

"They say Mennonites are abolition. You abolition? You a free
stater?"

"We're followers of Jesus Christ, is all. Not politics."

"That's not what I asked."

"Leave it, Drew," said one of the other men. "He answered."

"How do we know who this man is? That he's even a Mennonite.
Those are fightin' guns."

"They are that," said one of others.

"Maybe you ought to show 'em your diploma," said Charlie.
"From the seminary."

Butler glanced at the boy. Talk about your clenched stare of total
surprise.

"I have it right here in my haversack," said Charlie. I'd admire
very much to show it to you, sirs."

Charlie went about the task like the perfect son. The haversack
hung by its strap from the pommel. As he rummaged it out, Charlie
said, "It's from the Evangelical Seminary over in Marthasville." He
eased Stranger over to one of the men. "You know Marthasville?" He
offered the man the diploma. "See...John Slocum. That's my father.

They call me Jack."

Butler and Eadon watched the boy lie and lie and lie with the practiced assurance of a vested criminal. The men looked the diploma over one by one like they were staring at God's own words.

Then Charlie rode that diploma over to Drew personally. And as he handed it to him, he said, "My father's too private a man to tell you, but the money from the sale of them rifles are to pay the debt of my mother's funeral. Your mother alive, Mister Drew?"

And the look on that one eyed face. Where there was a moment ago the hawkish stare of bold command, there was now personal bitterness.

"His ma'am's alive," said one of the others. "But she don't talk to him much."

"Shut up," said Drew.

"Thanks to his dissolute habits," said another.

"Am I gonna hear it from you all…again?" Drew said.

"Well, you have been a drinkin' plague to the old woman."

He handed Charlie back the diploma. "I give it you are Mennonites in good and proper order."

And Charlie, having been taught by his father when and how to put the knife in someone where it would do you the most good, offered, "You best right it with your ma'am, Mister Drew. Once she's gone, she's gone to you forever. You don't want to be somewhere alone cryin' your eyes out 'cause you couldn't put your fangs away. I carry a picture of my mother in my haversack. Would you care to see it?"

He didn't want to see the picture and the last he said to the boy was, "Shut your mouth."

The boy had rendered him a defeat thanks to shame. Not by a fierce will or more vaunted opponent, but by the very same proxy that drove the boy and was more powerful than any moment of vengeance. Simple shame, if there was such a thing as simple shame.

Charlie saw, in that one eyed harrowing stare, how insolence and authority and hard edged ruthlessness were taken down. It surprised Charlie that he felt suddenly bad for the man, for they drank from the same well.

"Where'd you come up with that diploma?" said Butler.

"I stole it when I bought the clothes," said Charlie.

Alone on the road, they'd dismounted to let the horses rest and graze before the last push to Fulton. Charlie was squatting on his heels there in the short grass. He cut a cheroot, and was smoking part while Eadon smoked the other.

"They weren't gonna sell the diploma," said Charlie, "or the tintypes and such. Those were going with the money they raised from the sale to the seminary. It was wrong to do, but I did it anyway."

"Why'd you take it?" said Butler.

"My father taught me…the more truth you can add to a lie, the better the lie."

Butler glanced at Eadon. Were they both having the same thought about what was coming out of the boy's mouth?

"It was like when my father and I went to Brooklyn to skim Beecher and those decent colored folks. He had written to abolitionists in Missouri about their cause and joinin' up and raisin' money. He got back a handful of letters, including one from James Montgomery. That was important, so he could copy the man's handwriting. And he used all those real letters to seed the lie."

Charlie took a puff there on his cheroot then tapped ash in the dust and ground it out with a little dirt so as not to torch the field where they rested.

"Charlemagne," said Eadon, "you're the lyin'ist Mennonite I ever met."

Though a moment of humor, the boy was uncertain. "My father," he said, "used to say I had a natural talent for lying. He was even a little jealous of me and told me so once. 'Cause lies and schemes just came to me with no hard thinkin' at all. He said I was like a singer or a circus acrobat, a writer even. That I had a God given talent in that direction. If there is such a thing as a 'God given talent' in that direction."

CHAPTER 57

IT WAS DUSK when they reached the outskirts of Fulton. The road struck through a long swath of timber and where it began to thin away they could make out a stream of torches. The town had set up outposts on the roads into Fulton. Not only to keep watch on all those that came and went who might beset the place with violence, but also the roadhawks were on the watch for the black murderess who had sworn killings if her sister were convicted for the murder of her master, the master who had seen fit to rape her over a time of years.

They were already calling her a murderess from the story Eadon was told by the black workmen at Iron Mountain. He, in turn, had told Butler and the boy as they rode. How much of it was true, and not a white lie, no one could be certain.

Her birth name was Cassie, but she was known as Angelfire. Her master, the man who had been murdered by her sister, had bestowed the nickname upon her. You see, she had fiercely good eyes and a steady hand. She was a born shot with a rifle, so much so, the master had taken her everywhere. He trained her with every kind of long gun. She was better at bringing down game than any of his own boys, white or black. He'd rewarded her with her own Sharps carbine when she was ten. He used to brag that she gave him more pride than any prize dog or hog he'd ever had, and he'd only wished he had a white son who could match her.

She had run away after the murder and arrest of her sister. She had taken a saddlebag of ammunition. She had only the brown raggy dress she wore and no shoes. Witnesses swore they had seen her, or someone looking like her, on a scrub pony in the woods. Most of the slavers in Fulton were certain she was being hidden out by abolitionists or defiant blacks. The family of the dead plantation owner had put up a Special Notice -- "Anyone helping, hiding, feeding, or protecting in any way, the runaway known as Angelfire will be subject to severe penalty."

The story the blacks had told Eadon at Iron Mountain was that the dogs of slave catching brothers had picked up her scent near the state asylum. She wasn't on horseback so the dogs hunted her hard through the trees and the underbrush, savage, bared teeth, and on into an open trace of farmland.

That's where the killing took place. The brothers saw the dogs had caught up with the girl and were tearing at her dress. The brothers were sprinting through the scrub grass, shouting to their animals, when they discovered it wasn't her.

The girl had taken her dress and draped it over the remains of a scarecrow, and it was then they realized she had lured them into the clearing, and that she was out there somewhere with her carbine.

Before they could control their animals and escape, there came the report of a rifle and a small puff of dust jumped from the shirt of one of the brothers. He died there in the scrub grass calling to his brother, who'd abandoned him and the dogs. The other brother later found dying in the road by a man who said the brother had told him that the girl came along naked, waving her dress and screaming, and she killed the dogs that were huddled around the brother while he lay there.

The man who told the story was an illiterate miscreant who had been found prostrate in many a Fulton alleyway. And there was a feeling in certain quarters that he had murdered the brothers and the dogs himself, to rob them of their pittance, and then he'd created the story to play into the rage and revulsion of the "good people" of Fulton.

• • •

Butler was ordered at riflepoint to stop there on the road into Fulton. There were half a dozen men gathered up around the back of a flatbed wagon, drinking and playing cards, talking up the trial and that "black bitch" on the loose, as they performed their "legal duties" of guarding the sovereignty of the town. The man in the road with the rifle walked around Butler's horse and then Charlie's and Eadon's, taking measure of them.

"You here for the trial?"

Butler answered, "What trial?"

Charlie saw the man thought Butler a fool, and then the man turned his attention to Eadon. "This your colored boy?"

"I'm a freedman, sir."

The man certainly did not like being talked to directly, under the circumstances, by a black.

"You got papers, boy?"

Their measure having been taken, Eadon's papers coldly looked over, they entered what could only be called "the lion's den." The town was about half a dozen square blocks and it was all lit to hell with torches and fires. People had come for the trial and were camped out in open lots and empty fields, they'd parked their wagons right along the roadway. The last Charlie had seen anything like this was out front of the Barnum Museum and that might as well have been a lifetime ago, before the moral reckoning of the world had taken over.

The atmosphere here was something else altogether. There was an overwhelming sense of tension, a penetrating anxiety that encompassed everyone and everything. Innocuous as they were traveling down a street teeming with people, with placards, with the passing out of political pamphlets, with strident angry prophecies, they were stared at hard, as if they might be the threat that brings down the commonest decencies of organized society.

"You can feel it," whispered Eadon.

"What?" said Charlie.

"The violence. It's comin'. No matta' the girl gets convicted or not. That's not why people are here."

CHAPTER 58

In Missouri, most of the slavers lived in counties that bordered the Missouri River, which cut a pretty clear line east to west across the state. Callaway County was among them, and according to the clerk's records, had more slaves than any other. People knew their enemies well there, and they maintained a healthy suspicion of those they didn't. Some went about their political business with a clandestine efficiency that was more suited to the Borgias.

The home Butler brought them to was at the north end of the town. It was a proper two story brick, with a proper white washed fence and garden and porch and curtains and a proper shed behind it for horses and carriages.

They were ushered into a parlor by a young black woman and Charlie noted how quiet the home was and how gently appointed; and the scent of candles and the smell of cooking and perfume, and the voice of a woman a few rooms away with a touch of wisp to it and her clothes rustling as she approached them.

She couldn't have been much more than five feet tall standing there in the doorway. Her flesh, even in that light, looked to be little more than onion skin covering frail bone.

She gave Butler a hard going over, and said, "Are you a caution-ary tale…or are the Mennonites so desperate they have to count you among their number?"

Butler introduced Charlie and Eadon and the woman walked to them with gnomish steps and shook their hands.

She was introduced as Missus Genevieve Black. They would learn later that she was called by those in Fulton "Widow Black" because her actions in business had much in common with the illus-trious spider.

The old woman ran her fingers down the front of the boy's coat. "Do you know of Joseph?" she said. "And his coat of many colors?"

"No, ma'am."

"No matter," she said.

Charlie knew then that Butler must have written her of his plight. She fed them in the dining room. The settings were fine china and monogrammed linen. The boys grinned, star struck at so elegant a table, especially in light of their most recent travails. The woman's kindness and the décor of the room made Charlie think of the Glou-casters in Brooklyn, of them singing on their knees in a kind of shared prayer. In all the senseless fray going on around them, thought Char-lie, there was Christian goodness, willing to live with personal risk.

While they ate, Butler and the widow discussed plans for get-ting the girl and Charlie to the abolitionists in Pike County. The old woman was hoping that Butler could dissuade the girl from her reckless promise of exacting revenge if her sister was convicted and sentenced to death, as she surely would be. The trial, as they knew, was nothing more than a formalized act of corruption.

And Butler then said, "What will be harder, the finding or the convincing?"

The old woman got up and gestured for Butler to follow and Charlie and Eadon took it upon themselves to join them and there they were Indian file following the widow up a narrow staircase and down a narrow passage to a closed door where she knocked gently and a voice, after a time, said, "Yes, ma'am."

The widow opened the door and said, "Close the curtain and light a candle." And Charlie could see, even in the darkness of those few moonlight moments, a figure sitting in a chair by the window that looked out on the woods at the edge of the town. Then the shade was pulled and a candle lit. And in the first blush of light was the girl.

For that is what she was. Sixteen, Charlie guessed, seventeen, maybe. In a frayed dress made from poor quality tarp that hung like a loose rag from her knotty, fleshless shoulders. The Sharps rifle, so much talked about, leaning against the wall near her.

She looked too frail to even shoulder the weapon. Her face, boyish, fleshless as the rest of her and her eyes, huge eyes, challenging eyes—that's what Charlie saw there. And scorn, and untamed defiance, suffering, hunger, loss, loss most of all, loss that comes out of a person like water does from a broken river. The eyes had lived a lot longer than the body or the face, if you asked Charlie.

"This is Cassie," said the old woman. "Did you hear, child?"

The girl pointed to the open grate of the stove heart. Butler glanced at the widow to understand.

"I leave all the stoves grates in the house open. Voices carry through the pipes. She can hear everything downstairs. Slavers ever come, anybody ever come hunting, the girl will know and be gone." The girl was sitting in a chair with one leg up, barefoot, her arms wrapped around a knee. The light from the candle flitted with the breeze and her face seemed to glow as it went in and out of shadow.

"I know 'bout you?" she said to Charlie. "You come long way."

"From New York."

"Seen pic'turs. Grand lookin' place."

"It'll make you take a couple of breaths."

She looked Charlie over some. "I thought ya'd be bigger."

"I thought you'd be older," he said.

She laughed without constraint. "Know 'bout you, too," she said to Butler. "Say ya kilt some white men on Perryville Road."

Eadon realized, as did the others, there would be no going home now. That his life, mother and days in Cape Girardeau were lost to him.

"The story," said Eadon. He pointed to the rifle. "It true?"

The girl looked at the gun there in the soft shadows. She ran a hand through her unruly hair. During the telling, she rocked back and forth slowly, like a child.

"If I don' say I kilt dem brothers, they may beat sum'n nuff to bear witness 'gainst me. White folks want a colored person to done it…Even 'cause it makes 'em afraid. But I say nuthin'. Won' give 'em da satisfaction. As I tell it…those brotha's fools to be kilt that way… no matta who done it."

"Girl," said Widow Black, "Mister Phillips needs to talk with you."

"I know," said the girl. "I heard." She pointed to the open stove grate. "Wants me outta here 'fore I bring wrath down on 'em."

CHAPTER 59

THE OLD LADY MADE SURE all the downstairs curtains were shut tight, the lights few, the horses left out front stabled in the shed behind the house.

They had whiskey and coffee in the dining room. Charlie cut up a cheroot, and he and Eadon smoked while Butler did his best to convince this girl that if she were trying to commit suicide her plan was certainly daring enough. That the streets were crowded with ruffians and slavers waiting on her after the trial and there were people with no claim to politics of any kind who dreamed of a chance to squander the reward placed on her head.

But this was a woman child in a not so promised land, who murmured curses at every sensible argument thrown at her, who shook her head defiantly in the face of notions like caution or prudence.

She sat in the light like a lonely vigil candle and Charlie could understand her ardent and pronounced desires very well. They touched him so, and he saw that they were remarkably similar people. She being a better version of himself, who'd never been a lamentable pickpocket or confidence schemer. You take her, or Eadon—

Charlie wasn't sure he could ever measure up to either one for pure content of character.

He noticed the girl was staring at him. "That the coat?" she said.

He knew she meant about the money.

"That's the coat."

"Money is in the linin'?"

"Money is in the linin'."

She motioned that she'd like to feel it, where the money was. He grinned and nodded and stood up and she came around the table. She began to feel about tentatively, but wasn't sure where, and Charlie took her hand and placed it along the collar and then worked her fingers down through the lining. "All that...money?"

He nodded. She looked awed, joyous.

"Can I...?" She put her arms around her shoulders.

He understood. He set his cheroot down in the ashtray. He took off the coat and held it so she could slip her arms in one at a time. He'd never helped a woman on with a coat before, unless you counted a drunken bawdy girl in bed with his father, who was in dire straits when it came to getting dressed.

Well...when Cassie had that raggy cloth coat draped around her shoulders with all that money stashed in the lining she looked as if a heavenly glitter had descended upon her. She walked about the room, prancy, regal, a slight rusty sound to her breath. This was a child plunged into a wonder of personal dreams.

"'Nuff money here to get you a little paradise of your own. Maybe get to Canada. Or down to that neighborhood in Orleans where it all colored folks. And I hear, do they shine. Money...don't matter they hate you...does it?"

She glanced around the room waiting on some answer that didn't come. Was that thunder they all just heard from somewhere to the east? Faint tracings that would bring down rain on them soon enough.

"You ever think of runnin' away with da money?" She had been talking to Charlie Griffin.

"Yes," he said. "Many times."

"Why didn't ya?"

"I…was disappointed enough in Charlie Griffin."

"Who wants to be hated?" said the girl. She looked to the widow. "What we do wrong? Why my sister in jail for killin' a man been raping her for years? Could God hate us that much he created shackle and chain with our people name carved on it?"

She took off the coat and threw it on the table. She began to cry. "I'm goin' nowhere," she said.

She was in a demoralized state, trying to face down the iron conditions of life, armed only with pitiful sobs.

"Leave us," said the widow, rising.

Butler took the boys out back. They stood in the dark. You could smell on the breeze that there was rain in their future.

"I'm going to ride through the woods to see the best way of getting out of this town right from here" said Butler.

"What about the girl?" said Eadon.

"She's coming with us. If I have to gag her and tie her to a saddle. The old lady finances the underground railroad in central Missouri. Can't have things go bad here."

Butler walked down to the shed. Charlie followed after him. Butler left the shed doorway partway open, as there was just enough moonlight to help him locate his saddle and harness in the dark.

"I need to tell you something, sir."

Butler turned to find Charlie there in the doorway.

"Get out of the light, boy."

Charlie came into the quiet. He seemed unusually subdued.

"You're not gonna unveil another of your 'youthful transgressions,' are you?"

"Yes, sir."

"Christ," said Butler.

"I didn't slip a Dix into Dixie Jack's pocket. I made that up. So you...I wouldn't do anything that stupid."

"No," said Butler. "You'd just lie about doing something that stupid."

"Yes, sir."

"You got any more untoward lies in your pocket? I'd appreciate it if you'd narrow it down to just the ones I need to know about."

"None, sir...You need to know about."

"Charlemagne, if you can just stay alive long enough and keep from going to jail...You and Eadon, don't stray too far."

Butler got the horse blanketed and saddled only to find Charlie still standing there.

"What now, Charlemagne?"

"I had no idea, sir..."

"About what?"

"That a conscience was such a damn troublemaker."

CHAPTER 60

THEY WALKED THE STREETS OF FULTON listening to all the righteous barbarity of gentlemen and ladies and their astringent views of the world. Each side equally entrenched in every pretense of their cause, each with a pressing case of self defense, reflecting gravely on the other—the enemy.

Any fool worth his measure would know now that if there weren't slavery, there would be something else that worked equally well. Because the world is slavery, and slavery is inequality, and the world survives on inequality. Because without inequality there would be no wealth, and without wealth there would be no power, and without power there would be no control, and without control there would be no order. And order is man's highest aspiration, man's most precious commodity, because it serves his many greeds.

Billy Tule saw the world as moral nothingness. This was why he could turn a deaf ear to all that went on around him. Man, as he was, was grounded in misfortune and social depredation. Man was desperate. Man was worse than desperate, man was vainly desperate. And vanity lies at the root of all causes, and in the heart of all believers in a cause, and so Dixie Jack and his slavers hunted out of vanity. And, Tule hoped, that vanity would lead to their downfall, and his success.

But as he and Handy made their way up to the courthouse with the coming rain at their heels, they put on a proper show of allegiance, counting themselves among the ruffians, walking the town in the hunt for their quarry.

• • •

Charlie and Eadon took it upon themselves to trek the three blocks to the courthouse where a huge crowd had gathered. The girl was being kept in a second story jail cell. You could see her light from the courthouse lawn. She had been ordered to stay away from the window for fear the state would be cheated out of its justice by some earnest citizen.

Eadon wore an old slouch hat and his coat collar up, Charlie remained a Mennonite. They knew the risk. The widow had tried to dissuade them. But their youth dictated they experience the world, and they swore they would be vigilant.

The street fronting the courthouse was social mayhem. People were shouting up at the small square of second story light, cursing the girl, reminding her with monstrous descriptions of one's end at the noose. There was a lantern vigil on the lawn by abolitionists and free staters and those who felt the girl was right in what she'd done and should be acquitted. That the law as written did not differentiate between the rape of a woman and the rape of a black woman.

They were singing among themselves, but loud enough so their voices carried, and the girl in the cell could maybe hear, the song accompanied by a mouth harmonica and squeezebox.

"Let us pause in life's pleasures, and count its many tears... While we all sup sorrow with the poor... There's a song that will linger forever in our ears... Oh! Hard times, come again no more."

Charlie and Eadon kept to the shadows, clear of any group. The wind brought the first drops of rain and the night was growing dark as a stream of clouds began overtaking the moon. Charlie realized Eadon had slipped away from him, and alone now was looking up at that at the light of a prison cell.

"While we seek mirth and beauty and music light and gay... There are frail forms fainting at the door... Though their voices are silent, their pleading looks will say... Oh! Hard times, come again no more."

Charlie knew the song. He'd heard it sung at railroad depots and on street corners, wherever the poor or the broken, be they white or black, sang against the bitter travails of the world. He looked to Eadon and the cell window there in the great stone face of the building and he knew what the desperate are capable of, as he was among their number. It was then, as if the world were handing him a nightmare and telling him "test yourself against this, young Charlemagne," that he saw the white and the black who had hunted him across New York.

"There's a pale drooping maiden who toils her life away... With a worn heart whose better days are o'er... Though her voice would be merry, 'tis sighing all the day... Oh! Hard times come again no more."

Charlie thought he'd been stricken dead. He did not even feel
the first drops of rain hitting against his eyes. Through the drifting
landscape and a cast of shadows he kept sight of them a moment
longer. A shimmer of gold hung from Handy's neck in the shape of
a damaged cross. There, then gone.

*"Tis a sigh that is wafted across the troubled wave…Tis a waif
that is heard upon the shore…Tis a dirge that is murmured
around the lonely grave…Oh! Hard times, come again no more."*

Charlie backed into the dark. He looked for Eadon. He was gone.
He could not risk calling out. He wiped the rain from his face. He set
his gaze upon the courthouse lawn. There was a shot from back among
the crowd. A man's voice shouting, "I see him…Jack…I see him!"

There was more gunfire. People began to scatter. A woman took
to screaming. And then inexplicably, a Roman candle shot straight
up into a raining sky bursting apart above the courthouse roof.
Charlie and Eadon had agreed if there was trouble they would sepa-
rate and make for the Widow Black's.

Men raced past Charlie nearly knocking him down. They wore
badges and carried shotguns. Someone was yelling about a colored
man running away from the courthouse and brandishing a pistol.
Men came riding up the street, firing off their revolvers trying to
clear a path. It was Dixie Jack.

Charlie saw the two men who were hunting him shouldering
their way through the crowd. They had been close enough for their
shadows to pass right over Charlie. As they broke through the crowd,
Charlie saw a man lying on the lawn trying to keep from keeling over.
He recognized the man as one of the ruffians from Cape Girardeau.

CHAPTER 61

HE WANTED TO RUN, but didn't. He wanted to keep his head down and hidden from sight and cling to the shadows, but he didn't. Calmness can do more for looking innocent than actually being innocent—how many times had he been browbeaten with that by his father?

Another volley of gunfire the next block over. Even against the rain, you could hear the echo of pistol shots. More screaming. People were foolishly running to see what the cause was.

By the time he reached the widow's, the house was in a kind of organized frenzy. Butler had returned when he heard the shooting. Some of the widow's people were helping get all the mounts saddled and ready. Eadon was in the kitchen sitting at a table while two women tried to clean away the blood that covered his wrist and hand where he'd been shot.

"You made it!" he said seeing Charlie.

"Bad," said Charlie, meaning the wound.

"Bullet went through. I think a bone might be broken. One of the slavers from Cape Girardeau recognized me. I didn't mean to leave you—"

"Good thing you did. Where's—"

He pointed to the shed.

The widow was in the parlor, adamantly trying to convince the girl to leave with Butler and the others before it was too late for the girl to save herself, but she refused. A young black came tearing through the front door leaving it to swing wide open. He was soaked from the rain and out of breath. He yelled from the hallway. "They searchin' all da barns north da courthouse lookin' for da colored boy been shot."

The widow got up to go and tell Butler. "It's time," she said to the girl. Then, to the young man who'd run in, "Get that front door closed."

Charlie was alone now in the parlor with Cassie. She sat there silently on one sofa like some resolute angel staring at him.

"Da boy with that coat," she said.

Charlie nodded. He went and sat near her. Two children on a dark and rainy night, with the fangs of the world sharpening around them.

"You gonna try and soften me up?" she said.

Charlie shook his head no. "What you said. About God hatin' your people. Other people think God hates them. Some are white people. Poor people. There's even people who think they don't deserve God. That they're too bad of heart. I'm one of those people."

She looked at him now, surprised, unsure, questioning.

"I need to ask you something," he said.

• • •

Butler returned from the shed, his intention about the girl clear in the rope he carried. "Where is she?"

The widow was stitching Eadon's hand. She motioned with her jaw toward the parlor.

Butler was entering the room just as Charlie and the girl were coming out.

"I gotta get my rifle and my sack. I'm comin," she told Butler. Then she bounded up the stairs.

He looked at Charlie. "What happened in there?"

"Private talk," he said. And that was all.

Butler believed the roads to the north and east would be most heavily guarded, and so the most dangerous, as they were the direct way to Pike County. He decided they would veer to the west. Find somewhere to wait out the rain, then arc back toward the Auxvasse.

The girl knew of caves around Three Creeks where they could safely ride out the storm. The widow had given her an old infantry coat with a hood that belonged to her late husband. And it was this shrouded figure of a waif who led the way.

Riding at night, in a relentless downpour, the country black with hackberry and ash was an arduous nightmare. Her intention was to cross Stinson Creek just south of the bridge. They dismounted in the trees along the riverbank. They could see the bridge from there. It was alive with kerosene lamps and there were guards, churlish and drinking against the harshness of the elements.

Butler went to Charlie who was huddled up in that canvas tarp his father had made for him. The boy had exchanged that Mennonite hat for his cherished railroad cap.

"That coat is a precious commodity, boy. So you stay at the back of everywhere we go, unless and until I say otherwise."

Charlie thought that unfair and said so.

"Unfair or not. Do as I say or I take the damn thing off of you." He motioned for the girl to start the crossing.

It didn't take much for Stinson Creek to flood. The riverbank was a slop. Cassie stepped her mount down into the rushing current to show them the way. The horse's spindly legs were like an unsure spider's but she kicked the haunches hard and it made the far bank in one quick burst. Eadon was next. His mount buckled but righted itself, then lurched forward only to buckle again, and the girl waded out into the stream and grabbed hold of the reins to help him cross. He was to take up a position with his Hawken where he could watch the bridge. Charlie was next. He stepped that Spanish Jack right out into the stream keeping tight to the withers and that pony made it across like it was nothing, snorting out water, shaking its lean head.

It was left to Butler to bring the packhorse. He eased his mount into the current with the second horse in tow. It was a slow and unsteady going and he'd just about crossed when things went bad. Coming out of that black and wild current was a great mass of tree limbs and shore rot that hit the packhorse square and the horse bolted and cried out. Charlie and the girl charged into the current to keep that horse from going under.

Through the rain the men on the bridge heard the animal's cry of panic. Some of them swiftly took to the riverbank with lanterns. A voice yelled, "Who's out there?"

The words fell dead upon the darkness. A guard on the bridge had field glasses. He scanned the shoreline as best he could, rain streaming down the glass eyepieces. And there…well downriver… bluish shapes in the rainy nightworld of the river. "Someone is trying to cross." He pointed. "There!"

He had no sooner gotten the words out, than there was the heavy boom of a Hawken and the guard was blown back across the bridge. His field glasses caromed down the planking, all covered with blood.

CHAPTER 62

THEY MADE THEIR ESCAPE into a netherworld crowded with soaked trees and dark as ink. One of the ruffians at the bridge set off a Roman candle.

Dixie Jack was among those leading the house by house search of Fulton, when he saw a starburst in the wet sky west of town. Within the hour, he and his men were at the spot where the crossing had been executed. Billy Tule and Handy were among their number. They were to follow the tracks as best they could. These were Dixie Jack's orders. He would lead a small contingent of men. The rest would fan out a half mile in each direction. At dawn he would set off a Roman candle and all would converge upon that place. The guard and two others, who had been killed at the bridge, were left under the trees and covered by rags.

There would be no sleeping that night. There would only be the frail shadow of a girl leading Butler Phillips and his companions through a maze of forest and draws where the ground had become a spreading marsh. They walked their horses. There was only the sweeping sound of the rain and the dripping of it from endless branches.

The black timber, the rain. None of it existed for Charlie at that moment. He could only think of the two men who had hunted him from New York. And the black…wearing that cross… Missus Watters' cross…He couldn't bear to think how he came to have it. And by what cunning were they in Fulton? Did they tell Dixie Jack about the money?

Charlie's instinct told him they did not. And he didn't need instinct to know these men meant to see him dead. Their crossing half the nation was answer enough. By taking the coat and the task, he had inherited the evil that went with it, as well.

The caves were cut into a stony hillface where the roots of pine trees clung to the rock. The opening large enough for a horse to trot through and the cavern deep enough for a small fire to safely warm.

At the entry from where Butler watched, Charlie told about the two men who had hunted him from New York. All Butler said was, "We'll have to escape them, or kill them."

"You could have taken the coat," said Charlie. "And brought the money to Montgomery. Why did you labor yourself with me?"

Butler had a look Charlie might have said was melancholy, when he answered, "Men and women aren't born. They are created. And there's never enough to go around."

Charlie sat with the others by the fire. He took to looking through his belongings in the haversack. He cut up a cheroot and they all shared a smoke. He showed off the Mansion of Happiness game, with its trail of virtue and vice and beautifully painted people pictured there. Eadon had to laugh, going from one flowery image to another. "Doesn't seem like there's any colored folks on that road to heaven."

Charlie took out the paper photograph of his mother which passed from hand to hand with a quiet "very pretty." And the sealed letter from Missus Watters who Charlie believed now dead, for

James Montgomery, the abolitionist. And there, spread out on the cave floor, in the half light of a dusky primordial fire, his whole life. Meager to the world, maybe, but each memory rife with emotion.

And there was the page with the poem torn from the book, given him by the author himself. He took it up in the firelight. He read now with a different eye to the words about a child who went forth, and how everything that he looked upon became a part of him, and he, it. From he that fathered him, to she that conceived him, to the doubts of the daytime and the doubts of the night, and whether what appears so, is so.

And all that he had seen and felt had become the blood and bones of him, as the girl huddled there in that old infantry coat staring into the fire had sacrificed her desire for revenge to the needs of the greater good, to Eadon smoking a cheroot with his wounded hand knowing he would never see home again, and Butler Phillips who watched over them all, and Erastus Eels, wherever God had placed his unruly soul, and Missus Watters, and the cross she bore, even the auction, where he'd stood naked and in shame. He understood what the words said, and that what they meant were greater than any one heart ——

"We've got to get out of here," said Butler. And there was urgency in his voice.

They stood around him at the entrance to the cave. Dawn had come upon the rain. In the sky the remains of a Roman candle which Butler pointed toward, "Dixie Jack," he said. "He's gathering up his slavers. Been on the hunt all night probably." He looked to Cassie and pointed. "How far?"

She studied the last streams of phosphor and the dim marking of hills. "Headwaters of the river," she said. "Eight hard miles, even for those crackers."

• • •

Dixie Jack stood in a clearing in a grey cape. His ruffians reeling in from the countryside around him. They looked all to be there except the ones called Billy Tule and that "crazy nigger" with no thumbs who dogged behind him.

Billy Tule was anything but lost. He and Handy were on a forested ridge where Tule could watch Dixie Jack and his ruffians through a spyglass. The slavers were on the move now pressing into that grey downpour toward what they called Three Creeks.

"Well," said Tule. "This Butler Phillips has to either stay holed up and risk it. Or be on the move and risk it. What say you?"

The black breathed cold hard concentration. Not a bit of earthly sweat about him. He wiped the rain from his eyes with a thumbless palm. "He move. Sun gonna break. Mist all dey got. We catch 'em."

CHAPTER 63

THE SUN DID BREAK and too Goddamn soon for Butler. It came through the clouds hard and clean, and the rains stopped and the air filled with the sharp warmth of summer. They rode three abreast like guardsmen, with Charlie at the rear as Butler demanded. And Charlie, for the first time, saw the country that lay before them as they crossed the crest of a bare hill.

There had been fires the season before and as far as the eye could see was a ravaged wasteland. Vast tracks of wilderness stood burned. The cluttered trees charred and the branches at withered angles like disinterred black hands rising from the earth.

And that mist, crept along the river bottoms and grassland as if scarcely touching them and circling about huge sump holes, or dead still where the rains had turned the ground to marsh.

The first they knew they had been discovered was gunshots pinging off the hillface below them. Then came the howling of rifle fire and Dixie Jack and his ruffians appeared out of the deep shadows of morning like crazed yard dogs.

Butler pulled out his French rifle. "If they're too far, kill their horses." Angelfire and Eadon got out their long guns. Butler ordered Charlie, "Take the packhorse. Get out." He pointed to a starshaped configuration of hilltops. "Ride for there. Go!"

The girl fired her Sharps. The shot went through the skull of a horse. The blood spattered across the face of its rider. It crushed to the earth, the shoulder of the rider shattering against rock. A ball from Eadon's heavy bore struck the leg of a ruffian, the bone coming right through the flesh. As the ball continued on tearing apart his mount's haunch. The hilltop was immersed in smoke when the three escaped at a dead run.

Charlie was well ahead of them now and looking back. He could see Dixie Jack in that hat of his with a swarm of riders spread across the landscape giving chase, gunfire everywhere, the three ahead of them darting in and out of the mist, it parting before the chests of their animals, then swirling in behind them.

Their horses now leaned into a rising slope where there was a forest of devastated trees. Butler must have ordered them to wheel about, as they did, and dismounted and opened fire. Grey rifle smoke floated through the dead branches. Among Dixie Jack's number, a rider grabbed at his neck, another slumped in the saddle and his horse took off as if gone mad, its rider now dipping and tottering, and it was all he could do to hold on to the pommel.

Charlie was a ridge ahead of them and he slowed there and watched Dixie Jack have his men fan out like Charlie had been witness to in the killing down by New Madrid.

Dixie Jack gave the order and they charged, and as they did the riders broke into two bands veering away from each other, their intent on being to encircle Butler on the hilltop.

The men were barbarous in their yelling. An unshaved, reckless, filthy, exhausted company of wild and blood thirsty dragoons, ready to trample down the enemy with their own reign of homegrown brotherhood. But that solemn homeland they envisioned was about to gain a few more graves before they inherited the earth.

The air was now prosecuted with gun smoke. Another horse was shot out from beneath a ruffian. It had been charging head-long up the hillface and just keeled over. Dixie Jack must have been hit because his hat flew off as his body arced in the saddle, but he righted himself and he led the slavers on, booting his mount, shouting commands, fierce, unrepentant for his most horrible desires, dashing in his defiance of all risk, spidering his mount among the burnt and broken trees.

Eadon had been on one knee charging his weapon when he was shot in the back. He lurched forward spitting out blood. He was on his hands and knees when Butler came running over and slid to the ground beside him.

Charlie saw there were too many, just too damn many. They were on horseback, and they were on foot, even the wounded meant to make a bloody hell of it. The air had grown thick and grey and reeked of gunpowder. Charlie could hear the gunshots and distant cries of the suffering animals and men. They would have to abandon their position now, or now would be all there was.

He saw Butler grab the side of his face and reel backwards. A miniball had carved out a piece of his cheekbone. Eadon who was slumped over, his face pressed to the earth. He called to Butler, "I'm sorry."

Butler was reloading his pistol with a blood stained hand. "For what?"

"I'm just sorry, is all."

A rider came sweeping down on them and was shot dead.

Butler stood.

It was the girl. She was reloading her carbine on the run.

"We gotta try to get out," he said.

He led her to the horses, firing as he went. He gave her a boost to get her in the saddle quick when he was shot in the side of the neck. He cursed the pain. It was Dixie Jack. The girl had kicked her mount forward when she saw Butler had been hit. She came about and fired. She was close enough she could make out the blood on the front of Dixie Jack's coat. Her shot took him right through the belt buckle, but he kept hold of the reins and drove his mount right into hers and they both toppled over.

Charlie saw they were dying out there, where the sun bled down on a smoky hilltop, where the trees had been set afire, where the best of man and the worst of man had met for a few brief moments to determine the outcome of the future. They would be forever that moment, with only him and God as witness. They were being extinguished before his eyes, turned into dust, to be trampled under by the bitterest of boots and hooves.

He didn't want to leave them like this, he felt it a burning sin to leave, that no amount of suffering could forgive. But he knew. He had made a promise at the feet of the world that no passage of time would find forgotten, that had its roots in his soul and in the soul of his lost family. And when he turned Stranger about and put his brogans to the haunches, he was doing it for all of them. He was bearing it for all of them.

He sped down the far hillside leading the packhorse and as he leaned into the animal's withers, pleading for Stranger to go faster, crying into the beast's mane to please, please, go faster, he became that moment, and that moment became a part of him. And he became a part of the Spanish Jack, and the Spanish Jack became a part of him.

He was making for a sea of mist that clung to the earth far ahead there in the burning sunlight, the starcrest of hills Butler had pointed toward just beyond. He was racing across barren ground burned brown from fire. He was there one moment, alone in the blue and charged daylight, and gone in the mist the next.

CHAPTER 64

WHEN HE FINALLY GLANCED BACK, there looked to be nothing but dead trees rising up out of a mist as far as he could see. He slowed the animals to a walk to rest them on the chance he needed to run again. The country around him was silent and peaceful, but he remained vigilant. The landscape rose and fell in sharp contrasts and there were sump holes and marsh and stony islands and patches of dead leaves and branches at least a foot deep that crackled under the animals' hooves. He could see the hills he was heading toward through the trees, and he used them as a marker as there were no trails.

At one of the creeks, there was a plank bridge that somehow had survived the fire. He walked the mounts across, careful of the cracked boards or the loose boards. He stopped a moment. There were birds somewhere singing, and the water rippling along beneath him. It was as if earlier today had not ever happened or that the earth had absorbed it and moved on. He closed his eyes and foolishly rested his head against Stranger's neck.

The report of a shot carried from a long ways off. A fifty eight calibre ball from a Mississippi rifle and a shock of blood from the chest of the packhorse. It staggered and fell back on its rear legs then dropped over the edge of the bridge and into the creek.

Stranger bolted with Charlie standing beside him and holding fast to the reins. He was dragged down the length of that plankboard causeway. The crisp echo of a second shot stirred the air. Stranger cried out, Charlie lost his grip and a wounded Stranger took off into the brush and was lost to him in a swirl of grey.

The boy staggered to his feet. Two men on horseback—he could hear them. He took off at a run, keeping to the mist. He saw for a moment them coming downslope beyond the trees. The white and the black. Separating, the white shouting orders. The black was making for the bridge, the white crossed the creek further upstream in a thundering rush. He was yelling that the boy was on foot.

Handy drove his mount across the bridge. The wooden causeway tremored beneath him. One of his mount's hooves caught in a gap in the planking and went through. The leg was shorn apart at the joint and the horse went right over on itself. Handy was thrown headlong into the creek. The cries of the mangled animal were horrific in their agony.

Tule came sweeping into view and saw what had happened. "If we lose the boy," he shouted, "I will see you back in chains."

Charlie kept to the trees, he kept to the densest parts of the thicket, he kept his marking on those hills as best he could. They wanted the money, he knew that too.

Charlie could hear a horse being driven through the thicket. The mist ahead of him was thinning out, but still dense beyond a small clearing. The ground there was marked by open trenches where the creek had changed course over the years. There were fallen trees where the ground had crumbled away, great hulking things, whose roots had lost their grip. There were swaths of mud and marsh from the rains, and what might be a sump hole, but Charlie could mark out a thin path that took him partly over rocky ground. He would have to jump one of those trenches though.

He looked up into the barren treetops. The sun would burn off the mist and soon. He listened hard for the horseman. It sounded as if he was arcing farther away. He stared into the clearing. He was afraid. So he made himself think of Butler and Eadon and the girl there on the hilltop. He made himself remember he was a part of them now. And he took off at a dead run…and hoped.

Charlie was halfway across the clearing when this huge bear of a man came out of the wilds and hit Charlie like a locomotive. The boy was thrown across the clearing, splashing through mud and slamming up against the trunk of one of those fallen trees by the trench, so hard his arm broke.

He was on his knees, blood streaming from his nose. Billy Tule stood above him, his breathing sounded like it would tear through his chest. "I fooled you, boy. Wasn't on the horse. Baited you."

Charlie cradled the arm, his head swimming. He writhed with pain.

"You come a long way, you little thief. The money—"

Charlie shook his head. "Don't have it."

"Liar!"

"Gave it…to people in…Fulton. For—"

"Boy, I seen the act you and your father put on." Tule mocked Charlie, walking about like he had a crippled leg. From his coat pocket, Tule took out the Griffin Family Bible and threw it at Charlie. It caromed off his chest and landed in the mud before him. "Know how I got that from your father? Gonna get the money from you the same way, 'less you get Christian and hand it over. First the sack. Then I'm gonna strip you."

The boy's head was bowed, his broken forearm resting in his lap. He dipped his head to loose the strap, and he dumped the haversack on the ground in front of him. He was rocking back and forth in pain when Billy Tule bent to grab it up. As he did, Charlie's good arm came straight up with the deringer Erastus Eels had given him in hand, and he shot Billy Tule in the head. The bullet went straight up through the man's jaw. The bone tore through flesh and the jaw hung there like something from a broken hinge. The bullet continued up through the roof of the mouth and took out an eye. Tule staggered and fell. He was on his hands and knees with blood and brain matter oozing out of his eye socket.

Charlie gathered himself. He reached for the family Bible and forced himself to stand. The pain in his arm almost more than he could bear. He could hear the other one, yelling to Billy Tule from somewhere near the creek. But Tule was too busy to answer, gasping as he was for every last breath before the world went on without him.

Charlie stood over the dying man, and he leaned down and shook the Bible in his face most violently. "You may have taken the book from my father, but you forgot to read it. You know why...?" Charlie screamed out. "You know why? Because you'd a found out it was Goliath that got slewed... not David."

CHAPTER 65

When Charlie heard the other yelling, he slowly straightened himself up. The ground seemed to fall away—he was that dizzy—and the pain to his arm had him shivering. The other was closer, his voice more desperate, enraged. It carried high into the trees. Charlie had seen that face firsthand. He knew the dark force carried there.

Charlie walked over and bent down careful, not to tip over, and with two fingers of the good hand still holding the Bible, picked up the haversack. He slipped the strap over his head and put the Bible in the haversack, and using his good arm, guided the broken one through the strap so the haversack became a homemade sling. He then picked up the single shot deringer and put it in his coat pocket. It would be too difficult to load quickly with one hand.

He saw the other one for a moment far back in the mist. Then he saw him again where the sun breached the trees. Charlie went and knelt beside Tule. He was trying to move as quickly and assuredly as his will possessed.

Tule was lying on his side. That chest still pulled in the air, but the good eye had rolled up inside the head, and what was left of the mouth had become a sump hole for blood.

Charlie felt around the man's belt, his trousers. There was a revolver in one of his pockets. Charlie got it out and held it up to the light. He rolled the cylinder and counted three bullets.

When Charlie turned to confront Handy, the black was already racing toward Charlie through the mist, coming on with furious intent, a killing blade in each hand, eating up the distance between them as if he had God's own speed, silent as a mountain cat, and fearless beyond any human language.

Charlie took a few steps back. Each more tentative and uncertain than the one before it. He went down wobbly on one knee to marshal his strength, to steady his hand.

Handy would have to vault the trench to have at him. And when he did, there would be precious few seconds between Charlie and his fate.

They were all there with him. That's what Charlie told himself… Butler Phillips, the widow, Angelfire, good old Erastus Eels, crazy Jupe and Merc, kind Missus Watters, the Gloucasters in their Brooklyn parlor singing to Christ for His mercy and help, Ward Beecher… and his own mother and father, who were always with him, who had breathed into his body an incomprehensible call to will. They were in his trembling hand, in his defiant silence, his broken arm, his dry mouth, his bottomless fear, his fragile attempt at bravery. They would put their mark upon this moment as everyone who had ever lived put their mark upon the cross of sacrifice. And they would be there at the moment when Handy vaulted the trench.

Charlie could see now flecks of mud coming off Handy's shoes, he could see the sunlit sweat on his face, the narrow fire that was his eyes, and just as he went to leap the trench, Charlie fired and he fired again and yet again.

There was a flash of blood at Handy's right side, the shot just enough to make the body flinch, and instead of clearing the trench, he went into it. And the sound that came from that pit, the agony and rage.

Charlie used his good hand to brace himself and stand. He hesitantly approached that gouge in the earth. He looked over the edge. Handy was just feet away. In his fall, his leg had been impaled on the branch of a fallen tree. It had gone all the way through the muscle and he was hung up there like something skewered. He could not tear himself loose, he could not pull his leg back, he could not snap the branch and free himself. The blood coming from the wound was jetting out through his torn trousers. A long thin ribbon that sprayed the air. He still had a knife in each hand. He still had a look of furious intent. But he would die there.

"You killed my father," said Charlie, "and you killed Missus Watters is my guess, how ya have her cross. But they'll be here today when you die. I want you to know that." He shook the empty gun in his hand at the dying man. "And I want you to know…It was all for nothing. What say you to that?"

He looked to Handy to see if there was a realization of his deeds—sorrow, remorse, shame, fear, contrition. But there was none. There was only the tragedy of a man fighting against the edict of his world's history. Who even in his agony, was still tortured and defiant. He raised both arms and crossed them, and putting a blade to each side of his neck, he slit his own throat.

Charlie closed his eyes at the sight, and when he was sure Handy was dead, he painfully slid down into the trench. He tore the cross from the dead man's throat, and then he went and washed the blood from it in a puddle of rainwater.

ANNIE PIE

CHAPTER 66

ANNIE PIE AND HER YOUNGER BROTHER AND SISTER were gathering elderberries and flowers for their mother, who sold and bartered salves and infusions for the likes of such as colic and asthma, burns and fevers. Annie and her siblings were the children of freedmen who did work for the Bass family, which owned the Forest Hill Plantation, thought to be the largest west of the Mississippi.

Annie's siblings came running up from a cluster of trees yelling like some wild urchins. "There's a boy down there, and he's lookin' mighty bad."

Annie thought to go see for herself, and being a handful of years older than the other two, ordered them to stay put. When they refused, she threatened a whipping, and this kept them on a tight but angry leash. The mist had burned off, and there was a heady breeze. The dry grass bristled, the air coming down through that stand of poplars and scrub pine throwing up the dead leaves in a turmoil.

And there she saw a boy who had to be about her age sitting on a tree stump ruined with the years, his head drooping, arm cradled in a haversack.

"Hey, boy," she said, calling out. "What are you doing there?"

His head rose slowly. He was pale as could be. She stood before him with her placid face.

"Restin'," he said.

She took a cautious step or two toward him. She saw now there were spots of blood on his face. She brushed back her unruly hair.

"You better get away from here," said Charlie. "You don't need trouble."

"Get away? We live here." She pointed in the direction of her home. "Hey, you got blood on your face."

He wiped the fingers of his good hand across his face. He saw flecks of dried blood on the fingers. "I had to kill them," he said. "One I shot, and the other—"

"Kill them?" She sounded frightened.

He started to cry.

"Why you cryin'?"

"You don't need trouble. Just get out of here. But don't tell anyone I'm here. Or you saw me. All right? Please?"

The girl's sister and brother were calling out. "Annie Pie…Annie Pie…"

She screamed back at them to shut up.

Charlie covered his face to try and hold back a crying that he could not.

"Who don't you want me to tell?" said this Annie Pie.

"Slavers…ruffians. The men with Dixie Jack. You heard of Dixie Jack?"

He tried to move a bit, to get his hand in the haversack.

She saw there was something wrong.

"Your arm—"

"It broke when that fella tried to kill me."

She saw he had taken something from the haversack and now he had it in a clenched fist.

"A killing is a terrible thing." He said.

His crying seemed so deplorably sad, he looked so in need, so lost, and beaten. She almost wanted to cry herself.

"My friends...They're all dead back there on the hill. The ones who tried to help me. Butler Phillips...Eadon... and the girl from Fulton...Cassie...the one they called Angelfire. All dead. And it's my fault."

He put his good arm up to cover his face he was so ashamed to be crying like that. And this Annie Pie came over and sat next to Charlie. She did that slowly, and when she sat, she sat very close to him. "Nothing can be all one person's fault," she said.

"The money I have in my coat...I need to get it to the abolitionists in Pike County. That's why they were helping me. I've come all the way from New York. I've got to get the money to Pike County. To James Montgomery. They're meeting at a church there on the Fourth of July."

What kind of story, she thought?

He leaned toward her, half in need, half in exhaustion, his youthful tender face so full of wounds and she put her arms around him and pulled him toward her. She cradled him as she would a child or someone she loved. He wept against her chest. He kept repeating, "I've failed everyone." He pressed so tight against her she could smell the wood smoke in his hair. No boy had ever been this close, no boy had ever wept against her body. No colored boy, and no white boy, that was for sure. And her rotten, loud mouthed younger brother didn't count.

"Give me your hand," he said.

She did so with uncertainty. She saw his fist open up and she felt this wisp of anticipation. In the hand was a cameo. With a slave on one knee. She held it close. She had heard of these, but never seen one. Were they all this beautiful? The black so black, the white so white. She watched as he closed her hand around it. And then he passed out.

• • •

Charlie awoke to find himself on a straw mattress on the floor of a shed. Light through the slatted boards dusty and bright fell upon the comely features of a girl he vaguely remembered talking to in the woods. She sat on a straw mattress beside him. She seemed intent on his well being.

"Where am I?" he said.

"We brought you here. My mother set your arm."

Charlie could move some. Saw his forearm had been splinted, and was now in a better sling.

"Your name is Charlemagne Ezekiel Griffin."

"How do you know?"

She held up his family Bible. He saw his haversack was by her side. But his coat. He wasn't wearing it. He forced himself up. "My coat—"

"The one with the money in it." She pointed to where it hung from a nail on the wall of the shed above him. He eased back.

"Did I tell you that?"

"You told me a lot."

"I feel very warm."

"You have a fever. My mother is making you a tea of elder bark for it. Then she'll do one for the pain in your arm. You want to know my name?"

"No."

She seemed offended. "Why not?"

"It's Annie Pie, I think. Or something close to it. I heard some-one yelling."

"That's right."

"How'd you get such a funny name?" said Charlie.

"Talk about a funny name. Be careful, boy. Well…When I was born, Mister Bass…He owns the Forest Hill Plantation. He saw this white spot on my side." She lifted her shirt and showed Charlie a place below her breast with a spot about the size of a silver dol-lar where the pigmentation was white. "So he called me Annie Pie-bald… Like a piebald horse. But everyone just calls me Annie Pie. You want to touch the spot?"

He was certainly curious, but he couldn't believe he'd been asked. He ran his finger from the white flesh to the black. "It feels no different."

"It isn't, silly."

"I'm very dizzy," he said.

"You got a gash on the back of your head and it's mighty swollen there. You must a hit pretty harsh against somethin. Better sleep."

He slipped his head back down on the mattress, and then he remembered. "The cameo—"

She opened her palm to show him it was right there where he'd put it.

"Rest, Charlemagne. I'll keep watch on ya."

CHAPTER 67

ANNIE PIE'S FATHER RETURNED to their ramshackle homestead with news and leading a wounded Spanish Jack. Everything his daughter had said the boy told her was true...and much worse. He wanted the children out of the room while he conversed with his wife about what to do.

The younger ones were easy enough to threaten, but Annie refused. She was adamant and distressed for the boy's well being. Whatever she lacked in temper, she more than made up for in temperament.

And so it was, he told his wife and daughter of the fight on the hill where he had just been, that left about fifteen dead. Most were ruffians and slavers, and there was Butler Phillips from Cape Girardeau and a freedman who came from a good family there, one that owned an eating place on Water Street. And the girl from Fulton, the one they called Angelfire. Here's where things got plagued. She wasn't up there with the corpses like she was supposed to be. There was talk some of the ruffians had taken her alive, and what they did to the girl before they burned her body and buried it was not fit talk. But there were freedmen and slaves at Forest Hill who claim it was a lie…That the girl had escaped, she'd been seen, and the story was made up because the slavers were humiliated at being beat at their own game.

Then he got to the horse outside. By the length of the stirrups it might well be the boys. And where Annie's father found it, was just a few hundred yards from where Charlemagne was come upon by Annie Pie.

And that wasn't all. A short walk down the creek was where the father had come upon two men just like the boy had said. And it was a horrible scene, one that would chase you right out of the tomb. But what he had to say next was worse yet.

There were slavers and ruffians and them that hunt for reward looking for a fourth person that got away. And there were people combing the countryside for this person, and a pack of them were good friends of Dixie Jack and Dixie Jack was lying up there on the hilltop. And he'd been shot three, four times, easy. Now, you'd have thought Dixie Jack was just napping from the way he lay there in the dried and crumbling leaves, except for the birds picking at his eyes.

"The boy got to be got out of here," said the father. "Be a black cloud over this house till he gone. I know it's a bad thing. But sometimes a bad thing is all there is."

The mother was reluctant, even though she knew her husband was right, as the boy had a fever and a broken arm, and was worn to the bone. Annie was adamant they hide the boy there or somewhere close by so they could watch over him.

Charlie, on the other hand, had overheard the conversation from outside the house and thought the father entirely right.

Charlie had awakened upon hearing Annie Pie's father return with a horse, and he entered the little corral now and there was

Stranger. The animal had a nasty gash across the point of his shoulder and walked over to the boy with a slight limp. The animal nuzzled Charlie and all he could think was — he survived. Stranger had survived. Living things can survive, and Stranger raised his head and sniffed at the air with a kind of excited energy as if that bloodstained morning was less than a dream.

The children saw Charlie and started yelling and soon everyone was outside, and the father said, "That your animal?"

"Yes." And then Charlie said, "You were right."

"About what?"

"About me leaving."

The father realized Charlie had overheard them.

"Can Stranger make it to Pike County?"

"Can't push 'em, boy. Can't run 'em. But he's young and sound and strong."

No one suggested what Charlie was attempting to be a fool's errand, though they silently believed it was.

It was decided Charlie would leave in the morning so Annie Pie's mother would have time to make a poultice for the horse and some tinctures for fever and pain for Charlie to take with him. At supper they all held hands as Annie Pie's father said grace, and more than grace, asking God to make special watch over all his wounded and forsaken children.

Annie Pie was sitting next to Charlie and holding his hand and when it came time to let go, she did not. Not right away. She wanted this silent, invisible moment that was just between them, alone, as if some secret message were passing between their hands, and as self conscious as Charlie was, he managed the slightest hint of a smile.

Charlie sat in the dark later that night at the end of the porch, looking out upon the road that led away from there and waiting, hoping, the girl could come out. Peering in the windows from time to time—watching her pass, glancing out, obeying her parents' commands to get this and do that. And then as if out of nowhere, Annie Pie's mother said, "Go check on that boy, see how he's coming along."

She found him in the shadows beneath the rain leached porch roof, and when she sat, she sat close to him.

"My mother—"

"I heard."

"My father says even on that horse a yours, you'll make Saint Clements Church in about a week."

That would put him there in time for the Fourth of July gathering of abolitionists and the like. She looked out upon the road herself. The future waiting there in the moonlight.

"Annie Pie," he said.

She glanced at him. He hadn't been talking to her really. He'd just been saying the name.

"Your name fits you good," he said.

"It makes me seem different, anyway."

"You like seeming different."

She pulled her knees up on the porch and wrapped her arms around them and she thought about this and said, "I do. How 'bout you...Charlemagne? That—"

"It's too much name. Charlie suits me better."

He thought for a moment how darkness was a beautiful thing. How it was easier to hide there and be yourself. "Annie Pie," he said, in little more than a playful whisper.

She was taken with him saying her name again, and then she remembered. "Oh...I have this..." From her pocket, out came the cameo he had given her in the woods.

"No," he said. "I want you to have it."

"This?"

"I got it from an old colored gentleman at a church in Brooklyn. He brought it with him from England."

"All the way from there?" she said. "Where they have all those kings and queens? How would you like to see a real king and a queen?"

Charlie grinned at the idea of seeing them walk around with those heavy robes and big old crowns on their heads. "I wonder," he said, "if anyone ever tried to steal one of those crowns right from their heads and run off with it."

It was a storybook thought to be sure.

"Why give it to me?"

He looked at the cameo, and he could measure the silence around him. He was incapable of explaining emotions with the little he knew. If he'd been taught how to explain himself as well as he had been taught to be a pickpocket, he would surely have been able to tell her that the moment she sat next to him in the woods and put her arms around him, she'd saved his life. That he had lost all faith, that he was despaired, that the violence he'd seen had demoralized him, that he had come to believe he was an old man in a boy's body, and that his youth and life were gone and would be so, forever. And then she was there.

He had no way of saying this. He could only fold her fingers around the cameo and hold them there, and she saw that his hand was trembling.

CHAPTER 68

SLAVE CATCHERS ARRIVED THE NEXT DAY. They too had joined in the hunt for this "fourth rider" who had been with Butler Phillips in the murder of Dixie Jack and his ruffians. There were three of them, and they came trotting up to the homestead on big stud horses. One was white, the other two black. The white was known as Le Sans, Louisiana born and bred, and escutcheoned on his saddlebags—*sans loix ni discipline*, meaning without law or discipline. Le Sans was a small, swarthy man who wore spectacles, and who at one time had been a teacher until he found his calling.

They had traced a horse that showed signs of being wounded from a place in the woods near where two bodies were now victim to the will of nature. Le Sans ordered the homestead searched and Annie Pie's father could do nothing about it. One of the blacks found teardrops of dried blood in the dust of the corral. Le Sans wanted answers.

The father admitted a man had ridden through yesterday and bought grain for his horse, which he fed at the corral. Le Sans demanded the father describe the man.

"He was about twenty," the father said, "lean, dark hair, and he wore a railroad cap."

Annie Pie and her mother listened silently. It was all as her father and Charlie had plotted out on the chance something like this were to befall them. Le Sans looked to the women, and they could add nothing more to the rider's description. The father had had the foresight to send the younger children to a neighbor's, feeling that they would wither under such circumstances.

Le Sans spoke privately with his two blacks. One went to the corral, the other unholstered his revolver. "We'll be taking your daughter with us on the road for a few days," said Le Sans, "to identify the man when we find him."

Annie Pie's mother fell to frantic pleading for her daughter, and her father asked he be taken instead.

Le Sans answered, "God help you, if you've lied to us."

• • •

They pressed on hard, keeping to the main roads, sure this "murderous vagabond"' was making for the "big rally of white niggers" at Saint Clements Church. Le Sans questioned wayfarers, searched wagons, intimidated those he found suspicious, and flat out threatened if it suited his aims.

They hardly slept, they wore out horses, and the girl was little fed and treated hardly better than a mule. And all this to no avail until they reached Indian River just inside of Pike County. That is where they came upon Charlie Griffin.

He had stopped at the Paxton Store Crossroads to rest and feed Stranger in a field by the traders' stalls where half a dozen wagons were parked and campsites established.

Charlie had been listening to a flock of men around a wagon talking about the trial in Fulton, and how the "colored bitch" got convicted of murder and was sentenced to hang.

Charlie returned to where his horse was staked to find two blacks looking Stranger over, studying the wound, the hooves. A little swarthy man astride his mount, giving orders, and who there on a horse beside him?—Annie Pie, looking tired and filthy from days on the road.

It was as if it was starting all over again. Maybe that's the way of it, the way of all things until they are brought to their rightful end. Charlie must not with the slightest gesture, give himself away.

Le Sans said to the girl, "That the horse?"

She answered with a shrug. She couldn't be sure. She saw Charlie before any of them. She kept her eyes downcast.

Le Sans saw this Mennonite boy approach.

"Sir," said Charlie.

"Your horse?" said Le Sans.

"As of two days ago. Mine died. He's not much with that wound. But was all I could afford."

Le Sans swatted Annie Pie with his arm to get her to look up. "He the one?"

She stared at Charlie as if he were a stranger. "No sir...He just a plain boy."

"Yes, miss," said Charlie. "I'm certainly that. Just a plain boy." He smiled at Le Sans, the blacks, the girl. "No one ever mistake me for the king of England."

"You have papers to prove that's your animal?"

"Sure do, sir."

Charlie went through his haversack, slung over a shoulder, with his good arm.

"You a Mennonite?" said Le Sans.

"Yes, sir," said Charlie. "And a proud servant of Jesus Christ."

Charlie handed Le Sans the papers which he read carefully. A bill of sale from one Charlemagne Ezekiel Griffin to one John Slocum. The forgery a testament to the talents taught the boy by the late Zacharia Griffin, who had believed without reserve, there was a special place in heaven for good forgers.

Charlie did his best not to look at Annie Pie, in spite of the powerful emotions he was experiencing. His desires in conflict with the need to keep her and himself safe.

"How did you break the arm?" said Le Sans.

"Helping some immigrants with a sheared wagon axle. A crate fell on it. I've always been a clumsy lad."

Le Sans handed Charlie back the bill of sale. "Can you prove you're this John Slocum?"

"Sure. But my friends call me Jack." He put away the bill of sale and then from the haversack out came the diploma from the Evangelical Seminary for one John Slocum.

Le Sans gave it a quick glancing. He was beginning to look like a man facing defeat. "The fella who sold you the horse. Can you describe him?"

Charlie took a proper moment as if truly thinking. "Tallish… skinny…older than me but younger than you. Quiet."

Le Sans handed him back the diploma. His look of defeat turning to disgust. "Where did he sell the horse to you?"

"Where? Outside of Mexico township. Back there in Audrain County."

"Did he say where he was going?"

"Say?" Charlie shuffled a bit as if trying to recall. "No, sir. He just got into a wagon with a couple of loud fellas. I did notice on the canvas hood someone had painted 'Free Staters.'"

Le Sans cursed violently. He took a private moment with the blacks. They got out maps and went to work charting the quickest way back to Mexico, no matter how bad the country, so they might continue their pursuit.

"We takin' that one?" said one of the blacks pointing to Annie Pie.

Le Sans dismounted. "She'll slow us down." Then he went and dragged Annie Pie from the saddle. With her in tow, Le Sans made the rounds of the trading stalls and travelers, asking every black he came upon where they were heading.

A black with his wife and family in a flatbed wagon answered, "We headin' for Call'way County, sir. Jefferson City."

"Ever hear of the Forest Hills Plantation?" said Le Sans. "The Bass family?"

"Ever'one hear'd dem, sir. They out by Three Creeks."

Le Sans shoved Annie Pie toward the wagon. "This girl's mammy does work for the Basses. You take her home now, you hear. And Bass may take a shine to you."

Charlie watched as the man and his wife and children looked down at this pitiable girl sitting on the ground with her back to the wagon wheel. They knew they weren't being asked.

"And you tell Mister Bass, it was Mister Le Sans who told you to bring the girl home. You hear, boy? Mister Le Sans. You repeat that name now, boy."

"Mister Le Sans," said the man, repeating the name, "said to tell you he ask'd us brin' da girl home."

It's such the way of it, thought Charlie. Le Sans would lord it over some black or Free Stater, but he wasn't about to bring down the ire of a powerful family who may not appreciate him killing off one of their people, at least not without their say so.

Annie Pie was hauled up onto the wagon by the children. Charlie watched as the wagon trundled out onto the main road. Annie Pie climbed over a paltry stack of the family's possessions to get one last look at Charlie.

He put a hand up to wave to her, and she nodded. And for one ardent moment, a lifetime was spoken between them in the testament of a look.

CHAPTER 69

CHARLIE GRIFFIN ARRIVED at Saint Clements Church at dusk on the third of July, eighteen hundred and fifty five. There was a service in progress and that simple clapboard church was filled to overflowing.

There were many wagons and horses about, and tents and campsites had been set up all along the road from the church, and these stretched back to the forest and the river there. Singing came from within the church.

> *Let us break bread together, on our knees...*
> *Let us break bread together on our knees...*
> *When I fall on my knees with my face to the rising sun...*
> *Oh Lord, have mercy on me...*

Charlie dismounted and stood beside Stranger there in the dusty roadway. The light from within the church made the windows and open doorway glow as night fell. He knew this song. The Gloucasters had sung this in their home that fateful day. There was clapping to the music from within the church that Charlie could feel in the ground beneath his feet. How far, Charlie thought, he had come to be back where it all started.

Charlie approached the crowded doorway and singled out a gentleman and excusing himself, said, "I'm looking for James Montgomery."

The man nodded and stepped from the doorway and pointed to a flag, well down a ways, that rose in the sunset above a tent. "You'll find him there."

Charlie walked along with Stranger following behind him. They were a dusty portrait of roadborn youth, that's for sure. Charlie was no longer dressed as a Mennonite. He wore his faded trousers and railroad cap, and that ratty old coat he'd brought this far was slung over a shoulder.

There about a dozen men around a table in the tent from where the flag hung on a stanchion. They seemed in close conversation looking over a series of maps spread across the table.

He stood in the doorway to the tent where a couple of rough looking fellows were gathered around a table, and said, "Pardon me. I'm looking for James Montgomery."

Montgomery stood at the head of the table facing Charlie. A lean man about the same age as Butler Phillips, with a full beard and warlike eyes and shoulder holster bearing a Colt revolver. "I'm he."

"Sir…I've come from New York, Brooklyn…and Ward Beecher. And—"

"Charlemagne Griffin," said Montgomery.

Charlie's mouth was so dry from being nervous, he could barely get out, "Yes, sir. But how—"

"I got a wire from Erastus Eels to be on the watch for you."

"Erastus is alive!"

"Ghosts don't send wires, boy."

Charlie had a letter in his good hand, which he offered James Montgomery. It was the letter written by Missus Watters and addressed to him. Montgomery opened the envelope. He looked over the letter, and then he read it aloud, "Dear Mister Montgomery. You don't know me, but I have long been part of the movement. This is a fine young man, and will prove to be worthy of your good will…Missus Emmaline Watters." Once done, Montgomery folded the letter and handed it back to Charlie. "What can I do for you, son?"

"Do you have a knife, sir?" said Charlie.

A strange request to say the least. A bit of laughter from a few of the men. One in particular unsheathed an Arkansas toothpick and jabbed the blade into the tabletop. "At your service," said the man.

Charlie set the coat on the table. He would have done the cutting himself, but with one arm in a sling, it was too cumbersome a task.

"If one of you gents will cut away the lining along the collar and down across the bottom, you'll find over four thousand dollars hidden there. Money that was raised by Ward Beecher in New York for you to buy weapons. It was for me to help deliver it to you."

The men looked at each other and at the boy, wondering what in God's name had found its way into their presence.

Charlie pointed to where they should start cutting and the man took up his Arkansas toothpick and obliged, almost in jest.

As soon as he cut away those first stitches Charlie felt this sweeping relief, as if the burdens of his life had been lifted. Freed, he was suddenly, and no longer a slave to the shames that had haunted him.

He watched as the seam was ripped open and a packet of money was exposed. The look on the men's faces around the table began to turn from disbelief to bewilderment and the more the seam was torn and the next packet of money taken from the lining, and then the one after that, which Montgomery laid out on the table in a heap, there came over the men a remarkable silence.

And the boy there, with the last of a burning sun behind him, was glad to be done with the task.

"You came from New York?" said Montgomery. "All this way? With that much money in your coat?"

"Yes, sir. But...I had a lot of help along the way."

Now that the coat had been emptied, one of the men went to toss it aside, but Charlie grabbed for it. The coat, you see, was part of him, and it would go where he would go.

"You have a place, son?" said Montgomery. "People?"

Charlie shook his head no.

"Find this boy...I mean this young man...a place to sleep and some food."

Then Montgomery came around the table and offered Charlie his hand. And after they had shaken hands, the next man offered his hand, and then one after that. A succession of men passed before him. Thankful, resolute, tenacious men.

And as proud and satisfied as Charlie felt, he would have given it all up, and taken on again all the burdens, if he could bring them back—all the ones whose names were written on his heart in the ink of death.

They started the fireworks early, it being the evening of July third. It was Charlie's birthday. They were setting off Roman candles far down the road from the church. There was music and drinking and much merriment and Charlie walked the road with Stranger looking for a quiet spot from where to watch the night unfold and take in the fact that he was a year older.

There was a bench against the church wall, and Charlie took up there. He wore that ratty coat and his railroad cap. He got a cheroot out from his haversack and a bottle of beer he bought and he sat alone with Stranger picking at the grass and watched the bursts of color explode upon the Missouri sky.

He wanted to be alone with his thoughts, seeing how it was his birthday and his task completed. And what should come to mind, at a moment like that, surprised and perplexed him.

Where do I belong? thought Charlie. Where do I belong, and how do I get there? The question was so vast, he felt incapable of answering.

So he drank some beer and smoked his cheroot and pulled a leg up onto the bench and draped his good arm over it and watched the sky go electric with fierce streaks of red and gold and white and blue. And Stranger there, undisturbed by it all.

Charlie did not have an answer but what he did have was faith there was an answer. The future would demand an answer, and he would be up to the mysteries that came with finding the answer.

He thought back to that first day on the ferry from Brooklyn, with that flamboyant gent tearing a page from his book of poems. Everything the boy saw became a part of him. Charlie remembered, and Charlie understood. A child went forth that day, so a man could be born to follow in his footsteps.